WICKED WISH

MEGAN MONTERO

CHAPTER 1

ASTRID

"*R*ight, because friends know the way you taste."

Dead silence surrounded me like a bomb had been dropped and not a single one of them knew what to say. That needle sticking up from the pandora configuration called to me. I had to touch it, had to know once and for all if I was the Lockwood heir. I reached out and pressed my finger to the sharp point.

Throbbing pain shot through the tip of my finger. It ran down my arm like marching fire ants. Flames spread through my shoulder and across my chest. It knocked the breath from my chest. My lungs contracted painfully, and I gasped. My body felt like burning putty and I stumbled back off my stool. I couldn't breathe, couldn't see anything but that damn needle receding back into the top of that box. The metal clinked and folded in on itself and the book fell to the floor at my feet.

Pain like I'd never known flowed over me then something clicked inside me. Like all my life I'd been holding this part of myself back. The dam of my power shattered and it felt like a million little paper cuts covered my body. Magic flowed out of my hands like a waterfall.

Maze shot to his feet. "She's gonna blow!"

Beckett raced forward. "Hold on, just hold on, Astrid. Don't let it go yet. I'm going to get help!"

I tried to hold it back, tried to stop whatever was happening from coming. Tremors wracked my body, cold sweat broke out over my skin, and the more I tried to hold it back, the more pain shot through me. My knees quaked and my muscles gave out. My face rushed toward the ground.

A moment before I cracked my cheek on the marble tile, two strong arms wrapped around me. The scent of clean fresh linens surround me and my cheek pressed to his chest. Golden smoke poured out of me, flooding the room. I couldn't stop it. The pain was too much. Dots swarmed my vision, my body contorted of its own accord. I threw my head back and screamed.

I'm going to die.

CHAPTER 2

*C*old sweat broke out over my skin as I faced my queen, begging for her help. My throat closed around the words. "She's going to die."

Astrid, *my* infuriating girl, was lying in a pool of her own magic in my house while I was here trying to get help. So much power, her tiny body couldn't control or contain it. If we didn't do something, it'd kill her and most of Warwick Academy. Somehow over the past few days I'd grown accustomed to her challenging me at every turn. Now I didn't know what I'd do without it, without her.

There, in the middle of the witch court throne room, sat my queen and the only hope I had of saving *my* girl. I needed her power. I needed her to save Astrid.

Zinnia's crown was perched on her head and those wild midnight locks fell down the sides of her face. She jumped to her feet. "I'm coming!"

Tucker, one of my best friends and the lead knight of the witch court, jumped into action. Flames danced down his arms and his eyes widened at the sight of me. "Let's go."

He ran headlong into the portal without hesitation. Zinnia was hot on his heels with the other queens right behind her. I swallowed hard and stepped through my portal, the last man to go back to hell.

The instant I was back in my kitchen I saw things had gotten so much worse. Logan, Cross, and Maze were plastered up against the walls, trying to contain her power within the sphere they created. Their hands shook. Magic poured from each of them in an array of colors, but their skin was pale and soaked in sweat. I didn't know how much longer they could hold her.

Maze turned to me with black locks of his hair falling over his milky white eyes. "Stop this now or we're *all* finished."

Zinnia pointed to the circle. "Take up positions and hold that barrier!" Silver streams of magic wound up and down her body, sending her hair flying around her face, tangling with the gothic crown on her head.

Wind whipped through the room, making it hard to move.

Tabi staggered to Maze's side and threw her hands out. Ribbons of her yellow magic filled the room and wrapped around the sphere. Their magic was a smoky mix of green, burgundy, and orange that blended in with Astrid's massive golden cloud. The wind died down in the room but intensified within that sphere. Zinnia pressed her lips together and marched forward.

His honey-colored eyes sparked with burning embers as he grabbed her arm and yanked her back. "You can't go in there, it's too dangerous."

Zinnia placed her hand over his. "If I don't, she'll die. No one deserves to suffer like this."

He pressed his lips together and let her go. She took a step forward into the wall of magic and nearly fell back. I ran up behind her and wrapped my arm around her shoulders.

I yelled over the howling wind, "I'll get you to her!"

"You can't stay in there." She held her hand out to block the turbulent gusts from smacking her in the face.

Nova moved directly across from us on the outside of the circle and threw her hands up. Purple sparks hit the sphere and the ground started to shake. Serrina moved to the other side opposite Tabi. Her red magic seeped in through the boundary and over to where Astrid lay. It drifted over Astrid's face and nose yet nothing happened to her. Her body didn't relax a fraction.

Serrina threw her hair out of her face. "She's too strong. I can't get her to calm down."

I turned my shoulder against the wind and shoved forward with Zinnia wrapped in my arms. "I'll do what I have to do to save her."

"Get me on top of the island!"

"Serrina, hold that side!" Tuck ordered. "Nova, push in on the right. Hold it, Tabi! Hold the wind!"

Electricity sizzled through Tabi's hair, making it stand on end. Her hazel eyes burned with determination as more of those yellow ribbons of magic streamed out of her. "I'm trying!"

I pulled Zinnia forward. Inch by inch we made our way to the island in the middle of the room. A shock wave of energy pulsed out of Astrid. I grabbed Zinnia's arm and shoved her down to the ground and covered her. "She can't take much more of this!"

"Neither can the house," she screamed over the sound of the walls cracking around us.

She grabbed the edge of the counter and hauled herself up. I wrapped my arms around her legs and lifted, trying to get her to where she needed to be. I placed her on her feet on the island. Zinnia stood over Astrid with her feet on either side of Astrid's hips.

I didn't want to see her suffer through this. But there was nothing I could do, nothing I was capable of to take away her pain. Silver streams of magic wound around Zinnia's body and up her arms. She held her hand just above Astrid's chest and shot her magic straight into her. Astrid's back arched up off the island and a gut-wrenching scream broke from her lips. Another shock wave of power exploded out of her, throwing Zinnia through the air.

Tuck's fire wings shot from his back and he caught Zinnia. With one pump, he flew into the sphere of Astrid's powers. I scrambled to stand by her head.

Zinnia moved above her once more. "Hold her down."

Before I could place a single hand on her another wave of power rolled out of her. My feet flew up and over my head. I crashed into the wall and slid down. My vision wavered and then the blackness took me.

CHAPTER 3

BECKETT

The room was still. So still I could hear my own breaths, the thumping of my own thundering heart, and my footsteps as I turned. The room was sterile white with subway tiles on the floor and four walls. When I looked up, only bright shining light shone down on me . . . no roof? Even though it should hurt my eyes, it didn't. *Where the hell am I?*

I heard a soft gasp. When I turned, I found Astrid standing next to me. Her deep red hair was smooth down the side of her face, her cheeks were pink, and her lips were full like strawberries. When she looked up at me with those sparkling emerald eyes, I sucked in a breath.

"You're okay?"

She held out her arms, examining her hands and touching her face. "I-I'm not sure."

"What happened? Where are we?" It felt so real, yet somehow I knew it wasn't. I was supposed to be in my kitchen trying to save the girl standing next to me. Yet I was trapped in a room with no doors or windows.

"I have no idea." She pressed her hand to her chest and hunched over, hissing in pain. "But I don't feel well."

I grabbed her hands and dragged her to my chest. I threw my arms around her, pulling her in closer to me. The smell of strawberries surrounded me, and I lowered my face to run my cheek over the smooth strands of her hair. When her arms wound around my waist and her body pressed against mine, my pulse raced. I've wanted her so close for so long. To have her near me even for a second where we weren't fighting was . . . heavenly.

"Everything is going to be okay, I swear."

WAS I KNOCKED OUT? Was I dreaming this? Had that last hit of magic portaled us somewhere? Her small hands wrapped in my shirt, tugging me closer.

She pressed her face to my chest and shook her head. "No, Beckett. I really don't think it will."

"All you have to do is fight to take control of what is rightfully yours." I reached up and smoothed her hair back from her face, cupping her cheeks in my hands. I wasn't sure why, but here in this place I felt free to touch her, to be how I wished it were between us. Here there was no anger or frustration. If I was dreaming, I didn't want to wake up.

"Why are you being so nice to me?" She blinked up at me from under thick eyelashes.

"I always want to be nice to you." I ran my fingers over her cheek and brushed a lock of hair behind her ear. "I want to be way more than nice to you."

She stumbled back from me with her hand pressed over her heart. She hunched over, sucking in gasping breaths. Her body wavered from solid to ghostly white, nearly transparent. I reached out for her, and my hand drifted through her torso. I called upon my magic, hoping to hold her here with me, but nothing happened. No blue smoke, no orbs at my fingertips.

Where the hell are we?

When she peeked up at me, her face wavered and crumpled in pain. "I don't know if I can do this for much longer."

I wanted to hold her in my arms, to protect her. I needed her like I needed air to breathe. She wavered back to solid and I dove at her, wrapping my arms around her waist. I turned my body in time to take the hit from the floor with her on top of me. Electricity sparked between us, pulsing beneath my skin. Our legs tangled together and her silky hair fell over me. Our faces were only inches apart. I pulled her up my body and pressed my lips to hers. Heat flashed through me and I wanted her closer. I wanted her so much it ached deep in my soul. Her tongue danced with mine. I flipped her onto her back and levied myself over her.

"You're brave and strong. I know you can."

Black streaks forked out over her hair and for a moment, her lips flashed to an impossible blood red. She looked like an enchantress ready to consume my soul. Then her body started to fade once more, and she smiled at me.

"If you think so."

My arms dropped to the cold ground through her. "Just stay with me." I couldn't hide the pain or pleading in my voice. I wanted her always.

"It's my time." Her voice sounded so far away and then she faded to nothing. Was she gone? Was she dead? My heart nearly exploded with panic. The deafening sound of my racing pulse was like a beating drum.

I jumped to my feet. "Astrid!" I spun in a circle,

trapped in this room with no windows and no doors. "Astrid! Come back to me."

A wave of dizziness overtook me and I swayed on my feet. I glanced down at my hands only to see them fading to nothing. I pressed them to my chest . . . nothing, I felt absolutely nothing. *What the hell is going on?*

CHAPTER 4

I forced my eyes open, but I couldn't see Beckett anywhere.

My panic rose as the face of a terrifying girl came into view. Silver rivers of magic flowed into her from all different directions. It coiled around her like snakes, thick silvery glittering snakes. Her midnight hair fanned out around her face and mixed with the tornado of my magic. Perched on top of her head was a gothic looking crown with sharp points at the top of it. Her sapphire eyes glowed bright and terrifying when she looked down at me. I wanted to scramble back away from her, but my body wouldn't listen to a single command. Fear and pain paralyzed me. I lay there shaking and wanting nothing more than to get away from her.

She bent down and met my eyes. "This is going to hurt."

Hurt? I didn't want it to hurt, I didn't want to be here, and I didn't want to feel this. She held both of her hands over her head and more power flowed into her. Her skin glowed with it, and the others around us watched with wide-eyed amazement. She was about to kill me and they were going to stand by and let it happen. My chest heaved with breaths and I couldn't stop the panicked tears from leaking from the corners of my eyes.

I whispered, "Please don't kill me."

I would give anything for her to stop, anything but the powers that were rightfully mine. I didn't know what was about to happen, but this terrifying girl promised pain and I knew she would deliver. Would I live through it? The agony was so intense, my organs were boiling from the inside out. The drops I felt gathering on my body could've been sweat or . . . blood.

I tried to sit up, to fight back, to do anything but lie here in a pool of my own magic. Everything hurt and my muscles quaked with the effort it took for me to hold back. I gritted my teeth and met her eyes. If she wanted to take it, then she was going to have to fight me for it.

CHAPTER 5

"*B*eckett! Beck man, get up! We need your help!"

I blinked my eyes open and shook my head. *What the hell was that?* Grogginess overtook me as I lurched to my feet. I rubbed at my head and winced at the bump forming on the back of my skull. The throbbing pain snapped me back to the present in a rush. The wall behind me cracked even more, and a piece of sheetrock fell to the ground. Tucker was behind Zinnia, using his wings to keep her steady over Astrid.

His eyes locked on mine. "Let's go!"

I jumped back into the sphere of her power. The air was oppressive and thick with magic. The ground rumbled under my feet and I struggled to get to her. I leaped forward just as Zinnia stood over her. She threw her arm out and silver streams of magic wound up and down her body like snakes and shot right into Astrid's chest. Her eyes flashed wide-open and her back arched up off the table top. Golden magic erupted from her palms and flew toward the ceiling. A hole exploded through the roof. Like a vacuum I felt myself being sucked toward it.

Zinnia pressed her lips together and shoved more magic into her. "She's fighting me! Serrina!"

Serrina turned and blew a kiss across her palm. Streams of her red power flowed through the turbulent sphere of Astrid's magic. Her streaked blond hair blew out from around her face, and she narrowed her eyes, focusing her energy on Astrid. Those red ribbons flowed around Astrid but never touched her. Serrina took a step closer. "I can't get to her."

Tuck threw his arm out. "Don't move."

He pumped his wings, keeping Zinnia where she stood even though Astrid struggled against them. He met my eyes. "Hold her down."

"Shit." I fought my way back to her head and gazed down into her face.

Tears streamed from the corners of her eyes. Drops of blood gathered on her skin like beads of sweat. "Please, Beck. Please don't do this."

I didn't want to hurt her, didn't want for her to feel this pain. But I had no choice. It was either let her hate me today or lose her forever. "I'm sorry."

I held my hands up at my sides and called my magic to my palms. Blue smoke billowed from me and flowed over the table. I laced it around Astrid's wrists and ankles, holding her down. A look of sheer betrayal crossed her face and I wanted to stop, to throw myself over her and take this pain from her. But there was nothing to do. The only one who could help her was Zinnia and even now our queen fought to hold Astrid together. Serrina threw her arms up higher and red ribbons struck Astrid just as Zinnia's power covered her from head to toe.

The three of us used all that we had on her. The magic in the room glowed lighter, the thick fog of golden power thinned, and the wind grew still. Astrid sucked in a deep breath and let her eyes slide shut. It was at that exact second, I felt her stop fighting my hold, stop fighting Zinnia from helping her, and letting Serrina influence her. But I didn't know if she would wake at any moment and attack. She didn't know them, didn't know they were here to help. And if I knew Astrid, which I did, she would wake up swinging.

I didn't let my magic down. "Is she okay?"

Zinnia slowly let her magic dissipate as she bent down lower, hovering just above her face. "She's very powerful and it took all of us to break down her natural defenses. But I think she'll be okay."

The tension left Astrid's body and she lay there, sucking in deep, panting breaths. Her eyes fluttered open for only a second then they drifted shut. It was the first time I'd felt relief since she started to ascend. Her swirling magic slowed to a light fog that drifted up out of the hole in the ceiling. Everyone dropped their hold on her and sagged against the crumbling walls or just sat on the floor. I moved to her side and leaned in. She lay there completely dazed, her eyes vacant, staring at the ceiling.

"Shh, you're okay. Everything is all right." I brushed one of her tears from her temple. She sucked in a breath and let her eyes fall shut as if she'd fallen asleep.

The others gathered together and began talking about what they were going to do now, how they were going to fix the house. I let my forehead drop onto the cold marble countertop beside her. And that's when I felt it, the warmth surrounding my wrist.

No, it can't be.

A faint glow came from the cuff of my shirt. I quickly glanced at her wrist and the same faint glowing was there. Before anyone noticed, the glowing stopped and I wanted to slump into the floor even more. *How . . . how could this happen now? That's not how any of this works.*

Shit.

She was my . . . soul mate.

CHAPTER 6

BECKETT

innia began to walk toward me and I nearly dove for Astrid's wrist. I wrapped my hand around it and quickly mumbled a spell under my breath to camouflage the mark I knew meant something huge! Something I wasn't ready to face or handle right now. *Oh shit, oh shit, oh shit. I can't believe this. She is mine . . . my soul mate.* I sucked in a deep breath and straightened my stance to face her. My fingers never left Astrid's wrist and I wasn't about to take them away now. Her eyes still hadn't opened, and her breathing was erratic at best.

"Why isn't she getting better?"

Zinnia placed her hand on Astrid's other arm and took her pulse. "She practically hemorrhaged magic. Her pulse is weak. She needs a healer, Beckett."

I moved in closer and put my arms under Astrid and lifted her up. "Tell me where to go."

Zinnia changed her grip on Astrid's wrist then threw her other arm out. Streams of silver and gold magic left her and the wall to the kitchen opened up into another room that hadn't been there before. A sliding glass door stood between the kitchen and the new room. A hospital bed appeared, along with all kinds of monitors, tools, and shelves full of medical supplies. On the opposite side of the wall were potions, vials, and books of spells. Though I expected the walls to be sterile like a hospital, they weren't. They were the same dark wood that matched the rest of the house and floors. It happened in mere seconds.

My house just got its own hospital.

I rushed forward with Astrid lying limp in my arms. As I laid her out on the bed, her deep red hair splayed across the white cotton sheets. Panic like I'd never known rose up in me. She had to be okay. She had to survive this. *I can't . . . I can't be without her.* I smoothed my fingers over those silk strands. I knew the others were watching me, but I didn't care.

Zinnia moved to the other side of the bed. "Beckett, we need help to get her better."

I swallowed around the ball forming in my throat. She was pale. Her lips held an alarming blue pallor and her eyes were yet to open. I glanced up and met Zinnia's sharp gaze and whispered, "I-I can't leave her."

Zinnia lowered her voice. "You don't have to."

I gathered my magic in my hand, forming an orb. I tossed it to the side, letting it open right across from Astrid's bed. Without a word, Zinnia squared her shoulders and marched into the portal. For a moment, I took in the silence and Astrid's ragged breaths. Against the white sheets she looked so fragile, so breakable, so human. I'd known her as this fierce creature who fought me at every turn. *I can't believe I wanted that to stop.*

Now I didn't want to imagine my life without her fiery, sassy mouth. "Astrid? Astrid, can you hear me?"

She didn't move, didn't respond in any way. I leaned closer to her and ran the backs of my fingers over her soft cheek. "You're going to be okay. I know it."

Before I could utter another sentence, the portal shimmered, and I felt them moving through it toward me. When I glanced up and saw that familiar fire engine red hair, I sighed in relief. I stood straight and approached her. "Niche!"

I threw my arms around her shoulders and pulled her in for a quick hug. Her presence here was more comforting than I could ever say. "I'm so happy you're here."

With one finger, she pushed her glasses back up her nose. She pressed her hand to my arm and winked at me. Then she moved past me toward Astrid's bed. She titled her head, studying her, then closed her eyes and held her hand over Astrid for barely a moment. She took a small step back.

"Can you . . ." My breath hitched in my throat. "Can you help her?"

"Of course." Niche gave me a warm smile and for the first time in hours I felt comforted.

Just then Professor Davis walked through my portal. She swatted at her twisted brown robes and fought to keep her cap perched on her head. Her salt and pepper hair stuck out in fuzzy puffs. Her round face was red with exertion and when she looked up at me, she narrowed her eyes. "Dare I say this, but, boy, your portals downright suck."

Zinnia gave a light chuckle as she came out next. "Yup."

I sighed. "My apologies."

She shoved past me and stood on the other side of the bed across from Niche. She glanced down at Astrid then turned to the cabinet and pulled crystals out. She stacked them in her arms then placed them on the floor around Astrid's bed. Each one was the size of a small baseball yet all different colors.

She glanced at Zinnia. "This one is powerful, my queen. She'll serve you well in what's to come."

Now *that* had me chuckling. "Astrid will never serve anyone." At their wide-eyed looks I clarified. "It's not in her nature to follow orders. I would know."

Zinnia grimaced. "I don't need her service, I need her friendship. How can I win her over, Beckett?"

As Professor Davis placed the last stone on the ground, a pastel pink dome covered Astrid from head to toe. Her breaths went from ragged to deep in a matter of moments.

I sighed. "I'll tell you that once I figure it out."

Niche grabbed up a mortar and pestle on the bedside table and began to dump herbs into it and ground them together. "Zin, I'm going to need a cauldron with boiling water."

"I'm on it." She turned and walked out of the sliding glass door.

My feet were cemented to the floor. I was helpless to do anything but stare at Astrid and plead in my mind for her to wake. I crossed my arms over my chest. The only sounds in the room were Astrid's easy breaths and the grinding of the herbs. Professor Davis stood to the side, mumbling spells over Astrid, each one adding a new layer of color to the dome. The dome itself looked like a glass shell, but it shimmered and rippled like water. The more Professor Davis stood there chanting, the better Astrid's color got.

"Beckett!" Niche snapped.

I jolted. "Huh, what? Did you say something?"

She rolled her eyes. "I've been saying your name for at least five minutes now."

Shit. "Sorry."

"It will only get more difficult from here." She grabbed a vial of bright purple crushed something and added it to her concoction.

My heart jumped into my throat. "What do you mean? Is she . . . is she not going to recover?" I could barely swallow. Sweat gathered in my palms, and I wanted to grab her up and hug her to my chest.

"Oh, she's going to be fine. You need to go get some rest. Or at least wash up. You look like you got hit by a garbage truck." She looked me up and down then turned back to mixing her potion.

Had I just been dismissed? When I looked down at myself, I knew she was right. My sweater was torn in multiple places, my jeans fared no better, my hair stood on end, and I was pretty sure there was dirt smudged across my face. I wanted to stay by Astrid's side. I didn't want to leave her for a minute while she lay like this. But I knew deep down Niche and Professor Davis would do all they had to, to help her. They didn't even appear worried. Each of them worked methodically. There was no panic to their movements or their tones. "Beckett, go on." Niche urged me toward the door. I sucked in a sharp breath then blew it back out. She would be okay. I saw it in the rosy pink of her cheeks and how relaxed her body was. "I'll be back in twenty minutes."

In the kitchen Tuck, Cross, Logan, and Maze had each pulled up stools and were waiting just outside her door. "Where are the others?"

Tuck rolled his shoulders. "Zin went to get a cauldron. From where, I don't know. And the others are in the parlor relaxing."

Tuck sighed and sucked in a deep breath. When he turned to look at me, I did the only thing I could think of. I threw my arms around his shoulders and gave him a quick hug and patted him on the back.

"Thank you. I really mean it."

For a second, he froze at the unexpected contact, then patted me on the back. "Yeah, no problem."

I pulled back and shuffled from one foot to the other. It'd been years since I hugged someone. Now twice in one day. What was happening to me? It caught me off guard just as much as it did him. I cleared my throat. "Um, listen, can I talk to you for a sec?"

He shoved his hand through his hair, pushing it out of his face. "Yeah, absolutely."

"Great." I took a step toward the hallway, then spun around and pointed to Cross. "You too."

Without a word, he rose to his feet and followed us down the hall. The front door stood wide-open, letting fall leaves drift in. To my right Tabi, Serrina, and Nova sat lazily on the couch. Each of them looked like they needed a nap. My toe hit the bottom stair and I stumbled forward, barely catching myself. I grabbed onto the railing and righted myself.

Behind me Tuck chuckled. "Missed that step there?"

"Wiseass," I muttered.

At the top of the stairs I turned to my right and led them down the hall toward what used to be my father's office and was now mine. I shoved the door open and waved them through, making sure no one followed us. After a pause and pushing Astrid's cat out the door, I closed it and clicked the lock into place. "Both of you have to swear not to repeat what I'm about to say to you."

They nodded in unison and I sucked in a deep breath. "Okay, here goes."

I pulled my sleeve up, exposing the mark around my wrist.

Cross gave a low, long whistle and shook his head. "Oh, man, I'm sorry."

"Sorry? Psh." Tuck grabbed my wrist and yanked me closer, examining the mark. When he turned my palm up, there were two circles, one big and one smaller overlapping each other. Two solid black bands ran from the circles in parallel lines all the way around my wrist. "Astrid?"

I nodded. "Yeah, the second she fully ascended."

Tuck shrugged. "I wonder why so late. I mean, I got mine the second I saw Zin."

"I honestly have no idea why now. Though I always felt connected to her. Maybe because her magic was blocked? I don't know."

Cross dropped down into the chair across from my desk. "What are you gonna do?"

"What do you mean what *he's* gonna do? He's going to tell her, aren't you?" Tuck released my hand and sat in the other chair next to Cross.

I ran my hand over the back of my neck. "Yeah, I don't know. It might be too soon for this."

"Dude, take my advice on this one. Keeping it a

secret is a bad idea." Tucker and Zinnia didn't have the easiest of starts, but seeing how they were now gave me a little hope.

Cross shook his head. "You say that now, but you do not know how much she hates him. Don't tell her. Try to win her over first, so it won't be such a bad thing."

I leaned back against the desk. "You think she'll take it that poorly?"

"Oh, hell yeah. Have you seen her? She's a total badass. Just put her finger on that needle after you told her not to. Not to mention she almost leveled the house." Cross chuckled. "This is gonna be hilarious."

Tuck punched him in the shoulder.

"Ouch, what? What'd I say?" Cross rubbed at the spot.

"You're an idiot." Tuck rolled his eyes and turned back toward me. "Who are you gonna trust, the guy who has the girl or the guy who's still chasing his?"

"I'm not chasing her, we have an . . . understanding." Cross slouched farther down in the chair, making the leather creak under him.

Tuck scoffed. "Sure you do. Ophelia is about as understanding as a butcher knife."

"Hey! You might not get her, but I do, and that's all that matters." Cross motioned to me. "Now our boy

here is out of his depth with Astrid. That girl has
nothing but venom in her veins for him. I don't know
what the hell fate was thinking pairing you two
together, but you must've done something wrong."

"Don't be a jackass," I snapped. There was so much
to Astrid that he didn't understand, that he didn't see.
She was brave, strong, brilliant, and beyond beautiful.
She was *everything.* "You have no idea what she's like."

Cross rolled his eyes. "And you do?"

I folded my arms over my chest. "Um, yeah, I
think so."

"You know what your problem is?" Cross chuckled.
"You're so used to girls liking you from the get-go that
you have no idea what to do when they don't."

Tuck sighed. "Like you know what to do? Who says
O even likes you? As far as I can tell that girl has got
you wrapped around her little fingers and you aren't
even together."

Cross' lips thinned. "All I'm saying is maybe wait a
little while until you can win her over. Turn on that
Beckett charm, make friends with her, then you lower
the 'oh, by the way, I'm your one true fated mate'
bomb."

"Jeez, dude, make me sound like a punishment,
why don't you?" Things weren't that bad between
Astrid and me . . . were they?

"You couldn't be more wrong." Tuck threw his hands up. "Lying will only dig you into a deeper hole. Trust me. Zin was livid when she found out I didn't tell her the truth."

I was torn. Both of them had a point. "But Zinnia actually liked you. I'm not so sure about Astrid. She pretty much does the opposite of whatever I ask her to do, even if it doesn't make sense, even if she knows it's not safe."

Tuck rose to his feet and clapped me on the shoulder. "I know, isn't it great? This is what we get when dealing with the most powerful women in Evermore."

He had a point. "It's damn exciting, that's for sure."

Cross moved to stand beside me. "Speak for yourselves. Your two girls are kittens compared to O."

"Only because O is feral," Tuck teased.

Cross nodded seriously. "You have no idea."

"As much as I want to disagree, I can't. But I still have no idea what I'm going to do." I wanted to run downstairs and tell Astrid what we were to each other. What we could be. But as of two hours ago she was pissed at me and with good reason. Just because I wanted her didn't mean she'd want me in return.

Tuck stood on my left. "Just tell her the truth."

Cross was on my right. "No way, at least not yet."

With an angel on one shoulder and a devil on

another, I had no idea what I was going to do. I couldn't help but wonder how Astrid would react or feel knowing we belonged to each other. The last conversation we had didn't go well. I'd told a room full of people we were just friends and her response was pricking her finger on that damn box and making all hell break loose. Worst of all, her words echoed in my ears . . . *Right, because friends know the way you taste . . .*

I'm so screwed. What am I going to tell her?

CHAPTER 7

*A*ll they did was confuse me more and more. One minute, it was a good idea to tell her and in the next, it was the world's worst idea. Astrid was unpredictable and feisty. I both liked and hated that about her. If only I knew how she would feel about this, about me, I'd tell her right away. As it was now . . . I might have to wait.

When we hit the landing, the parlor was empty. Not a single one of the queens sat there. I spun around. "Where are they?"

Tuck pointed down the hall back toward the kitchen and the infirmary room where Astrid lay. I quickened my steps toward her. I clenched and unclenched my fist at my sides. Tuck muttered, "Deep breath, man."

I sucked one in and blew it out hard as I came to the sliding glass doors. I froze mid-step. Astrid lay motionless with Zinnia, Serrina, Tabi, and Nova surrounding her. Niche stood close to her head while Professor Davis stood by her feet. The crystals on the ground glowed a rainbow of colors. They all held their hands out to their sides, their palms nearly touching with only an inch between them.

Niche closed her eyes. "Repeat after me. Sky above, earth below. Let our healing magic flow."

Each of them closed their eyes and repeated her words over and over again. Magic flowed from their palms. It mixed together in an array of Zin's silver, Tabi's yellow, Serrina's red, and Nova's purple. It rose in a cloud over the bed and swirled together, gently melding and twining.

The cotton ball cloud above Astrid held an array of colors that reflected down onto the white cotton bed. The colors covered her from head to toe, then all at once the cloud burst and an array of sparkling magic rained down on her, covering her from head to toe. It settled over her like a blanket and her cheeks pinkened. She sucked in a breath and her eyes fluttered for a moment.

I forced the door open and was at her side in an instant. "Astrid, are you okay?"

"Hmm." Her eyes shut and she curled onto her side. "Astrid?"

Niche placed her hand on my shoulder. "She's just sleeping now. She'll be okay."

"Yeah, Beck." Tabi caught my eye. "They had to do the same thing for me. I nearly caused a dormant volcano to erupt, so this was all good."

I gave them a single nod. I knew she'd be okay, but I'd feel better once she was wide awake and giving me all hell.

Niche placed the mortar and pestle back on the shelf along with the empty vials. "In any case, we have to be going back. There are . . . things that need dealing with."

"I understand." I summoned my magic to my hand and tossed an orb at the wall across from Astrid's bed. "That'll drop you right into the library at Evermore Academy."

"I think I'll stay." Zinnia sighed and looked around the room. "Beckett, could you move one of those couches in here from the living room?"

"I mean, sure. But you don't have to st—"

"I'm staying." Zinnia crossed her arms over her chest.

"All righty then."

Serrina grabbed my shoulder and gave it a little

squeeze, then walked past me right into the portal. Tabi gave me a little wave then followed quickly behind her.

Professor Davis pulled her cap down tighter over her fuzzy hair. She adjusted her robes, tightening them around her waist. She jabbed her finger at me. "Right, okay. I'm ready. Mr. Dustwick, honestly, perhaps you should take a class on portals. I feel like I'm about to go on a roller coaster ride. You are aware that I am not as young as you all. This is not fun."

"I'll work on it, Professor."

As she stepped through, I tossed a puff of my magic in after her. It would catch her and carry her through the portal smoothly at least for a while.

Niche dusted her hands off and rubbed them down her lab coat, leaving a trail of green smudge down the front. She tossed her mane of long flaming red hair over her shoulder. "All will be well, Beckett. She will make a full recovery by tomorrow. This kind of ascension can kill a warlock, but she is strong and I know she will be fine."

"Niche, I can't thank you enough."

"No need for thanks. I know she will figure her way out. You're the calmest, most level-headed of all the knights I've known. You will help her. I know it." With that she too walked into the portal.

No pressure or anything . . . My head felt like it was going to explode. My body ached and at any moment I was going to crash with exhaustion. We'd just gotten back from a quest to open that damn book, then everything happened with Astrid and now she was my soul mate.

Nova sauntered up to me and placed her glove covered hand on my chest. "She's going to be okay."

"I know."

"Do you, because from where I'm standing you look like you're about to fall apart." Her eyes were a deep all-seeing onyx I couldn't deny. In another life, another time I might've dated Nova. We might've even been a good couple, yet now I couldn't picture myself with anyone else but Astrid.

I sighed and ran my hand through my hair. "It's been a long few days."

She rubbed her hand over my chest for only a second then dropped it. "Sometimes as the Queen of death I see things others can't. You'll figure it out."

Without another word she left my side and disappeared through the portal. When I looked up at Zinnia, she stood there studying me. I squared my shoulders. "What?"

She chuckled. "Nothing." She turned and leaned against the wall. "I think the couch would be good here." Then she pointed to the other side of the room. "And one over there."

"Fine." With the wave of my hand, I closed the portal and sucked the energy back into the palm of my hand. Blue smoke drifted up my arms and seeped into my skin, melding back in. I rolled my shoulders and cracked my neck while I let that darkness settle into the pit of my stomach. I headed out the door toward the sitting rooms.

Maze was perched on the couch with a box of cheese flavored crackers in his hand. Crumbs and powder covered his chest and the cushions around him. Odin, that one-eyed cat, sat perfectly still next to him, watching YouTube videos of more cats.

I pinched the bridge of my nose. "Why do you keep showing him cat videos?"

Shrug. "Because he likes them." He shoved a handful of crackers in his mouth then patted Odin on the shoulder as if he were talking to a friend. "Oh, man, watch this one, it's hilarious."

"How do you know he likes it?" *What cat likes to watch TV?*

"He meows at me until I put it on. So I just do and he stops. We sit, we chill." He tossed a cracker at Odin. That damn cat caught it and ate it, creating his own pile of crumbs on the couch.

I shifted from one foot to the other. "Okay, both of you up now."

"What? Why?" Maze slouched farther into the couch and I swear that cat did as well. He leaned back on his hips and let his belly stick out. He kicked his legs out and leaned his shoulder against Maze as if he were human. That long tail of his whipped back and forth and I swear when he looked up at me with his one eye, he was challenging me to make him move.

"Because Queen Zinnia is staying in Astrid's room tonight and so am I. We need the couches." I felt my magic rising to my palm.

"That's what chairs are for, bruh." Half of a fist full of crackers made it into his mouth and the other half landed on the couch.

"Okay, enough." I opened up my hand and let my blue smoke seep onto the ground. "You can either move or I'm going to move you."

Odin meowed at me, but I wasn't about to stop. My smoke drifted under the couch and with the flick of my hand, it lifted up off the ground.

Maze grabbed Odin and hopped down before it got too high. "Such a buzz kill."

"Yeah, okay." I turned toward the other parlor where Logan sat on the couch next to the fire with a book in hand. "Do I have to convince you to move as well?"

He held his hand up in surrender and rose to his feet. "No, I'm sure I'll be quite comfortable in my room."

"Good." With my other hand I shot my magic under the couch and lifted that one as well. I guided it toward the hall. With one couch floating in front of me and one behind, I walked back toward the infirmary room.

The door slid open and I placed a couch on one side of the room and one on the other side with Astrid's bed in the middle. Tucker had made his way back to Zinnia and the two stood facing each other with their hands intertwined.

Tuck pressed his forehead to hers. "You sure you don't want me to stay? This will be the first time we haven't been in the same bed in a while."

"Whoa, guys, I don't want to hear this." I dropped down onto the couch.

"Don't worry, Beckett is here to keep an eye on me." Zinnia smiled up at him. They looked at each other like I wasn't in the room.

Tucker narrowed his eyes at me. "Yes, he will."

"She's safe with me." I sighed and glanced toward Astrid as she lay sleeping curled on her side.

"Oh, I'm not worried, because if anything happens to her, I'll kill you." He gave me a deadpan look and I knew he meant it. "You're one of my best friends, so I'm trusting you."

Zinnia gave him a little shove. "Hello, I'm a queen! I think I can handle myself."

Tuck smiled down at her. "I pity the fool who challenges you. Sure you don't want me to stay?"

"I want you to stay, but I need you to go to Evermore and deal with . . . well, all the things going on. Okay?" She went up on her tiptoes and pressed her lips to his. Tiny flames danced up and down his arms.

I rolled my eyes. "It's only a couple of hours." I pulled my phone from my pocket and checked the time. "It's already three in the morning. And what things?"

Zinnia stepped away from Tuck and faced me. "There are those who aren't pleased Alataris is dead and they're rising up against me, challenging my right to rule."

I leaned over and placed my elbows on my knees. "Are they warlocks or witches?"

Tuck and Zinnia shared a look, but neither of them answered.

I rose to my feet and gritted my teeth. "Are they warlocks or witches? Tell me!"

Zinnia sighed. "They're warlocks."

I curled my fist at my side. "This is my fault. If I could just get the council in line, then the rest of the warlocks would follow."

Tuck shook his head. "Nah, man. We can't expect miracles. And we think Dario is behind most of it. You know he was Alataris' right-hand man."

I started pacing. I was letting my friends down. They were being attacked because I couldn't get this shit together. "I'm so sorry. You sent me here to do a job and I'm failing."

"Beck, no, you are not." Zinnia shook her head. "Things like this take time. And will take a lot more than a couple rogue warlocks to unseat us. I have all the queens behind me. Until you are ready, we can handle this. Just focus on getting Astrid better and teach her to learn control."

I crossed my arms over my chest and sucked in a deep breath. "I swear to you, I will do this. There has to be a way to get us to take over the council faster. Some kind of warlock loophole in the law."

"I mean, as far as we know, the only rule is a council full of founding members can take over. These other hoops they make you jump through might just be excuses to keep them in control. But, Beck, if we could get to them sooner, that would be better." Zinnia shrugged. "If not, then we continue on the planned route."

"From what I remember our laws are much different than Witch Law. I have to check into it." I crossed my arms. "And soon."

"Well, no pressure. Just do what you gotta do." Tuck let his wings pop from his back. Flames flickered, filling the room with warm light. "I'm going to head out."

I wanted to be fighting at his side, to help them the way they helped me. "I'll be here if you need me. Want me to portal you?"

He shook his head. "Nah, I like to stretch my wings, see what kind of trouble I can get in on my way back to the school." He leaned in and gave Zinnia one more kiss then walked out the door.

It was silent with just the two of us watching over Astrid. "Thank you for staying."

She kicked her boots off then fell back on the couch. She hadn't tried to tame those wild locks after dealing with Astrid's tornado ascension. Instead, she lay back on the couch and tossed them over the arm. "Better get some rest. You're gonna need it."

I dropped back down onto my couch. "If you say so." As exhausted as I was, I couldn't even think about closing my eyes. "Yeah, okay."

As her eyes drifted closed and her breath grew deep and even, I sat with my back ramrod straight, staring at Astrid. I needed to find that book about warlock law that my father used to keep. Maybe it could help Zinnia or even Astrid . . . *Astrid. What the hell am I going to tell her? How will she take it? How am I going to get the council together to help them? How will I teach Astrid all she needs to know?*

But most importantly . . . *Astrid is my soul mate . . .*

CHAPTER 8

BECKETT

 *M*y eyes felt dry and bloodshot. I rubbed at them with the palm of my hands. Early morning sun streamed into the windows in the kitchen. I hadn't slept a wink and I was fatigued down to my bones. I couldn't really remember the last time I'd actually slept. The heavy book sitting on my lap only reminded me of all the things I'd read and all the things we were going to have to overcome to become the council. I didn't know how Zinnia could sleep there so peacefully, with warlocks going after her to challenge her. But my head was splitting and to say I was on the verge of cracking was an understatement. The warlock codex ran through my mind.

No witch shall ever rule.

The council shall be comprised of the five founding lines.

Should the lines falter, an interim council shall be appointed.

All members of the council shall complete their education at Warwick Academy.

Only pure lines shall rule.

No two lines may cross or intertwine in any way.

No alliances will be made between the lines.

A crossing of lines will result in an interim council being appointed.

Translation to all of that: I am so screwed. The warlock world would not accept a tainted council. The only way we would be accepted as the leaders of this world would be to follow the codex. It was bad enough that we were trying to take over, but now we had even more hoops to jump through. I shoved my hands into my hair and tugged at it. We couldn't add one more thing to this, not a single one.

Astrid needed to learn to control her powers. There were opposing warlocks rising to attack us. We were going to have to challenge the interim council and, assuming we won that challenge, we would still have to bring the warlock world together under Zinnia. Something others were sure to resist. No, we couldn't add one more thing to that list, not even a fated pairing. As I gazed over at Astrid, there was only one thing I could do to make this all easier . . . *lie.*

Or at least wait to tell her we were soul mates until it was better for everyone. I didn't want to lie to her, not even for a second. But all the world was stacked against us. I would have to wait until the right time, which wasn't now.

"You look like shit." Zinnia sighed and stretched her arms over her head.

"I feel like shit." I slid back onto the couch and let my head hit the wall behind it.

Zinnia rose to her feet and shoved her hair out of her face. At some point during the night she took that crown off and tossed it back onto the couch. She turned her gaze to Astrid. "She looks much better than she did yesterday. You need to go get some sleep."

I shook my head. "I want to be here when she wakes up."

"Last I checked, you two were fighting before this whole thing happened. And I need some alone time with her." Zinnia held her hand out and shot a ball of magic into the corner of the room. It swirled with glowing silver and golden power. It reminded me of one of those crystal balls that fortune-tellers liked to use when they lured in humans looking for a thrill.

"What is that?" I rose to my feet and took a step toward it.

Zinnia blocked my path. "That is a gift for Astrid. She and I will need to discuss it and it'll be better if it's just her and me. It's about time we became friends."

CHAPTER 9

Did I just die? Pretty sure I'm dead. I had no idea. But Beckett wouldn't let me. He fought for me when I didn't want to fight for myself. Fresh tears fell from the corners of my eyes and rolled back. This had to be what getting hit by a truck felt like. Every fiber of my body ached, and all my muscles were one big cramp. I stretched out in a . . . bed? *When did I get in a bed?* The sheets were cool and crisp against my sensitive skin. The pillow cushioned my head and I wanted to snuggle in and not get up.

An unfamiliar face loomed over me. Her hair was wild and tangled in all different directions. Glittering magic lingered over her skin and in those midnight locks. A sharply pointed gothic crown sat perched on top of her head and a dark olive-green scarf hung from her neck like it'd nearly been blown off. She held her hand up to me with a swirling ball of magic sitting in her palm. "It's yours, you can take it. If you want."

The muscles in my stomach protested as I sat up. My entire body quaked from head to toe with the effort. "What is it?" I glanced around the room, taking in my unfamiliar surroundings. "Where am I?"

"This"—she tossed the ball up and caught it—"is some of your magic. And you're still in Beckett's house. We just expanded it a little."

She pointed toward the sliding glass door. "See, there's the kitchen. Well, what's left of it. Anyhow, this is yours." Again she wiggled that glowing orb at me.

I'd never met Queen Zinnia before, but as she stood in front of me with my magic in the palm of her hand, she was nothing short of terrifying. All my life I'd thought witches were fake, but with her next to me with her wild hair, sparking blue eyes, and insane magic she was very real. They all were. I wanted to reach out and grab that ball of magic, but I hesitated.

"Oh, um."

"It won't activate unless you do it the right way. It's safe within the sphere." She extended her hand out toward me.

"What the hell did I miss?" Ophelia walked into the room, looking at us with wide eyes. Her hair was loose and flowed straight down her back. It was slick and smooth, nothing like Zinnia's and mine, who looked like survivors of a horrific storm. She glanced over me and then back out the door toward the destroyed kitchen. "Ohhhhhh, I see what happened here."

Zinnia tilted her head at Ophelia. "Where were you?"

"Hunting . . . so many things."

A dark look passed between the two of them before Zinnia returned her attention to me.

I didn't know what to do. All I knew was I needed to get my shit straight. "Can I just . . . I need a second." I glanced through the glass door toward the windows in the kitchen. "Is that a phoenix sitting in the window?"

"Oh yeah, he's protective to a fault." She waved to the bird, motioning for it to come into the house.

"Um, are you supposed to bring more animals in the house?" I sat up in the bed and crossed my legs. "My cat might try to kill it."

Zinnia and Ophelia both erupted into fits of laughter.

Ophelia pressed her hand to her chest. "I'd really, really like to see it try."

Zinnia gave her a playful slap. "Are you saying you'd like to see Tuck get eaten?"

"No, I'm saying it'd be hilarious."

The bird soared in through the hole in the ceiling. Its wings were a deep burgundy that was nearly dark enough to match my hair. Its long tail feathers were twice the size of its body and a flame danced at the end of it. Once it landed in the middle of the kitchen just outside of the door to my room, it looked directly at Zinnia and . . . *winked?* Then in a cloud of smoke and flames it shifted. The feathers faded away and, in their place, stood a deadly looking boy with literal sparks in his eyes. He stepped in through the glass door and stood there looming and huge.

I scrambled back on the bed. "Who the hell are you?"

"My Tucker." Zinnia stood up straight and left my orb of magic floating in the air. It drifted into the corner of the room and hovered there.

"Tucker Brand. Pleased to meet you. I've heard a lot about you." His voice was low and rumbling with a harsher rasp than Beckett's.

I rolled my eyes. "I can only imagine the things you've heard."

His lips pulled up into a smile. "All good things. I can assure you."

Yeah, right, if he heard it from Beckett. "I bet."

He chuckled and I couldn't help but wonder if all

the guys Beckett hung out with in this world were this delectable. I mean at school they weren't all good-looking, but damn if all of Beckett's friends weren't drop dead gorgeous. Even Maze with his craziness was good-looking in his own way. If I was being honest, Tuck was fiercely hot. So hot he gave Beckett a run for his money. Where Beckett was blond, bad, and surfer like, this guy was dark, haunting, and down-right dangerous.

Not that I cared what *Beckett* looked like. At all. I cleared my throat. "Where's Beckett?"

Probably bossing some people around, walking around the school kissing girls and pretending like they're "just friends." Probably being all hot somewhere anywhere but here.

Zinnia sighed. "I forced him to go take a nap a little over an hour ago. He didn't sleep all night."

"What? Why not?" I leaned back on the bed, feeling tired even now.

"He depleted himself helping you through the ascension. Then he sat here all night keeping an eye on you. I mean, he looked awful, so I had to send him away. He tried to fight me on it too."

What was that supposed to mean? Beckett stayed with me all night long? I didn't know why, but that made me feel warm in all kinds of weird places. Did it mean he actually cared about me or did he care about the power my bloodline brought? I didn't want to hope for anything from him. I knew what it felt like to hope for things that didn't pan out. My absent dad was evidence of that, and when Beckett had denied things between us, even I had to admit it stung. Stung enough that I put my finger on that needle.

"Oh, what happened to my book?"

"It's right here." Zinnia pointed to a thick book on the shelf. It was old, with a dark leather binding, geometric shapes carved into it, and there was a depiction of Medusa with all the snakes, a triquetra, a sun, a moon, and so many other beautiful things. I wanted to dive into it and read everything I possibly could.

The book disappeared and reappeared in my waiting hands.

My eyes widened. "Cool."

Zinnia placed her hand over the top of it and smiled. "Perhaps we could talk before you dive into that rabbit hole?"

When she smiled at me like that, I wanted to trust her, to maybe even be friends with her. So, I placed the book on the bed next to me and gave her a single nod. "Okay."

The thud of familiar footsteps came from down the hall. *Since when do I know what his walk sounds like? Ew.* I hated the way my heart did little flip-flops knowing he was coming this way. When he walked into the room, his hair was damp from a shower. He was just pulling a shirt over his head, giving me the barest glimpse of his chiseled abs before his sweater fell over it. He shoved his sleeves up to his elbow, showing me all that tan skin. My eyes were drawn to that thick black tribal tattoo that seemed to match Tucker's. Though Tuck had a phoenix and Beckett had a half sun, half moon, each of them were on the sides of their necks and ran just under their jaw lines. *Sexy.*

He narrowed those ocean eyes at Zinnia. "You told me you'd wake me when she was up."

CHAPTER 10

*B*eckett's ocean blue eyes bore into mine. "I-I'm so happy you're okay."

Was I okay? My body was sore like I'd run a marathon I hadn't trained for. So much power seethed beneath my skin. If I called upon it, I knew it'd rise without question. Before all this my power was questionable. Now it rolled within me like an angry tide. Golden magic seeped from my hands and all I could do was stare down at it.

"How do I make it stop?"

Beckett placed his warm palm over mine. His skin was rough from handling his blades, yet his touch was gentle. He lowered his voice. "Just take a deep breath and try to pull it back. However you picture it, think about it calming and rolling back into you."

I closed my eyes and sucked in a breath and pictured that calm ocean. It was the same vivid blue as his eyes and when I looked at it, it made me think of his steady gaze.

He hummed with approval. "That's it, you're doing it."

I peeked my eyes open just in time to see him lifting his hand away from mine. He gave me the barest hint of a smile. "See? You got this."

I blew out a shaky breath. "Yeah." And then I remembered what I'd done to his childhood home. "Oh, Beckett, I'm so sorry. Your house . . ."

"Nothing a little magic can't fix."

"Yes, but that brings me to my point." Zinnia moved in closer to me. "Now that you're fully ascended, you'll have to learn to control those powers."

She held her hand out and summoned the ball back to her palm. It floated over to her the way a balloon would. It stopped just above her fingertips. "Astrid, if I didn't take out some of your power, you might not have survived the ascension. Your body was built to hold all of this but not when it's all exploding at once."

Some of my powers weren't even in my body. Zinnia was holding them like a decoration. They were mine. I was supposed to have them. Did that mean I was deficient in some way? That I wasn't supposed to be a warlock? No, it couldn't! I was the last in the Lockwood line. My blood unlocked the pandora configuration. Emotions warred within me. I was terrified of what my powers did to this house, to the others standing around me, but most of all my own powers almost killed me. How could that be right?

The house was covered in dirt, and a hole the size of a swimming pool gave a whole new meaning to the word skylight. Even Zinnia still looked a bit like she'd been in a battle. I could only imagine what I looked like.

"Wasn't it like that for the rest of you?"

I wanted them to say yes, to tell me their ascension went as poorly as mine had.

Instead Ophelia ducked her head to meet my gaze. "You're a very powerful warlock, Astrid. Everyone's ascension is different."

Had Beckett just winced at that? I was exhausted down to my bones and a heavy feeling sat in the pit of my stomach. "That doesn't make me feel any better."

"Look at it this way. You got your powers and we all survived it. Best to keep moving forward, learn how to use them properly than worry about things that couldn't be helped." She shrugged it off as if destroying property and nearly killing people was no big deal.

I ran my hand through my hair. "I feel like I got hit by a train."

Tuck gave a humorless chuckle. "You pretty much did. A magical school bus . . . welcome to the big leagues."

Beckett cleared his throat. "Maybe we should let her get some rest?"

"I agree she needs to rest, and the queens and I will be back to check on her soon. But I have to explain this first." Zinnia held the ball up. "A piece of your magic is in here. As you start to master what you have, then you can come and grab more here. Just place your hand on it and picture it coming to you. It will only work if your hand is in contact with the orb. But be careful. This is a lot of magic and there are many people who would love to own it."

I reached for the orb and Zinnia placed it in my hand. The outside of it felt like cool glass, but inside the golden magic instantly swarmed toward my hands and gathered there yet didn't seep through the orb. I could feel it wanting to come to me, to come home. But I knew I wasn't ready. There was so much in me already. It seethed within like a dark tide ready to rise up and drag me under. Would this little bit finally do it?

"Okay. Thank you."

"You're welcome. And, Astrid"—she ducked her head to catch my eye—"I know you will get this, just one day at a time."

I nodded. "Right, yes, one day at a time."

"Beck, I really have to get back now. There's no telling what could've happened while I was gone."

Tuck ran a hand over the back of his neck. "Yeah, about that. Two words. Matteaus and fountain."

Zinnia pressed her fingers to her temples and began rubbing them in rhythmic circles. "Not again. He's going to kill me this time. I swear. Who was it?"

Blue magic seeped from Beckett's hand and gathered into a perfect ball. He tossed it at the wall and an oval-shaped portal opened up. "That'll put you right back at the scene of the crime."

"Ugh, thanks. Duty calls." Zinnia leaned over the side of the bed and gave me a quick hug. "I'll see you soon."

I knew she meant it as friendly, but I felt nervous for our next meeting already. I plastered a fake smile on my face. "Till next time."

Ophelia jumped up from the couch. "I'm going to

go too. I love it when Matteaus loses his shit. It's so great."

The three of them disappeared through the portal, leaving only Beckett and me . . . alone. For the first time since we came back from our little quest. Silence hung heavy in the air between us. I didn't know what to say or do, but I did know one thing. I wanted out of this room. But I wasn't sure how my body would do walking up the stairs. "Um, Beckett?"

"Yeah?"

"I'd really love a shower and to be in my own bed. I'm still kind of tired." I peeked up at him.

He shuffled from one foot to the other then hesitated to come closer. "Oh, um, okay, I can go get one of the girls to help you."

I didn't want one of them, though they were all nice and yes, girls, but I didn't know them. I knew Beckett and though he pissed me off, for some reason I felt comfortable with him down to my core. "Maybe you could help me?"

CHAPTER 11

BECKETT

hen she peeked up at me with those hypnotic emerald eyes, I couldn't say no. If only she knew the power she had over me. Astrid slid off the bed, but the second her feet hit the ground, her knees gave out and she collapsed. I jumped forward and caught her before she hit the ground. Her body trembled. This close I felt her every move. I wrapped one arm around her back, holding her up.

"I can carry you if you like?" *Did my voice just dip lower?*

She shook her head. "Can we just take it slow?"

"Sure." I guided her toward the door. Though her steps were slow going, she was stronger than she thought. *My strong girl.*

"I shouldn't have touched that needle." She shook her head and the faint smell of strawberries drifted up my nose. This close my body thrummed with awareness for her.

"No, you shouldn't have."

We started down the hall leading toward the foyer. Her footsteps were light and shuffling. She was so small, so fragile. Her head barely came up to my chin and yet she had so much power I could already feel it seething within her.

She made a sound in the back of her throat like a groan. "You're supposed to say it's okay."

"Okay." I chuckled.

At the bottom of the stairs in the foyer, she looked up at it like it was Mount Everest and sighed. I pressed my fingers to her back.

"You want to give the stairs a try?"

She slowly lifted her leg and placed it on the bottom step. As she forced herself to step up, she groaned. "Ugh, yeah."

I held her arms, helping her take the next one. "You're alive. Some warlocks don't survive the ascension." Golden smoke seeped from her palms and I could tell the effort it was taking for her to climb these stairs was taking its toll on her. Her arms quaked and she had a death grip on my hand.

"Screw this." I tilted her to the side and swept my other arm under her legs. I scooped her up close to my chest and held her there. "Better?"

She sighed and relaxed her body. "Better, but once I'm good, don't think you're just going to pick me up and carry me places."

"I wouldn't dream of it." I chuckled and walked up the stairs with ease. She was so slight, yet so fierce. Deep down I was glad we were fated. Even if I couldn't have her.

I walked with her in my arms down the hall and around the corner to her room. The rightness of the moment coursed through me. When we stood outside her door, I suddenly grew nervous. What was I supposed to do now? I didn't know. All I knew was she was going to tell me how she wanted this to go down and I was going to keep *every* feeling I had to myself. Astrid reached down and turned the knob to her room and shoved the door open. The morning sun peeked in through the sides of the shades. It gave the room a warm, dim look. To my right stood her bed with a multitude of pillows all clad in black sheets. Directly across from me up against the windows was a single desk with a pair of jeans hanging off the chair and to my left was the door to the bathroom.

"You sure you want me to help you?" I whispered even though it was just the two of us and Odin.

She swallowed. "Yeah."

All righty then. I squared my shoulders and carried her to the bathroom. Again she reached out and opened the door for both of us. I stepped in and stood there for just a moment, unsure of what to do next. When Astrid first got here, she'd manifested her room into what she wanted it to be. Black and white marble tiles ran the expanse of the bathroom. To my right was an oversized soaker tub. To my left was a vanity fit for a queen complete with mirror and lighting. Across the way on the entire back wall was a glass shower with multiple shower heads, matching marble tile, and a stool.

In the middle of the bathroom there was a white fluffy carpet. I placed Astrid on her feet on top of it. She swayed, then grabbed a hold of the sink. "I feel so awful. I should be able to do this myself."

"I remember what it was like to get my full powers and, trust me, I was just as bad off." I shrugged.

She held the counter with a death grip. "Perhaps a bath instead of a shower?"

Do not be an idiot. Keep it together, do not look! I swallowed and shook myself. "A bath might be easier."

I moved to the tub and turned the knobs until

steaming water began to flow. I ran my fingers under the water. "Okay, got that going."

A blush colored her cheeks and she smiled at me. "Is this as awkward as I think it is?"

Oh hell yes it is. "No, not at all."

"How about some bubbles?" She tucked a lock of her hair behind her ear.

Before I could reach for the bottle of bubble bath, the tub filled with them. "Your magic is already showing."

Her eyes widened. "I did that?"

"Oh yeah." I glanced around the bathroom. "Do you, um, want help getting undressed?"

She arched her eyebrow at me and her cheeks pinkened. "Did you just ask to see me naked?"

"No? Yes? I mean no." I cleared my throat. *Shit.*

She turned her body and leaned back on the sink then unbuttoned the top button of her jeans. My eyes locked on hers with laser focus. Her fingers were nimble as she opened the fly. I glanced down at my own fly. *Stand down, soldier, or I will chop you off.* The only things I could hear were my own breaths and the sound of that zipper inching down. I swallowed around the nervous ball in my throat. Astrid pushed her pants down to the middle of her thighs, revealing cute black panties, plain yet sexy as hell.

"Can you get them from here?"

My palms were covered in sweat. My insides twisted with nerves. *Keep it calm.* "No problem."

I will cut you off, you traitor. I squatted down and hooked my fingers in the belt loops of her jeans and slowly pulled them down her legs. Her skin was pale and smooth. She was so soft, like silk. Goose bumps broke out across her skin. *I'm not the only one affected here.* I hooked them from her ankles one at a time then tossed them aside and rose.

She stifled a pained flinch as she lifted her hands over her head. "Off, please."

I grabbed the hem of her shirt. *Do not look down. Do not look down.* I locked eyes with her and yanked her shirt up and over her head with one quick movement. *I can do this.* My eyes bore into hers. Tension pulsed between us. "Anything else?"

"Yeah, close your eyes."

I shut them tight, wanting to do at least this right for her. I'd messed up by calling her just my friend in front of the others when she was so much more. I felt her small hand on my forearm. I stiffened, helping her to keep her balance. "Are you okay?"

"Yeah, I'm just taking my bra off."

Leave it to my brain to try and picture exactly what

that looked like. I shook my head. *Don't go there.* "Okay."

"Just hold still."

"Got it." I wanted to whistle or hum, anything to take my mind off the fact I was standing in a room with my soul mate naked in front of me for the first time . . . and I couldn't look.

"Whoaaaaaa." Astrid's hand slipped from my arm and she tipped forward, falling into me.

I didn't open my eyes, but I reached out, catching her so she wouldn't fall. With her arm in one hand and something warm, soft, and firm in the other, I held her close. "Astrid?"

"Um, Beckett?"

"Yeah."

"Does that feel like my arm to you?" She giggled.

I gave both my hands a squeeze. In one hand I definitely felt bone, but in the other was something soft and delicious. "Not really."

"Then maybe you should, you know, not keep holding it." She laughed out right.

"Shit." I dropped that hand as if I'd burned her. *I'm an idiot.* "I didn't mean to."

"Oh, I know. How could you know? You're being a perfect gentleman." She guided me to the right toward where I pictured the bath. "I mean, all the queens were gone and who else could I trust with this? Maze? Cross?"

Over my dead body. I would kill them both. "No."

She tilted to the side and the sound of sloshing water hit my ears. Then her weight shifted back and she went down even lower. When her hands fell away from mine, she signed. "You can open your eyes now."

I looked at the ceiling. "You sure?"

"I'm sure."

I drew my gaze down and took in Astrid lying back in the tub covered in bubbles. Only her knee and head peeked out from within the bubbles. Everything else was covered. "You look . . ."

"Like crap? I know." She ran her hand over her face, washing away some of the dirt smudges from her cheek.

"I was going to say lovely."

She smiled up at me. "I've never been this sore in my life."

"I know. It's like every muscle in your body has been ripped apart and put back together." I took a step back toward the door. "I'll leave you to it."

"Beckett?"

I hesitated. "Yeah?"

"Can you stay for a few mins longer?" She bit her

bottom lip. "I just want some company. I almost died and I don't want to be alone right now."

"I'll stay with you." *Always.* I swallowed around the ball in my throat.

If I had lost her, I didn't know what I would do. Life would never be the same now and whether or not we were together, I wanted her here with me. I walked back toward the tub and sat on the floor across from her. All I could see was her dark locks hanging over the side of the tub and her delicate face. Her features were so beautiful, with her small pert nose and too full lips. Her wide emerald eyes stood out against her pale skin. She slid under the water and came back up. Her hair was soaked and clung to her face. She ran her fingers through it then twisted it into a knot at the top of her head. I grew entranced watching her running her fingers through those strands. Everything about her was distracting, so much so that we sat in silence for long moments before she spoke.

"Did it hurt?"

I shook myself. "Did what hurt?"

"Did I hurt you when my powers came out? The others, they looked like they were in rough shape. Especially Zinnia." She bit her bottom lip.

"It wasn't easy, but no, I wasn't hurt." I lifted my knee and rested my arm across it. The same arm where, if I hadn't been wearing a glamour, my soul mate mark would show. Those two perfect lines running next to each other with two small circles intersecting.

"Can I ask you a question?" She lifted her arm and let it rest on the side of the tub.

My eyes locked on the lingering bubbles on her skin and I watched as each of them popped and faded to nothing, revealing more of her skin to me. "Yes."

"I thought I saw a mark on my wrist earlier."

My heart shot into overdrive. I thought I'd glamoured it before she could see it. I forced my voice to be steady. "What kind of mark?"

"I don't know, it was like two black lines, one thicker than the other, running around my wrist almost like a tattoo. Do you know what it was or is? Sometimes I kind of think it's still there even though I can't see it. Does that sound crazy?"

"Not crazy at all." *Be cool, be casual . . . lie.* I waved my hand and let the glamour drop from her wrist.

She sucked in a breath and held it up to me. "How did you do that?"

"I glamoured it earlier."

"What's a glamour?" She examined the two little circles, tracing them with the tip of her finger. Would she trace the one on my wrist too? I wanted her to.

I could almost picture lying next to her while she did it. "It's a kind of magic to hide things. You can do anything from little tricks like change your hair color to big things like hide an entire building."

"Okay, so why are you hiding this mark on my wrist? What does it mean?" She held it out to me to let me look.

Oh, I have looked at it. All night long. I'd thought about it and all the things I could've made up and the answer only came to me ten minutes before she slipped her little body down into that water. "I wanted to hide it so no one knew about it. It's a tie to that orb Zinnia gave you. A tie to your magic if you will. But I don't want anyone knowing that thing even exists. If they did . . ."

Her eyebrows rose with concern. "You think they'd go after it?"

I waved my hand and muttered the spell once more. The mark vanished from her wrist and part of me hated the fact it wasn't there. The part of me that wanted to claim her for my own. The part I couldn't give into. "I know they would."

CHAPTER 12

ASTRID

I expected Beckett to sneak a peek at something, but not one time did his eyes waver from mine or drift downward. Either he was a gentleman through and through, or he had no interest whatsoever in me. He dropped my robe on my shoulders and I quickly tied it around my waist. Then I turned to face him. Though I ached all over, I felt my strength returning quicker than I expected. "I'm surprised how much better I feel after the bath."

"And your newfound power. I suspect it's helping you heal faster." He held his hand out to me. "Let's get you to bed. At least for the rest of the day."

I crossed my arms over my chest and the movement felt stiff. "Is that an order?"

"No, it's a recommendation." He held up his

fingers, only an inch apart. "And maybe just a little bit of an order."

He held his hand out to me. "To bed then?"

Yes, please? No, down, girl, down. I took his hand and let him guide me to my bed. He pulled the ball of covers off my bed and motioned for me to get in. I quickly lay down and huddled into my robe. Beckett raised the blanket up and over his head, then let the air catch it and drift down over me. "Thank you for helping me out. You didn't have to."

"I wanted to." He sat at the foot of my bed. "Astrid, now that your powers have come, we're going to have to step up your training." Locks of his blond hair fell into his eyes. I wanted to reach out and brush them back, but I lay still as stone. When he looked at me like that, all soft with concern, I felt myself wanting to do whatever he asked.

My pillows were so warm and cushiony behind my head that I relaxed back into them. "I know."

He rose to his feet. "I'll go get your grimoire and maybe you can take a look at it later today after you've had more time to rest."

"No need." I held my hands out and pictured my family book within my grasp. The grimoire appeared right on top of my hands. I placed it on the bed in between us.

"Impressive." He reached out and flipped the book open. His eyebrows rose and he turned them one after the other. "Ummm, Astrid, why are the pages blank?"

"What do you mean?" I leaned forward with my heart in my throat. We hadn't come all this way for a blank book of nothing. I reached for the book and pulled it into my lap. Golden smoke poured from my hands the second my fingers touched the pages. They flooded with writing, pictures, and geometric shapes. "Holy crap. Is that supposed to happen?"

"When it comes to being a warlock, there are no rules." He held his hand out. "May I?"

I dropped the book into his hands and the pages immediately went blank. "Maybe it's some kind of protection."

"Exactly." He held it up to eye level, examining the weathered pages. They were an aged cream with spots of brown on them. When I reached out to take the book back, he held it away from me. "Hold on a sec. Let's see if you can make them appear from there?"

"How?" I didn't know if I was capable of doing what he asked. My magic was operating on its own at this point. Control might be asking for a lot right after my ascension.

"You're overthinking it." He turned the book

around to face me the way teachers did when reading to the class.

I held my hand up and called upon my magic. It rose like a tidal wave in me. Darkness crashed and I felt smoke pour from my hands. It seeped over the sides of my bed and up onto the book in Beckett's hands. The pages glowed like the rays of sunshine, and Beckett closed his eyes against it. He turned his head away as the words flooded back onto the pages along with everything that'd been there before.

"Astrid, I think that's enough." He held the book away from his body. The muscles of his arms shook and he rose to his feet and held the book out in front of him while he lunged to keep his balance.

But I didn't want to stop. It felt good to let the magic flow. My sourness disappeared, my energy increased, and I felt ready to take on anything. I smiled and watched as the pages flipped of their own accord. Each one filled then flipped to the next one.

"Astrid, stop!" Beckett shoved the book closed then threw his hand out. A pulse of blue magic pressed against my chest, like a gentle hand forcing me to lie back on my pillows.

I closed my hands and smothered my power. I sucked in a deep heaving breath and some of it still seeped from me, but I was back in control.

Beckett smacked the book together and tossed it onto the bed next to me. He hunched over with his hands on his knees and sucked in deep breaths. "That was interesting."

I wanted to shy away from the power that'd exploded out of me so easily, but it was warm, comforting. I felt strong, almost unstoppable when I called upon it. "You told me to."

"Control, Astrid. You need to learn control." He tapped the cover of the book. "Time to start practicing."

"Beck . . ." I wanted to tell him I was sorry, but I wasn't really sorry.

He waved my words away as he stood up straight. "Get some rest and I'll come back later."

Before I could say another word, he walked toward the door and wrapped his hand around the knob. He paused and glanced at me over his shoulder. "Read and rest."

So much for not being bossy. "Okay, boss."

His back stiffened, but he didn't say another word and simply walked out of the room. Just as I was about to open the book, Odin wiggled out from under the covers beside me. "That was intense."

I pressed my hand to my head. "I know, right?"

Odin lay down and spread out next to me. His

voice was low and hissing. "I like him. He gave me this stuff called fried chicken last night. We're now best friends."

"Don't you hop on the I love Beckett train." I pulled the book into my chest and little puffs of smoke drifted from my hands.

He rolled over onto his back and extended his legs out. "Too late. Tomorrow I'm going to see if he'll give me potatoes."

"Potatoes? Cats don't eat potatoes."

"I am the wrong animal." He sat up and started to lick his paw. "Ew." Lick. "Yuck." Lick. "Blah."

"If you don't like it, then why are you doing it?" I stifled the urge to laugh.

He put his paw down and flipped over to a sit. "Cat videos. I have to be a cat. Cats lick." He jumped up onto my headboard and walked across the edge to my nightstand where he stood before my cell phone. "This buzzy thing buzzes a lot. I found it in the kitchen and brought it up here."

"Thanks." I grabbed my phone off the dresser and quickly punched in the code. "One hundred and thirty-two texts? Damn it."

It'd been a little over a week since my birthday and I hadn't talked to Tilly, not really. She was more than my best friend, she was my sister and I all but disappeared. I wanted to text her so bad and tell her about this place. About Warwick Academy, about Beckett, about nearly dying. At some point I was going to have to figure out a way to handle all this. I just didn't want to lose her or lose us. She was the only family I had. *No, wait, one text from my dad.*

Hey, pumpkin, headed to Bora Bora for a week or two. Everything okay at school? They called a week ago and said you hadn't been there.

"Way to be concerned about where I am, Dad." I quickly hit my reply. *Found a new Boarding School in CT. I'm loving it. Decided to stay. Have fun in Bora Bora. Xoxo- A*

Those three little dots popped up and his response came a moment later. *Okay, honey. Have fun.*

That just isn't normal. Aren't parents supposed to, I don't know. Care? He spent most of my life in court rooms around the country and leaving me to my own devices. But just one time I'd like him to show some concern. But without him being absent I never would've gotten so close to Tilly. I sighed and moved to the next set of texts . . . Tilly.

There were exactly one hundred and twenty-two messages from her. The last one ended in, *I have a certain skill set I have acquired over the years. Skills that come in handy for these types of situations. I will hunt you down and I will find you . . . watch your back, hooker. I'm coming.*

We had officially reached Defcon-Tilly. She was going to kill me when I finally did see her. I opened up the text and started to type out some kind of lame excuse, but we were beyond that now and I had no idea what to say, so I went with the simplest answer I could.

I knew I shouldn't have let you watch that movie. I hit send.

The bubbles appeared right away. *Human trafficking is a real thing, Astrid. It's a real thing. You could be dead in a ditch somewhere texting me in your ghost form. Are you a ghost?!?*

Definitely not a ghost. I wanted to tell her I was a warlock, but I couldn't. Those bubbles appeared on her end once more and I just wanted to hit that call button. Instead, I sent a quick text. *GTG, text later, good luck on the hunt . . .*

My phone buzzed with more messages, but I couldn't do this. I knew avoiding her wasn't the answer, but until I figured out what the answer was, I needed to step back. I wanted to keep her safe and this world, hell I, was dangerous to be around. Instead, I opened up a text thread to the only girl I could actually talk to.

Sooooo I ascended last night.

At the top of the screen with two little snake emojis was Medusa's name. She replied instantly. *OMG!!! That's exciting. Was Beckett there? I bet he was.*

Yeah, he was there . . . I almost died. I still don't feel great.

My FaceTime immediately began to ring and I hit the little green button, accepting the call from Medusa. "Hey."

She held the phone so close to her face then smacked one of her snakes out of the way. "Oh, honey, you do look like death. Are you okay?"

I cleared my throat. "Yeah, I survived." I pressed my hand to my head. "Barely, I put a hole in the ceiling and nearly destroyed Beckett's house."

"Bet he wasn't mad, was he?" She wagged her eyebrows at me.

"He didn't seem mad. He even helped me . . ." I lowered my voice. "Take a bath."

A high-pitched squeal came through the phone. "Oh . . . my . . . God. Did he sponge off your back?"

"Nooooo."

"Your front? Girl, you are naughty!" The picture on the phone moved like Medusa was walking around her cave. Then she jumped and flopped back on her bed.

I shook my head. "No, he didn't even look. I'm one

hundred percent sure he's not even the littlest bit interested."

"Girl, you are not seeing what I saw. He was probably just trying not to pop a boner. It would be frowned upon if he did."

I pulled my blankets up and curled on my side. "I'm not sure and to top it all off I can't even talk to my best friend, who's more like a sister. I just miss her."

"What's this friend's name again?" Medusa tickled one of her snakes under its chin then pushed it away.

"Ugh, Tilly. And she's so upset with me and I can't leave here. I could really hurt someone with this new crazy power I have."

"You couldn't hurt me."

"I'm sure I could. I'll probably be locked in this place for the rest of my life." I gave a humorless chuckle.

"Nah, Gregor used to come here all the time and mess around with that book of his." She sat up straight and squealed. "Did you unlock the book?"

I turned my phone and gave her a shot of it sitting on the bed next to me. "It's right here."

"Oh, Astrid, this is going to be fantastic! You should bring it here and we can mess around with it."

I chuckled. "You're like the only person who wants me to mess around with my powers."

"Yeah, let's do it and pizza too. Okay?"

I yawned and though it was morning I felt like it was midnight. "Yeah, for sure."

"You look tired, so just text me when you're coming over, okay? I'm available at any time."

"Oh, I definitely need girl time with pizza." My eyes felt heavy and exhaustion ate me.

"K.K. chat later." She disconnected the call and I rolled onto my back.

Odin walked up next to me and curled on his side against me. "Sleep. I will keep watch."

For some strange reason that made me feel better and I let sleep take me under.

CHAPTER 13

I paced back and forth in my room. The grimoire sat on the foot of my bed wide-open. After I slept for nearly a whole day it was late afternoon and I'd already spent the past few hours reading my grimoire trying to make any of it work for me. But nothing was happening, nothing but a blown-up pillow, a ton of smoky magic, and frustration coursing through me. And I was only on page two.

Odin sat on my desk and knocked a bottle of nail polish on the floor. Then he moved to a cup full of pens. "What's wrong with you?"

"I'm a cat now, it's what we do . . ."

"You like being a jerk? Seriously?" I shoved the pens back into the cup. They clattered together when I slammed them back on the desk.

"I am a demon, so yep." He licked his paw and ran it over his head.

"I'm going to ban you from videos, mister." I turned back toward the book and leaned over it. "Just have to figure this out."

A knock sounded on my door and I called out, "Yeah."

"Can I come in?" Beckett called back.

"Sure. I'm dressed this time." I didn't turn to look at him. My eyes were locked on the pages of the book. I bit my bottom lip. "But how do I . . ."

Beckett leaned in next to me and his clean fresh scent hit me. "Anything I can help with?"

I shook my head. "No, I can get this. I know I can."

He pressed his hand to the small of my back and electricity shot up my spine. He leaned in. "Don't put too much pressure on yourself. Just let it come naturally."

I turned to face him. "How can you say that? Last night I blasted you with power. Who knows who else I'm going to hurt! And did you see the hole in the ceiling in the kitchen, because I sure as hell did."

He took a small step back and held his hands up in surrender. "Think I know what you need. Just give me like an hour and we'll get this all straightened out."

CHAPTER 14

ASTRID

A short time later the sun had gone down and I'd spent the whole day trying to do one little spell and it just didn't freaking work. There was another knock on my door, but I just didn't have time for it. "Beck, I-I just want to be left alone, okay?"

The door flew open and smacked into the wall with a loud thump. Odin flew off the bed with a start, his back arched and his fur puffed out in straight spikes. My head snapped up to see Ophelia standing in the doorway. "Wrong answer!"

She had a big sack hooked over her shoulder. "Where should I put my stuff?" She stepped into the room and walked in between the side of my bed and the windows. I opened my mouth to ask her what was going on, but she cut me off with the wave of her hand. "Never mind, here is good."

She grabbed the bottom of her bag then turned it upside down and dumped the entire thing on the floor. Vials, clothes, a pillow, and several books spilled out. She dropped the bag then hopped on my bed. "Okay, I'm good."

"Jeez, O, don't you have a room down the hallway?" Zinnia strolled in with a small backpack on her shoulder. She dropped it on the ground just beside the door and looked up at me. "Is this okay here?"

"Um, yes?"

Nova came in next in a pair of baggy black men's sweatpants that swallowed her tiny waist and dragged on the floor. She too dropped her bag down on top of Zinnia's. "Wow, Astrid, you have a nice room."

"Thanks?" I turned to face them.

Serrina followed behind Nova. She had her hair pulled into a messy bun on top of her head, a ripped up Guns N' Roses T-shirt and a pair of dingy worn-in leggings on. Though she wore no makeup, she was still one of the most beautiful girls I'd ever seen, with model good looks. She smiled down at me. "Hey, what's up?"

"Um, nothing. What's up with you?" I sat on the foot of my bed and watched Tabi enter next. She wore a tie-dyed shirt and pants matching set. "It's been a while since we've had one of these."

I looked at them all. "One of what?"

"I do believe this is what the ladies like to refer to as a sleepover, love." A boy walked through the door with so much grace I had to do a double take. His hair was shorter but fell back from his face in unruly chocolate waves. He was as tall as Beckett but had an air of class about him that I hadn't seen in any of the boys here. When he smiled at me, I felt the blood rush to my face.

Are those fangs?

"I-I didn't plan a sleepover." I didn't know what to make of all these people in my room. No one had warned me and I really had no idea what to do.

With so much speed I barely saw him, the boy raced across the room and lay out on my bed with his hands behind his head and his ankles crossed. "No need to plan. I think we've got the right of it. We come over and we sleep here. Isn't that right, ladies?"

Oh God, that British accent was delicious and those deep brown eyes with mahogany in them. This guy was *fine.* Though he lay in my bed, he didn't rumble his black jeans, the white shirt, or that black jacket. Beckett strolled into the room, and with the wave of his hand, he picked up a pillow with his magic and tossed it at the boy, hitting him right in the face. "Grayson, I don't recall you being invited."

"He can stay if he wants to." I threw my hand over my mouth. *Did I just say that out loud?*

The muscle in Beckett's jaw ticked yet he said nothing. Grayson hunkered down on my bed and sighed. "See that, mate. I've been invited." He waved his hand toward the door. "Now sod off and leave the rest of us to it."

"Grayson." Beckett growled in a warning tone.

"All right, all right." He gracefully came to a stand and walked over to me. He held his hand out to me. "Grayson Shade, from the House of Shade at your service."

I placed my hand in his. "What's the House of Shade?"

"Vampires, love." He winked and brought my hand to his mouth and pressed a light kiss to the back of it. "And you are as lovely as Beckett said."

"All right, that's enough." Beckett grabbed Grayson's shoulder and yanked him back then shoved him toward the door. "Aren't you supposed to be home dealing with things? I do recall Matteaus sending us both back."

Grayson shrugged. "Things are *complicated*. Besides, with you here we were one knight down. I couldn't very well leave the lot of you shorthanded, could I?" He ran his eyes over me then over Beckett. "Perhaps we should stay?"

"Out." Beckett chuckled as he shoved the vampire toward the door.

"Bloody hell, man, I'm going." He took a step down the hall. "You're a right git for spoiling my fun."

Beckett rolled his eyes. "Sorry about that. He kind of goes where the queens go."

I took a step toward Beckett and lowered my voice. "What are they all doing here?"

He leaned in closer to me. "You were kind of freaking out, so I called in reinforcements." He took a step back and grabbed the doorknob. "Have fun."

With that, he shut the door, leaving me alone with five girls I barely knew and apparently we were having a sleepover? When I turned to face them, I plastered a smile on my face. "Um, hey, guys. Thanks for coming. I didn't know Beckett called you."

Ophelia bent down and looked Odin in his eye. "Your cat has one eye."

"Yup."

"I like it." She scratched him under the chin. "So are we all sleeping on the floor or what?"

"Oh, I could go out and look for some air mattresses or something?" I honestly had no idea what to do here. The only sleepovers I'd ever had were with Tilly and she wasn't here. If she were, this would be going a lot smoother.

"Do you think you have to?" Zinnia sat on the floor and crossed her legs. "I think you can do it from there."

I glanced around at the others and they all sat expecting something from me. "What do you mean?"

"I mean you have all this power. It's time to use it. Hell, have a little fun once in a while. You just have to relax and let it, you know, flow."

If only they knew . . . *that's what I'm afraid of.* This churning darkness in me just waiting to come out. But I didn't want to embarrass myself in front of the most powerful witches in the world. I closed my eyes and pictured five cots set up in a circle to include my own bed. There was a round of "nice, sweet, whoa, and thank God, I did not want to sleep on the floor."

I peeked my eyes open and sighed with relief. There were five perfect beds, each with white fluffy blankets and huge pillows. Zinnia sat on hers the same way she'd been sitting on the floor. Tabi stood in the middle of her bed for a second before she dropped down. Serrina lay out on hers like it'd always been there.

Ophelia picked up the stuff she'd dumped on the

floor and threw it all on top of the bed she claimed. "Why did I bring so much crap again?"

Zinnia rolled her eyes. "So was it as difficult as you thought?"

I shook my head. "If only the book were that simple."

"All right then, you want us to look at it and give you some pointers?" She looked so normal with her crazy hair and sitting there in her pajamas and yet she was a freaking queen of all witches. People followed her, followed her rules, and she was going to sleep on a cot in my room. If anyone could help me, it was these girls.

I reached back on the bed and grabbed the book then walked in the middle of them all and opened it up. "Honestly I keep trying these spells and nothing is working."

"You know what would really help this situation?" Ophelia leaned in closer to the book. "If I could actually see the pages."

"Oh, right." I opened up my magic and my palms warmed as golden smoked seeped from them.

The pages filled with words once more and there was a collective gasp from the queens.

Tabi chuckled. "It's got built-in protection. Cool."

I raised my eyebrows. "Your grimoires don't do this?"

"Honey, we don't have grimoires just stacks of books that we have to filter through. I wish we had grimoires for our casts. It would've made learning our powers much easier." She sighed then sat down on the floor in front of her bed. "Circle up."

They all grabbed pillows and blankets from the beds and dragged them to the floor. In a matter of minutes we had a soft lounge on the floor and were hanging out. Nova curled her legs under her. "You know what we need? Pizza with extra cheese."

Ophelia shook her head. "Nah, we need French fries with melted cheese. You can't go wrong with anything potato."

"Popcorn." Serrina laughed. "All fun nights include popcorn."

Zinnia pulled her cell from her back pocket. "I don't think we can get delivery out here. This isn't the City."

"No need." I didn't know why, but I figured if I could make beds for them all, why not a mini buffet? I waved my hand and let my smoke pour over the floor and an array of food appeared: four boxes of pizza, bags of piping hot steak fries with multiple dipping options, bowls of popcorn, and cookies.

"Is this like one of those play pretend things and it's there or is this legit?" Ophelia grabbed a bag of fries and reached in. She shoved them in her mouth and groaned around her bite. "Oh, it's real."

Zinnia shook her head. "Leave it to my sister to shove things in her mouth and ask questions later."

Ophelia threw a fry at her. "I'm not the one sleeping with a bird."

"No, you're the one torturing a deadly warlock until he goes crazy." Zinnia grabbed the fry off her shirt and popped it into her mouth.

This was all so normal and not at all what I expected. "You guys are not what I thought you'd be." I grabbed up a slice of pizza and took a bite. The cheese was nice and hot with a crispy crust, just the way I liked it.

"What did you think we'd be like?" Zinnia held a slice of pizza in each hand and took turns taking a bite from each one.

"I don't know, dancing around under a full moon making blood sacrifices or something like that." I shrugged.

Ophelia turned dead serious. "Oh no, Astrid, that's not what witches do . . . that's what warlocks do. Didn't Beckett tell you?"

I nearly choked on my pizza. "What? Sacrificing what? Like animals?" Panic rose up in my throat.

"Oh yeah, there's a barn in the woods behind the house where they keep the animals. I can't believe he didn't tell you." Ophelia shook her head and sighed. "Yeah, lots of goats."

I dropped my pizza. "I think I'm going to puke."

The others broke out into fits of laughter. Serrina reached into her bowl of popcorn and tossed a few pieces at Ophelia. "She's messing with you. There aren't ritual sacrifices in the warlock world. At least not while Beckett is around. I can't say what the resistance is doing, though. That's a whole other breed of bad."

"Why are they resisting?" I knew Zinnia had killed her father, their leader, only a few weeks ago. But from where I was sitting, she didn't seem like the bad guy.

Ophelia cleared her throat. "There are those who oppose Zinnia's rule. Only because she is a queen witch and not a warlock. There are others who wish to claim what's left of our father's followers for their own greedy needs. But don't you worry, I'll be handling that soon enough."

A dark smile crossed her face and a shiver went down my spine. Whoever was on Ophelia's shit list really had it coming and soon. "So am I the reason the warlocks have resisted so far? Like are you all waiting for me?"

I suddenly felt an immense amount of pressure to become all-powerful to help these girls.

Zinnia shook her head. "Nah, they're just crazy. And Ophelia is overprotective because we are all each other has."

"Oh, I know how that is. My mom is gone and, well, my dad is pretty much MIA. Is your mom gone too?"

They all froze and glanced from Zinnia to Ophelia and back again. Zinnia's gaze fell to the floor and her eyes held a sheen of unshed tears. "My mom is very sick and she hasn't been conscious for a while now." She sniffled. "We are really close and I miss her a lot even though I go to see her almost every day. It's not the same when she can't talk to me. But I have faith she'll get better soon. Beckett is helping me and so is O."

Silence hung in the air around us and I instantly regretted bringing it up. "I'm so sorry."

How was Beckett going to help? It just made me that much more curious as to what exactly he was supposed to be doing for Zinnia besides get the warlocks under control. I didn't know how I felt about it, knowing he had so much on his plate yet still tried to help. Somehow it made me feel softer toward him.

"Let's not talk about it, okay?" Zinnia shook herself and plastered a smile on her face. "Come on, let's play with that book a bit?"

I sucked in a sigh of relief. I wasn't the best at getting myself out of socially awkward situations, especially ones that I caused. I grabbed the book and pulled it back into my lap. "I just don't get how this works. I keep saying the spell and nothing happens."

Nova reached over and took a handful of popcorn and shoved it into her mouth. "Let's hear it."

Glad to put on a show for you. I was the noob in this group and I felt like I was standing in front of a classroom . . . naked. I cleared my throat. "Eyes to see, ears to hear, touch and taste as my senses do appear. Change it now by fire light and appear to the world which I envision as my sight."

I glanced around and shrugged. "See, nothing happens."

"There's a rhythm to a spell. You need to have feeling behind it, believe in what you're saying." Zinnia motioned for the book and I handed it over. She thumbed the page I was looking at then turned toward me. "Okay, so this is a glamour spell, right? But what were you picturing you were changing?"

"I don't know. I was thinking about making myself blond or something."

She wrinkled her nose. "Don't ever go blond. Red suits you. But let's make it more fun. How about you give Serrina a beard or something?"

Serrina giggled and sat up straight. "I was hoping for a smaller ass, but I'll take a beard. Hit me."

"Okay, now here's something different I'm seeing in your book. Apparently because you're part of the manifestation class, once you master this spell you won't need to say it. You can call it to your powers and let it flow. Which means once you master the spells in this book you might master your powers." Zinnia's eyes were bright with excitement. "That's cool."

It actually really was cool. "Okay, so I have to say it with conviction?"

"Close your eyes and really picture Serrina with that beard." Her voice was soft yet commanding. I closed my eyes and pictured her with a long full beard. Like a lumberjack who hadn't shaved in years. Zinnia continued, "Now let your magic go, don't be afraid of what it can do, especially in this room. We will all be fine."

I sucked in a deep breath and spoke each word carefully.

"Eyes to see.

Ears to hear.

Touch and taste as my senses do appear.

Change it now by fire light.

Appear to the world which I envision as my sight."

I felt it flowing through me, my power. It rose up and crashed in my chest. I peeked my eyes open and Serrina sat across from me with a beard that ran down to her knees. She broke out into laughter and started braiding it. "This is hilarious."

"See, Astrid, sometimes you just gotta breathe." Zinnia handed the book back to me. "You'll get it. I know you will."

I accepted it back and sighed . . . *no pressure.*

CHAPTER 15

*A*strid sat on the couch in the parlor with her grimoire lying across her lap. After last night's sleepover, her stress level dropped and she smiled while reading. Odin lay beside her flat on his back. She absently ran her fingers over his stomach as little puffs of magic drifted up from her hands. It felt right, that she was healthy and happy. And here with me. I loved seeing the color in her cheeks and the life in her eyes. Her magic made her strong, stronger than she knew. Just three days after her ascension and she was back to being healthy. I knew her power had something to do with it. I'd seen others take weeks to recover. But here she was looking all cute in her black leggings and off the shoulder black sweater.

Her hair spilled in long, thick waves over her

shoulder and fell down to her elbow. She was beautiful and she was mine. She just didn't know it yet. The corner of my lip pulled up of its own accord and I couldn't stop it if I wanted to. "Feeling better?"

She tore her eyes away from her book for barely a second. "Yeah, the queens really did help."

"They're not so bad, are they?" After being with the queens for months and fighting against Alataris, I knew each of them had something to bring to the table for Astrid.

"No, I really liked them." She tucked a lock of her hair behind her ear. "And I'm not so scared of this."

She held her hand up and that orb appeared, floating just above her palm. The power swirled within it and even from where I sat across from her I could feel it. "You think you're ready for more?"

She shook her head. "No, but I'm not so terrified of it."

"Good." I leaned back on the couch and crossed my arms over my chest.

"Try not to look so satisfied with yourself," she teased then turned back to her book.

The sound of a ruffling bag came from the hall along with hurried footsteps. Maze rounded the corner like his ass was on fire. He crumpled the bag of chips in his hand and they exploded. His feet slid as he came to stop in front of us. "Incoming! Don't say I didn't warn you!"

Then he took off right up the stairs just as fast as he came in the room. I jumped to my feet. "What does that mean?"

The hinges on the front door creaked as it swung open and banged against the wall. Headmaster Ridge stood in the doorway, looking like he'd not only pressed his own clothing but pressed himself. He wore a three-piece suit made for a butler, complete with pinstripe pants, a gray vest, and a suit coat with tails that ran down to the back of his knees. His wingtip shoes were polished to a shine that matched the oil slicked on his head. He looked down his hooked nose at me and his lips wrinkled in distain, giving me a view of his crooked teeth.

"Professor Ridge, I would say it's nice to see you . . ." I shrugged. "Well, that's it."

"Watch your tone, boy." He stepped over the threshold into the foyer.

Behind him stood a woman who had her hair pulled into a tight bun on top of her head and wore a thick black velvet robe that covered her from neck to toe. Streaks of gray streamed back from her temples and wound in with the rest of her hair. Her face was wrinkled like a prune. Even her lipstick was prune purple. She reminded me of a bullfrog, with the way her eyes bugged out of her head and her bottom lip pushed out farther than her top lip. Even her skin held a greenish tint. Ridge turned and extended his hand out toward her. "May I present Cora Ferguson of the warlock council and Jiovanni Archer."

Jiovanni walked through the door next. He was a slight man with worm-like features. He was barely five and half feet tall, with a bald head, big nose, and small beady eyes. He too had wrinkles from head to toe. Though he was a smaller man, his power was world-renowned, as was his evil. His specialty was punishing those who went against the warlock law, by any means necessary.

I extending my hand out toward him. "Jiovanni, a pleasure to meet you. I've heard so much about you."

He sneered at my outstretched hand. "Yes, young Dustwick, I am sure you have. Though I hope the things I've been hearing about you are a scandalous falsehood."

He brushed past me and walked around the foyer, examining both parlors. His eyes landed on Astrid and he sucked in a breath. "Is this the Lockwood?"

Astrid rose to her feet and walked over to the foyer. "Hello, I'm Astrid."

Cora groaned in disapproval and moved to Jiovanni's side. "The one who caused all the commotion only days ago." She looked her up and down. "I hardly believe *you* are the Lockwood."

"No, I'm *the* Astrid and, yes, the last of the Lockwood line." She held her chin up and met the woman's narrowed gaze with one of her own.

That a girl! I crossed my arms over my chest. "What can I help you with, Headmaster Ridge?"

"Well, there have been rumors going around that things have gotten out of control in this house. Naturally since it's on school property, I felt inclined to"— he tilted his head, looking up the stairs and then down the hall—"check in."

I held my hands out to my sides and motioned to the house. "Well, there is nothing going on. As you can tell everything is calm, the house in clean, and we are all healthy. No need to *intrude*."

Logan walked in from the hall. "Hey, Beck, Maze was supposed to get me a hammer, but he . . ." His words trailed off once he spotted the council. "Mrs. Ferguson, Mr. Archer, nice to see you."

Jiovanni folded his hands behind his back. "Logan Whitmore, you are the image of your father. Hopefully with the same loyalties. Which is more than I can say for Mr. Dustwick here. Your father would—"

"My father would say nothing. Because he isn't

here." I ground my teeth together. Of all the times for him to walk in for construction help. "There's one in the shed out back, Logan."

Logan gave me a tight-lipped nod then headed back into the house. "I'll find it."

"You are quite disrespectful." Cora huffed at me.

I shrugged. "Respect is earned. Not a single one of you has earned mine."

Beside me, Astrid sniggered and pressed her fingers over her mouth to hide her smile. Cora straightened her already pristine robes and huffed at me. The distinct sound of a tapping came from the wooden planks on the front porch. Tap, step, step. Tap, step, step. A large figure filled the door and my heart sped up. Though I didn't show it on the outside, the presence of this man made rage boil in my veins. The last time I saw him was the night my father disappeared and this was the man responsible for it.

"Beckett Dustwick." My name was a growl on his lips and I stiffened.

"Damiel Edwards." I ground my teeth so hard I bit my cheek. The taste of blood filled my mouth.

He stood eye to eye with me. His thick black hair was pulled back from his face and bound together by an old-fashioned black cord. His beard matched the thickness of his hair. The most alarming thing about him were his stark yellow eyes. He tapped his cane on the ground and walked farther into the room. Tap, step, step. I remembered that noise like it was yesterday. I was that young boy again hearing that noise on that horrific night. With every fiber of my being I HATED him. It took everything I had in me not to use that stupid silk cravat he wore to strangle him.

He gazed up at the chandelier in the foyer then into the parlor where Astrid had been sitting. His eyes locked on her orb. "It's come to our attention that a dangerous amount of power exploded here only three days ago. Is that true?"

I curled my hand into a fist at my side. "What would you know about truths?"

A snide smile crossed his face and he gave a humorless chuckle. "Tread carefully with me, boy. I've known you since you were this big." He held his hand at his hip.

I took a step forward and came nose to nose with him. "I'm not so little anymore, am I?"

My magic rose to my hand. I felt it like a second skin, ready to use if I need it. A small hand slipped into mine and I felt her tug me back.

Damiel titled his head to the side and looked her up and down. "What have we here?"

I pulled Astrid behind me. "She's none of your concern."

"On the contrary. That explosion of power is the council's concern. You endangered the rest of Warwick Academy. The students here are under our jurisdiction, our protection." He took a step to the side and once again his eyes locked on Astrid. "You, my dear, are a danger."

She held her chin up and gave him a level look. "Am I the only warlock to ever ascend?"

He looked from me back to her. "Have you taught her nothing?" He shook his head. "No, you are not."

"Right, so if every student who ascends is a danger to the school, seems to me you'd be lacking in students. No matter how powerful they are. Unless there's some school rule I'm missing about not accepting students who ascend, then I think I'm well within my rights to be here." She tapped her finger on her cheek, making an exaggerated thinking motion. "As a matter of fact, I am the last of the Lockwood line, an original founding family. I do believe I have a house here and a place in this school according to your laws, isn't that right, Beck?"

I nodded. "It is indeed."

"So the way I see it, I belong here more than, well, you." She gave him a blank, pleasant smile.

"You might, but that doesn't." He pointed toward the orb.

"It's mine." The smile dropped from her face and I felt her palms begin to warm. I squeezed her fingers silently, willing her to calm the hell down before she blew him up. Though I would love to see that.

Damiel turned toward the other members of the council. "Whether or not it's yours, power like this can't be left lying around. It needs to be safeguarded, protected. Something you're not capable—"

The sound of clanking metal filled the room. A cage dropped around the orb and slammed into the floor. Thick metal poles wound up from the ground through the bars like thorn covered vines. They jutted out with razor-sharp glinting points. A thick metal chain wrapped around the cage then a padlock snapped closed around it.

Damiel chuckled. "Isn't that cute."

He held his hand out and dark navy smoke shot from it at the cage. It wrapped around the bars. The sound of groaning metal filled the room, but a moment later the smoke exploded away from the cage and the orb.

I wanted to scream with triumph, but instead I kept my cool. "Problem solved. The power is protected."

Astrid took a step to stand in front of her orb. "Aww, wasn't that a cute attempt. Now back off."

"I couldn't agree more." Cross came in from the kitchen. He leaned up against the wall and crossed his legs at his ankles. "Back off."

Damiel straightened his stance and whirled around. "Cross Malback."

Cross held his hands out to his sides. "The one and only."

"I recently had the pleasure of speaking to your father. Such an example of what a true warlock should be." He glanced at Ridge. "Isn't that right, Ridge?"

The headmaster nodded like a bobblehead on a dashboard. "Indeed."

Cross took a menacing step forward. "Where is he?"

Damiel shrugged. "Why would I tell you that?"

"I plan on having some . . . *words* with him."

"Well, I'm sure if he wanted to speak to you, he'd find you." Damiel sighed and took a step toward the orb, his eyes flickered with want.

Enough was enough. "It's time for you to go."

All four of them stood there looking at me like I'd sprouted eight heads. Ridge cleared his throat. "You overestimate your importance, Beckett Dustwick."

"This is my house, isn't it? We have all five lines

united together, don't we? So I think it's you who overestimates your importance." I walked past them to the door they hadn't bothered to close. I waved for them to leave.

Damiel stopped just in front of me then glanced over his shoulder at Astrid. "For you to have any claim, you all need to be in control of your powers . . . your full powers. Good luck with that."

Cora tittered and huffed as she followed. "Well, I never in all my years."

"Bu-bye now."

Jiovanni chuckled and shook his head. "You poke the lion."

"He poked me first." I pulled the door open farther so he would get the hint to leave.

He strolled out with his hand behind his back.

Ridge stayed in the foyer for a moment. "I will be watching your every move and if she takes one step out of line, I will be there."

I glanced at Astrid. "She's ready."

But was she really? It didn't matter how much bravado I showed them. Shit just got real. The council knew the lines were uniting, they knew I was heading it up, and above all they knew we had a weak link. Without another word, he walked out the door and I slammed it shut behind him. *It's time to play . . .*

CHAPTER 16

*M*aze came halfway down the stairs with that damn bag of chips in his hands. He reached in and pulled one out. "I warned you."

"Barely, next time details would help, you ass." Beckett ran his hand through his hair and began to pace. He looked more stressed than I'd ever seen him.

"I felt my warning was sufficient." He shoved the chips in his mouth.

Logan strolled in from the hallway with the hammer in hand. "Okay, what the hell did I miss?"

"The council has just drawn war lines." Beckett moved to stand in front of me. When I looked up at him, I knew the easy lightness he'd shown me for the past few days was over. This was a warning shot from the council, and we all heard it loud and clear. They weren't just going to hand over their place to us. They were going to fight. By any means necessary. And Damiel alone was terrifying. I didn't know what the connection was between him and Beckett, all I knew was I could see the hate in Beckett's face. But why was it there?

Beckett curled his hand into a fist. "We need to be ready and soon."

I blew out a breath. "Yeah, no pressure there, bossman."

"I mean it. It's time to study. You need to learn control to be ready before we get more than just a visit from Damiel Edwards."

I crossed my arms over my chest. "What is the thing between you two?"

"I don't know what you're talking about." He walked past me toward the hallway.

I turned and followed closely behind him. "Oh really? You both looked like you were going to kill each other on sight."

"The guy is an ass, Astrid. He will act like your friend one second then stab you in the back the next. For his own greed." He stepped into the kitchen and debris from the roof littered the floor. It crunched under his feet when he turned to face me. "He would kill his own mother and steal her powers if it made him ruler of all warlocks."

"You know this would be a lot easier if you stopped keeping secrets from me."

He wrinkled his nose at me. "What are you talking about? All I'm saying is that we can't afford to waste any more time."

"There is tension between the two of you." Just then Maze, Cross, and Logan walked into the kitchen and I stood between them all. "For that matter you all have known each other since, I don't know, birth. I've been here for a few weeks and you just expect me to learn my powers and fall into line right behind you? I'm not a machine."

"Hey, I was just trying to fix the roof. Don't lump me in with these insensitive fools. I'm in touch with my feminine side." Maze pressed his hand to his chest, trying to look all innocent.

"Oh please, you're just as crazy as the rest of them." I raised my hand toward the room and shot my magic at it. Piece by piece it connected together like doing a puzzle in fast forward. The cabinets righted themselves, the debris cleared, and everything went back to the way it was before I'd ascended.

Beckett arched his eyebrow at me. "If only you could do that all the time and not just when you're

MEGAN MONTERO

pissed at me. I'd hate to have to pick fights with you for all eternity."

"Why not? It's what you do best." How could he have been so considerate, so caring the past few days, and then gone right back to bossy jerk. His mood swings were giving me whiplash.

"If you can't see by now that everything I'm doing is to protect you, then you need to open your eyes. We aren't dealing with some New York socialite threatening to take away your high-class status. These are real warlocks. They kill the ones they love." He sucked in a breath and his face grew bright red. His eye shimmered. The muscle in his jaw ticked as he ground his teeth. "They kill them for no good goddamn reason."

"Right, because I'm playing at being a warlock. In case you forgot, I almost died a few days ago."

Logan stepped in between us. "Maybe we should just relax and take a step back."

"Shut up, Logan." I felt his power rolling over me, but I didn't let it in. I didn't want to relax. I was angry, and nothing, not even Logan's low-key cool, was going to take that away. He snapped his mouth shut and held his hands up in surrender. I pointed at Beckett. "You should calm the hell down. I am doing the best I can."

The red in his cheeks suddenly subsided. "I know you are."

"Do you? Because from where I'm standing I get three days of reprieve from all"—I waved my hand over him—"of that and we're back to battle axe Beckett when some hoity-toity big deal warlocks walk in."

"Don't take them so lightly."

"Yeah, well, are you forgetting who we are?" I put my hands on my hips. I wasn't the leader of this group, he was, but if he needed to be reminded of what was happening, then I would remind him.

He groaned and leaned up against the counter. "What are you talking about?"

"Why would they come here if they thought we were just a bunch of kids? If they weren't threatened, they wouldn't bother with us. But no, we get the headmaster and the council standing in our foyer making threats. Seems to me we shouldn't be worried about what we're doing wrong. But keep on doing whatever it is we've been doing to make them that scared."

Cross chuckled and perched himself on a stool at the island. "She's got a point."

"They didn't come here because they feel threatened. They came here to scope out the competition. So you need to study . . . now." Beckett ran his hand through his hair. "Please, Astrid."

"Fine." I spun on my heels and headed out of the kitchen.

"Dude, you know when a girl says fine it means it's anything but fine, right?" Maze whispered to Beckett loud enough for all of them to hear.

"He's not wrong!" I yelled as I walked into the foyer and up the stairs.

Odin silently ran up the stairs at my side and jumped onto my shoulder. "I think you should give me a hammer."

I sighed. "What do you need a hammer for?"

"Odin's son has a hammer . . . I should have a hammer. You know, to smash things." Once in my room, he hopped down onto my bed and sat perfectly still.

I shook my head. "The last thing I'm giving a demon cat is a hammer that wielded lightning."

"Suit yourself, but I think that'd really scare the crap out of the council."

"The only thing that'll scare them is a united line of heirs ready to take over." I held my hand out and cleared my mind, picturing the book in it. A moment later it appeared, and I sat down on the bed with it. "There's only one way for me to be ready."

our hours later and my eyes were dry and burning from staring at the pages of my book. The sun had long since gone down and when I picked up my phone to check the time, it was two minutes to two in the morning. The house seemed quiet, but that didn't mean anything when dealing with the other heirs. *Tink.* I snapped my head up. "Did you hear that?"

Tink. Odin pointed his paw toward the window. "From there."

Tink. Was that a pebble hitting my window? *Tink tink.* I rose to my feet and walked over to the window in time to see the next tiny stone hit the glass pane. *Tink.* I grabbed the window and hauled it up. Cold air rushed in, flooding my room.

"Astrid, oh, Astrid, let down your hair or some shit."

"Leo?" I peeked my head out to find him and Cassidy standing behind a bush with a handful of tiny pebbles.

"Who else is gonna come free you in the middle of the night?" He took a step out from behind the bushes and waved for me to join him. "Come on, let's go."

"Where are we going?" I glanced back at the book, knowing I should just keep my nose buried in it.

"To have some fun." A light flickered on, on the first floor and Leo dove to hide.

"I'm supposed to be studying my grimoire."

"Hold up, the lost Lockwood grimoire, you found it? Girl, bring it out to play!" A wide smile spread across his face. "Do that leaf thing and come on."

"I don't know." I bit my bottom lip.

"Are you a warlock or what?" He crossed his arms over his chest.

I wanted to be under the full moon. I wanted to play with my powers. Most of all I wanted out of my room for just a little while. "Be right there."

He high fived Cassidy. "That's what I'm talking about."

I walked into my room and grabbed my winter coat. We were more than halfway through November and the temperature dropped a lot over the past few days. Thanksgiving would be here soon and I paused while shoving my arms into the wool coat. Tilly would need me for the holiday. We always had Thanksgiving together. Sneaking out with Leo and Cassidy was just what she would've done. *I miss her.*

I pulled on my black beanie and headed for the window.

Odin lay on the bed next to my book. "Have fun."

"Cover for me, okay?" I swung my leg out of the window.

"Meow?"

I giggled. "Right, good job."

I swung my other leg out of the window and sat there for a moment. I reached my hand out and pictured the giant leaf I'd used to sneak out only last week. Except this time it wouldn't be an accident and I would control the way this went. The tree on the side of the house bent and twisted its branches until a thick bare one drifted right under my feet. I placed both of my feet on the branch and came to a stand. I held my arms out to the sides for balance like I was surfing. Golden smoke poured from my hand and into the limb. I steadily lowered myself to the ground where Leo and Cassidy waited.

I stepped off of it and waved. "Hey, guys."

Leo walked out and scooped me up into a hug and spun me in a small circle. I laughed when my feet finally hit the ground. "Well, good to see you too."

Cassidy came up and gave me a quick hug. Though she only came up to my chin, she was fierce. In fact, she was a commander in the Malback House, the house of warriors. She had her bomber jacket zipped up to her neck and a knitted black cap with a hydra on the front of it. The mark of the Malback House. She was tiny with pin straight black hair that fell to just below her chin. She had a wide round face that lit up when she smiled. "I'm so glad you're okay."

"Why wouldn't I be okay?"

Leo threw his arm over my shoulders and guided me away from the house. "Because everyone heard about your ascension."

"You mean everyone saw it." Cassidy fell into step beside us as we walked out onto the sidewalk that wound its way through the whole school. She held her hands up and made them arch over her head like a rainbow. "Pyrotechnic light show, dude."

I rolled my eyes. "Tell me about it. I was lucky the queens showed up when they did."

Both Leo and Cassidy stopped dead in their tracks, and I walked a few steps before I spun around. "What?"

Leo glanced at Cassidy then at me. "You met the witch queens? Like all of them?" He removed his thick black glasses and rubbed at his eyes. "Was she here? *Zinnia?*"

He said her name like she was the boogie man. Cassidy nodded. "Even I wouldn't mess with that witch. She's hella powerful. Like wipe your powers out in a matter of seconds powerful."

Leo looked over his shoulder, like it wasn't two in the morning and nothing but dark woods surrounded us. He whispered, "I heard a couple months ago she took a warlock's power and put it in another warlock . . . it killed them both."

The girl they were talking about and the girl I knew didn't sound like the same person. "I met her and she was cool. I mean, she did take some of my power out, but she gave it back."

Leo's stepped forward and looped his arm with mine and we started walking. "What do you mean?"

Cassidy walked on his other side and looped her arm with his. The three of us strolled around the bend and my thoughts returned to the night of my ascension and how my body had been torn apart. "My, um, my power, it was too much. If she hadn't stepped in, I would have died."

"Noooo shiiittttt." Leo squeezed my arm. "Then I'm

glad she was there to help you. Doesn't mean I want to meet her, though."

Cassidy shook her head. "Me neither and I'm not afraid of anything, but that witch scares me."

I scoffed. "She's not even close to as bad as the warlock council. Now those guys have got some serious evil going on."

They both stopped again. Cassidy looked up at me with panicked eyes. "You met the warlock council? You met Damiel Edward?"

I rolled my eyes. "Oh yeah, that guy is a complete jerk and there is some serious tension between him and Beckett. If the rest of us hadn't been there, I'm pretty sure there would've been a fight. It looked like Beck wanted to kill the guy."

"Makes sense." Leo nodded.

"What makes sense? What happened between them?" I looked from Cassidy to Leo and back again. They just stared at the ground, not saying a word. "Oh come on, guys, tell me."

Leo shook his head. "Astrid, this is something we can't tell because we don't know all the details of what happened. You need to get it right from Beckett."

"Okay, but not even a hint?"

Cassidy tugged us to keep going. "The only thing I

can tell you is on the night that Beckett's mom died, Damiel was there . . . in the house."

I quickened my steps to keep up. "You're not going to tell me what happened to his mom or his dad? And why was Damiel there?"

"Can't tell you, now shhhhhhhh." Leo pressed his finger over his lips.

As we came closer to Lockwood House, they pulled me into the woods that encroached on all sides of it. The building was a light baby blue today with bright white shutters. The black dahlia flowers that I originally loved about this house were now bright white daises . . . in winter. It was a beautiful imposing two-story house, with a giant porch. Over the front of the porch stood the giant metal face of Medusa with her mouth wide-open in a scream, the snakes all tangled around her head, each one baring their fangs. It was so different than the real Medusa I knew.

"First of all, what are we doing here? Second of all, what the hell happened to the house? It looks like a family of four belongs here with a freaking minivan."

"Kitty has been telling everyone that the power that exploded from the heir's house the other day wasn't yours. She's saying you're trying to make yourself look like the Lockwood heir and no one really thinks you are. That you made the whole thing up."

Leo pointed to the house. "She says that she's the only one the rest of the students can trust because you have Beckett and the others tricked. I'm not going to say what she said you did to trick them, but it was bad."

"What the hell did she say?"

Cassidy crouched down lower next to me. "He might not tell you, but I will. Basically she called you a ho. One girl in a house with four guys. She keeps telling everyone to do the math."

"That little bitch." Golden smoke flowed from my hands and seeped onto the ground.

Leo placed his hand on my shoulder. "Oh, we don't get mad."

"We get even." Cassidy finished for him.

"What did you guys have in mind?" I eyed up the house, trying to think of any and all possibilities.

Leo pointed to the side of the house where there was a small opening in the woods that hadn't been there before. A brand-new porch 911 turbo was parked in the small clearing. It was a pristine silver with black trim. *Too bad.*

"How did they even get a car on campus? There aren't roads between the houses."

Leo chuckled. "Rumor has it that daddy Kalarook paid Professor Charles a small fortune to have her simply manifest it here from the Kalarook estate. I don't know why since they can't really drive it anywhere."

"Yeah, but that hasn't stopped Kitty from telling everyone she brought it here with her own power and that *you* better watch out because she's powerful enough to take your place with the heirs. She keeps telling everyone how her father is going to have a place on the council too. You know, once she and Beckett go public."

I swallowed down the rage in my veins. "Go public with what?"

"Their relationship." Leo chuckled. "As if that boy would look at her."

"That car is nothing but an ornament, a decoration . . ." An idea lit my mind and Beckett might not be mine, but he definitely wasn't *hers*. *Ew.* I held my hand out and thought of my grimoire. It was getting easier and easier to manifest the more I did it. The book sat heavy in my hand and I flipped the pages open.

Leo leaned over my shoulder. "I thought there were supposed to be spells in there. How is that going to help us?"

I pressed my hand to the page and let my power flow. The words slowly appeared the way vanishing ink would. "It's got built-in protections."

"Cool. But what are you thinking about doing?"

Cassidy pointed at the page I'd just opened. "Ohhhh, I like it."

"The ice queen wants to put on a show. Let's give her the spotlight." I rose to my feet and held my hands out to my sides. My power poured from me and seeped across the ground like a poisonous fog. The wind kicked up behind me and my hair flew around my face. It felt good to let my magic go, to let that tide rise within me and not worry about who or what I was going to hurt.

Leo held the book up for me to see all the while chanting, "Do it, do it."

Cassidy clapped her hands together and practically bounced with excitement. My power seeped into Lockwood House. It went under the door and through the windows, though they weren't open. I looked down at the book and recited the words the way Zinnia taught me, with feeling and a steady rhythm.

"Sky above, ice below.

Feel the freeze and make it flow.

By power of night and flaking light.

Let the snow fill this site."

The moment I spoke the spell I felt it imbed into myself. I knew what it felt like to create it, to unleash this madness. Now I could manifest it anytime. I crouched back down next to Leo and Cassidy. "Now we wait."

"How long?" Leo peeked at the house just as the lights flashed on in two rooms.

I giggled. "Not long."

The rest of the lights flickered on and the front door flew open just as Kitty ran out screaming with Kyle hot on her heels. Beyond them inside the house the snow piled up at least two feet high. It blew around like a true blizzard. Ice formed on the railings and dripped from around the door. Kitty and Kyle stood out front watching as I went Elsa on their asses. But it didn't feel like enough, not nearly enough.

My power was flowing, and I wanted more. "You guys ever heard of a Whomping Willow?"

Leo nodded. "Yeah, why?"

"How about a Punishing Pine?" I opened my hands and my powers seeped into the woods and found the biggest pine tree it could.

A crashing sound came from behind the house and I chuckled. "I'm suddenly feeling so Christmassy."

The pine tree marched out like a soldier then stabbed its roots deep into the ground, planting itself beside that ornamental car. The ground exploded up and chunks of earth flew over Kyle and Kitty, coating them in dust. The branches of the tree vibrated and lifted like a hammer over the car and slammed down. It crashed onto the roof of the car, crumpling it inward.

Kitty threw her arms around Kyle and screamed, "Noooo, my baby."

I wanted to feel bad about it, I really did . . . *sorry, not sorry.* The tree lifted its branches once more and slammed them down again. The sound of crumpling metal filled the air, glass exploded outward, and the alarm blared to life.

With that same thick branch, the tree slid under the car and tossed it up into the air. It flew end over end and came back down right into its waiting branches. Where it stayed hanging like an ornament on a Christmas tree. I dusted my hands off. When Leo and Cassidy looked at me with wide, proud eyes, I shrugged. "What? I'm from New York. I like decorating for Christmas before Thanksgiving."

CHAPTER 18

"*A*nd then it beat down my car. Crunched it like it was an aluminum can." Kitty sat at her lab table before potions class started. Though the class was set up like a standard classroom with rows of desks, I knew at any moment the professor would walk in and transform everything. I found myself looking forward to seeing the most experienced manifestor at work. I sat next to Leo, waiting for her to get here.

The other students all sat enthralled with her story. Kyle nodded along with everything she said. "And our entire house is an ice castle, covered in snow. We can't even get to our clothes."

Kitty examined her nails. "Not that it matters. I just

saw my father on campus. He'll have it all straightened out in no time. He even brought us more clothes."

I glanced at Leo, who sat opposite me. His lips were bursting with held in laughter. He was dressed impeccably with his gray button-down shirt and perfect black cardigan with the siren on the back for Whitmore House. He looked well rested and ready to go. He mouthed the words "oh my God" at me then pretended to flip his hair.

A giggle burst past my lips and everyone turned to look at me. Kitty narrowed those dark green eyes. Her hair fell in waves down the sides of her face, giving her high cheekbones a softer look. In New York she'd be considered beautiful. Hell, anywhere she would be beautiful. Then she tilted her head and sneered at me, and any sign of her beauty was lost. "You two belong together."

I winked at Leo. "Good friends are hard to find."

"Well, I for one think it's so cute that the two people nobody wants became friends. Kind of like an outreach program for losers. Losers helping losers." She chuckled.

I opened my mouth to snap back at her when the professor walked in. "Pardon my tardiness. I had some"—she eyed up Kyle and Kitty—"some unfinished business to handle on campus."

Kitty preened and smiled. "We can't thank you enough, Prof—"

"Like I had a choice. Your father and Headmaster Ridge are very chummy." Professor Charles waved her away and turned her attention back to the class. "Now if all of you would open your books to page two hundred and fourteen."

She lifted her hands and her light smoky blue magic seeped from her palms. Her magic matched her flowing shirt. It was chiffon, with a bow tied on the side of her neck, the sleeves billowed and snitched in at her wrists. She wore black dress pants and sparkle covered sneakers. Every time I saw her I couldn't help but think I wanted to be just like her when I grew up.

The room lifted and changed from the classroom to a bowl-shaped stadium seating. The desks vanished and on each rise was a set of lab tables. I moved to where Leo and I worked together.

The professor began to walk around the room. "Now if you will, we are working on a love spell of sorts. Though magic cannot create real love, it can create infatuation, for a short time. In the warlock world this used to benefit many of our former great leaders. Like Cleopatra, who many men claimed to love. Or Helen of Troy. Some say she was a love witch, but others claim it was her power with this very potion that brought men to their knees."

I raised my hand and the professor pointed at me, giving me the floor. "If this spell enchants people beyond what their free will, will allow, then why let us make it?"

She arched her eyebrow at me. "Can anyone answer Ms. Lockwood's question?"

With all the attitude she could muster, Kitty turned to me. "Because we're warlocks, duh."

I wrinkled my nose. "Not sure that's an actual answer."

The professor chuckled and shook her head. "In short, no, that is not an answer. Because we as warlocks are inclined with the dark arts, what we do with them is entirely up to us. But this particular potion is very complicated to brew and I highly doubt any of you will master it. What I am looking for is your skill set."

She flicked her wrist and the cauldrons all appeared on each of our tables. Small fires flickered beneath them and I opened my book up to the right page. I pulled the ingredients out from under the desk and placed a multitude of vials on the table. "There is a lot to this potion."

Leo nodded. "I'm not going to help you out much . .

." He lowered his voice. "But enough so you'll kill it and learn what the hell you're doing."

"Nice." I stood over the cauldron and read the first line. "Three quarters distilled water."

I rested my hand on the side of the cauldron and the water filled to the right point.

Leo looked at me with wide eyes. "I don't think I'll ever get used to that."

"You better start." I shoved my sleeves up to my elbows. "I plan on getting really good at it."

Leo nodded toward where Kitty was carrying her cauldron across the room all the while the water sloshed over the side of it, leaving drops on the floor behind her. "Right, and *she's* the most powerful of the Lockwood House."

Kitty placed her cauldron over the small flames then bent down low and blew on them, forcing them to burn higher. "Better get started, losers. I have a good idea who I'm going to use my potion on, do you?"

I rolled my eyes. "I don't plan on using it on anyone. Why would I?"

"Because no one would love you otherwise?" She batted her eyelashes at me.

Professor Charles walked up the steps and stood between our two tables. "Astrid, I suggest you go get the water you need to get started. This potion will take the whole class period."

Leo pointed to the cauldron. "Oh, she did it"—he cracked his knuckles—"with her powers. You know how easy it is for the most powerful Lockwood to manifest things."

Such a pot stirrer.

Kitty growled low in her throat yet said nothing.

Professor Charles' lip tugged up at the corner. "I'm not sure about most powerful, but I see great things for you, Ms. Lockwood. And good job with the water."

I turned my attention back to the cauldron. "Okay, what's the next ingredient?"

Leo read from the book. "Four drops of rose water according to the compass. Then stir opposed to the clocks, thrice times the points of a pentacle."

I snapped my head up. "Say what now? That doesn't make any sense."

"You're not baking a pie here, Astrid. This is potion making and some of these potions were written a long ass time ago. You have to translate the meanings."

I bit my bottom lip. "Okay, so four drops by the compass. Means four drops of rosewood oil, by the four points on a compass? North, south, east, and west?"

"Precisely."

I grabbed up the eyedropper and dipped in into the oil then sucked up the liquid. I pulled my phone out and opened up the compass app. Then I held the dropper over the cauldron and placed one drop to north, south, east, and west."

The boiling water turned to a soft pink color and the smell of roses wafted up on the steam. I smiled at Leo. "Okay, what's next?"

"Shhh, look." He didn't look up from his book, but I knew what he was saying.

From the corner of my eye I spotted Kitty copying my every move. *Well, I'll be damned.* "Okay, I guess we'll have to be slyer about how we do this."

He moved his chair around to the other side of the table to sit next to me. "At least this way when we talk your back will block her."

"Okay, next line." I tapped the pages with my fingers.

He turned to face Kitty and made a show of pushing his glasses up with a certain finger. "Try doing your own work."

"Come on, don't engage. They're not worth it. Let's get this done." I lifted a small dish with ground up snail shells and pinched the dust between my fingers. "It's like sticky sand."

"Yeah, you don't wanna know what makes that stick."

I dropped the crushed-up shells and turned my attention back to the spell.

Leo continued, "Then stir opposed to the clocks, thrice times the points of a pentacle."

"Okay, so there's five points in the pentacle, but three times that would be fifteen. And opposed to the clocks? Does that mean counterclockwise?"

"You are getting the hang of this." He handed me a large wooden spoon.

I dipped it in the cauldron and stirred it counterclockwise fifteen times. Then I pointed at the book. "Okay, hit me."

"The diamond of the seas wrapped in the octopus' grip does the result need a dip. By the clock and months in the year stir until the mother appears."

"For the love of the creator, Leo. That is not English." I dropped the spoon down on the tabletop.

"It is, you just have to break it down and listen. What is the diamond of the seas?"

I glanced down at my supplies. "The pearl."

"Right, and what happens if it's held too tight?"

"It gets crushed?" I shook my head. "That can't be right. You can't crush a pearl."

Leo handed me a mortar and pestle. "Give it a go. But if it's an octopus, how many pearls do you need?"

"Eight. Thank God you're my partner. I would not have been able to do this without you." I dropped eight pearls into the cup and started grinding them up. They rolled around, making it difficult, but I did it.

Leo slammed the book shut. "You know what, I am so tired of them getting away with everything."

"Just ignore them." I dumped the powder into the pot.

"You don't know what it was like before you got here. The things they did to me, to everyone." He leaned in closer. "I can't believe I dated him. I was an idiot."

"Don't be so hard on yourself. You can't help who you love." I stirred the cauldron and the liquid turned to a mother of pearl shimmering essence.

"But you can damn well try and I just let him . . . ugh." He looked away.

I reached out and placed my hand over his. "Sometimes when things happen to us in our past, we need to think of them as separate events. They happened and now it's over. That hurt can't hurt you anymore unless you let it."

"Where you learn that from?"

Too many years of being disappointed by my father.
"I've just been there."

When I looked over at Kyle, he blew a kiss to Leo and snickered. Leo jumped to his feet, about to walk out. I grabbed his arm and pulled him back. "Do not give him the satisfaction . . . they'll get what's coming to them."

Kitty's arm shot up. "Professor Charles, what happens when we finish it?"

The professor walked up the stairs over to Kitty's table and looked into the cauldron. "If you do finish it correctly, I will let you keep it. But I wouldn't use it lightly."

My head snapped up and something in my gut told me to pay attention. "What would happen?"

"Well, once the potion is consumed, whomever the victim is will be obsessed with love and the pursuit of it. It will be relentless, and it will be difficult to combat when that person decides who they want. And once the effect wears off, the poor victim will fall ill and show signs of withdrawal. Cold sweats, shivers, vomiting. In the extreme cases some of them need to be restrained."

"Why would you let us keep that?" I took a small step back from the cauldron.

"Because, my dear, this is Warwick Academy, not

Evermore. Survival of the fittest is practically our school motto." She moved on to the next table.

Kitty held up her wooden spoon dripping with potion. "I know exactly who mine will be for. Someone who needs to wake up and see the potential right in front of him."

In the pit of my stomach I knew she was going for Beckett. I just didn't know when or how. But I would stop her.

CHAPTER 19

ASTRID

*C*lass ended and of course Kitty and Kyle were the only other group besides Leo and me to get the potion right. Which just pissed me off. The cheaters had no right to that potion. I knew she would go for Beckett as soon as she got the chance. He may have only kissed me twice in the time I'd known him, but there was no way in hell he'd be anywhere near her against his will. I threw my backpack over my shoulder and marched toward the door. Kitty and Kyle had already made their way out and I was going to beat that potion away from them if I had to.

"Ms. Lockwood. A word." Professor Charles leaned against the desk at the front of the room.

"I really have to—"

She crooked her finger at me. I sucked in a deep

breath, hoping Beckett hadn't shown up outside my classroom like he'd done before. Leo waved to me as he exited the room.

I waved back. "Later."

Professor Charles looked me up and down. "May I offer some advice?"

"Yes, please." *And be quick about it.*

"Your powers are more than you know. Don't hold them back. No matter what you think will happen. The only way you're going to know their limits is if you test them." She turned away from me and walked to sit behind her desk. "You are a warlock, not a mortal. There is no place for fear in this world."

"I-I understand." I didn't want to tell her I was worried about hurting someone or what my own powers would do to me. That didn't seem like the warlock way. I felt the darkness in me, those desires to do whatever the hell I wanted, consequences be damned.

"Practice with the Lockwood grimoire and then come to see me." She waved me toward the door.

I started to leave then I paused and looked at her over my shoulder. "How did you know about the grimoire?"

She ran her hand through her pixie gray hair. "When you're as old as I am and have no one around who shares your powers, research is imperative to learn your craft. I'd very much like to see that book, but I've waited this long and I will wait until you trust me enough to show it to me."

I gave her a single nod. "Okay."

What more could I say? All the adult warlocks I'd met in this world had been questionable at best, but there was something about Margarite Charles that I admired. I opened the door and stepped out into the crowded hallway. There was a traffic jam of students stopping and staring. I immediately knew who and what they were looking at. It happened whenever he came out on campus. To them he was famous. To me, he was . . . *more.* I pushed past the throng of students toward the little circle of people surrounding him.

There he stood looking more delicious than ever in his dark blue jeans, white shirt, and leather jacket. He leaned up against the wall with one leg propped up behind him. Those tousled blond locks fell into his eyes and for a moment my heart skipped a beat. He gazed off down the hall and I wanted him to look at me with those ocean eyes of his.

"Excuse me." I moved past the last person blocking me from his view and stepped into the circle of people surrounding him.

He smiled. "Astrid, hi."

"Hi. What are you doing here?"

He shrugged. "I was in the building. Figured I'd stop by and maybe walk you to your next class." He popped a piece of something into his mouth.

I reached out and grabbed his hand, yanking it toward me. "What did you just eat?"

"Oh, um, Kitty gave it to me." He motioned to where she stood. "It's really bitter for chocolate, though."

My anger spiked. The audacity of this bitch, to drug him in public. She snickered and winked at me. Beckett didn't belong to her. He belonged to . . . *never mind who he belongs to!* "You *witch.*"

Gold smoke drifted up from my shaking hands. "How dare you."

"It's no big deal. Calm down." Beckett shoved away from the wall to stand in front of me.

Why do people always tell me to calm down when I'm in a rage? Like that helps!

"Don't tell me to calm down. She bespelled you." I lifted my hand with my magic, picked him up, and put him down beside me.

I stepped up to Kitty and came nose to nose with her. "Isn't that right?"

She shrugged. "Sometimes love needs a little push."

Beckett unleashed a violent curse then grabbed my

shoulder and turned me to face him. "You need to look at me for the next ten seconds okay?"

"What, why?" I tried to face Kitty, but he held me there.

"Because I need to choose an object of obsession or everything will be it and I choose you. Not *her*." He stared into my eyes for what seemed like long moments.

"Ugh, Beckett. No!" Kitty protested from right beside me, yet his penetrating gaze didn't waver. When she stomped her foot, her heel clicked on the wooden floors.

I was sinking into his gaze and sinking fast. They flooded with so much desire it staggered me. I wanted him and for however long he was going to want me.

He shook his head and backed away. "I'm so sorry. Just remember I had no choice."

"I know you didn't." I rounded on Kitty. "You did this to him! You selfish, spoiled ass!"

"Astrid, we should go." He wrapped his hand around my elbow, but I shrugged him off.

I took another step toward her. I didn't know why, but I felt more rage than I ever had before in all my life. He loved to boss me around and be an ass at times, but he was my piece of ass. *Wait, no, not piece of ass, he was my ass to deal with. NO! He was mine. Also NO!*

I shook my head. "No, she has to pay first."

The students all plastered themselves to the walls of the hallway. Kitty rolled her eyes. "You think you have any power over me, think again. You're a newbie. What can you possibly do?"

I lifted my hand and shot a bolt of power right at her chest. She flew up off the ground and slid ten feet down the hallway. "That."

I stomped forward and my power rose like a tsunami, the darkness overtaking me, and all I could focus on was how she wanted to hurt what was *mine.* Kitty staggered to her feet and held her hands up. She fired a shot of her light pink magic at me. With the wave of my hand, I deflected it into the wall. "Adorable."

My hair stood on end and my golden smoke filled my senses. "You know what? A good taste of your own medicine would do . . ." It tilted my head to the side. "Don't you think?"

She held her hand out in front of her. "You're such a freak, Astrid!"

"No, I'm a warlock." I marched up to her and pushed her up against the wall and leaned in. "You will feel all the effects of the potion used on him. You will love everything you see. Your obsession will last as long as his does and when the withdrawals hit him, you will feel them."

"Y-you don't have that power."

I snickered a deep dangerous laugh that sent goose bumps down my own spine. "Watch me." I relished in the darkness I felt. It was euphoric, and I didn't want it to end.

Beckett ran up to me and yanked me away from her. "Astrid, we need to leave now."

"Astrid Lockwood! My office now!" Ridge's voice boomed down the hall and everyone's heads snapped toward him but mine. I continued to stare down Kitty until she turned to the garbage can next to her and began to pet it . . . lovingly.

I kept my feet planted watching what I'd done to her, watching my power take effect.

Ridge yelled again, "Now!"

Beckett dragged me down the hall toward Head-master Ridge's office. As I passed the other students, they all looked at me with wide eyes, dropped jaws, and . . . fear? Leo was the last one I made eye contact with. He gave me two thumbs up.

Beckett pulled me against his chest and threw his arm over my shoulder then pressed his nose to my hair and inhaled. "Oh God, you smell so good, it tortures me." He sighed. "Your lips taste like strawberries, did you know?"

I jabbed my elbow into his ribs. "Beckett, focus. I think I got us in trouble here."

He shook his head and turned his eyes on the door we were about to walk through. "Right, yeah."

"Look, let's just make sure I don't get expelled then we can deal with this thing happening to you." I followed Ridge through his door and into his office.

The interior of the office was seeped in traditional style dark wood. The desk took up half the room, big and heavy with carvings in the front of it. Behind the desk stood wall to wall shelving littered with too many antiques to be stylish. Ridge took his place behind his desk and motioned for us to sit in the chairs facing him.

I dropped down into the chair and folded my hands in my lap. This was bad, very, very bad. The council had just been in our house the day before and here I was making a scene. I wanted to feel bad about it, but strangely I didn't.

Beckett grabbed the other chair and pulled it right next to mine, so the armrests were touching. He dropped himself down into the chair and rested his arm against mine. The tips of his fingers brushed against my skin in little circles, sending goose bumps skittering over my skin. I pushed his arm back onto his side of the chair and faced Ridge.

"Look, I know that—"

He waved his hand, cutting me off. "We are waiting."

"For what?"

The door to the office swung open and I jumped in my seat and turned to see Damiel Edwards stroll through. With that cane tapping on the ground with each step he took. "For me."

He moved to stand beside Headmaster Ridge. "I hear there was a disruption in the hallway today."

"It literally happened ten minutes ago. How could you be here that quickly?" I slumped down in the seat.

Beckett shook with the effort to sit up straight. "This isn't any of your concern."

"I offered Mr. Edwards our hospitality at the school here so the council could have the personal touch when dealing with things of this nature." Ridge steepled his fingers and pressed them to his lips. "Now to deal with the ground of your expulsion, let's begin, shall we?"

"Expulsion? You can't be serious." Sweat covered my palms.

A wide smile broke out over Damiel's face. "He's

deadly serious. You assaulted another student and used a potion on her to boot."

I crossed my arms over my chest. "I didn't use any potions on her."

"Then why is she outside kissing a water fountain?" He motioned to the window. "I saw her on my way over here."

Beckett grabbed a lock of hair and rubbed it down his cheek. "And what are you doing to Kitty for using a potion on me?"

He sighed and reached out to run the back of his fingers down my cheek. I swatted him away. "When I was in Professor Charles' class, she said Warwick was survival of the fittest. Is there a precedent for other students being expelled for what I did?"

They glanced at each other and Ridge cleared his throat. "If you are part of the council, you must be held to a higher standard."

"But I'm not part of any council as of right now." I swatted Beckett's hand away from my cheek again. "I'm just a regular student."

Damiel shook his head. "Nonetheless, Ms. Lockwood. Your behavior—"

"Warrants nothing." Beckett cut him off as he took my hand in his and kissed the back of it. "She's only a student."

"You don't seem that affected by the potion." Ridge sat back in his chair. "Perhaps you're faking."

I pulled my hand from his. "Trust me, on a normal basis I drive him crazy. He can barely stand me."

Beckett jolted in his chair. "What? Astrid, that is not how I feel at all. I like you, so much. It pains me really."

I motioned to him. "I rest my case. Normally he's snapping at me."

He took my hand in his and this time I let him. I tried to ignore the way my pulse quickened at his touch, and how much I liked it.

This isn't real, this isn't real.

"That had better be true. We do not condone fraternization between the house lines. Something like that would be catastrophic to your cause, I fear." Ridge had the audacity to smile. I wanted to leap across the desk and smack him.

Someday.

"No matter, you and this Kitty girl will both be expelled," Damiel said as if it was nothing. "And no one in the warlock world would accept an uneducated warlock as our leader. This position must be earned."

Beckett scoffed, "And yet our laws state it's a position that the heirs are to have, not just any old, lying, backstabbing son of a bi—"

"What I think Beckett is trying to say is that I will accept my punishment, but it should fit the crime. So you plan on expelling Kitty Kalarook along with myself? Then so be it."

Damiel opened his mouth to speak when Ridge shook his head, cutting him off. "Two-day suspension, for now."

"What?" Damiel's bright yellow eyes flared with anger.

Ridge sighed. "The Kalarook family contributes favorably to this school and to the council. These two young ladies have obviously learned their lesson. Two days, Ms. Lockwood."

Beckett jumped to his feet. "You can take your two days and—"

I hopped up and grabbed his hand. "I will see you in two days."

I pulled him out the door before he could get us in more trouble and get me expelled for real. I tugged him down the hall and out the set of double doors leading to the path that would take us back to the house before this spell got worse.

The cool air bore down on me and I shivered in my Lockwood jacket. Beckett threw his arm over my shoulders and pulled me against his body. "I'll keep you warm, Astrid."

I put my arm around his back and pushed him forward through the crowd of students watching us. As we passed Whitmore House Leo came jogging out the front door to catch me on the sidewalk. "So what happened?"

"Two-day suspension. I think it's a good thing, though. I have no idea how this is going to affect him." Beckett pressed his lips to my cheek and heat rushed to my face. I loved the way his lips felt against my skin.

Leo chuckled. "This is going to be interesting. The boy got exactly what he wanted."

"Oh come on, Leo. You and I both know I drive him nuts. I'm just hoping the potion isn't that bad."

Beckett grabbed my chin and made me meet his eyes. "I would never do anything you didn't want me to do."

Leo laughed. "Yeah, Astrid, just tell him what you want him to do to you."

"Shut up." I pulled Beckett forward. "Come on."

"A bit of advice." Leo stopped and called after me, "Give the man what he wants and it will be a lot easier on him . . . and you might like it."

Give him what he wants? "What does that even mean?"

"I want you, Astrid." He ran his hand down my arm and laced his fingers with mine. This far on the path and we'd passed all the houses except Lockwood and Beckett's house. We were alone. The sound of my racing heart filled my ears, his ocean scent filled my senses, and his skin against mine sent heat flooding through my body.

"I know you do, for now. Once the potion wears off we'll be back to normal, don't worry."

"Not for now . . . for always." A mischievous smile spread across his lips and he glanced into the forbidden woods. "Come on, I have an idea."

CHAPTER 20

ASTRID

 eckett tugged me through the woods into a small clearing. Twigs crunched under my feet and the rustle of leaves mixed in with the pounding pulse in my ears. His big hand swallowed mine completely. He spun on his heels and I almost collided with his chest. "Beck, what are you doing here? I think we really need to get back to the house. The others will be able to . . ."

His lips pressed against mine, cutting my words off completely. They were firm and warm and just perfection. He threw his arms around my waist and walked me backward until my back pressed into the trunk of a tree. Fire ignited between us and I wanted him more. He groaned as his tongue dipped into my mouth and danced with mine. My stomach did little flip-flops and

I wound my hands in the back of his jacket, pulling him closer to me. Our bodies melded together, and I was lost to everything that was Beckett Dustwick, his touch, his taste.

I wanted his hands all over me and his mouth on mine. Our bodies melded together, and his every muscle rippled under my touch. When he cupped my face with his hands, I sighed at how right it felt. His hands ran down my neck, then my arms. He intertwined his fingers with mine and raised my arms over my head, pinning me to the tree trunk. His ocean blue eyes bore into mine. "I want you so bad."

"I-I . . ." I freed my hands from his. "Beckett, we can't."

He leaned in and ran his tongue up the side of my neck and my mind went blank. I titled my head back, letting him rain kisses all over my skin. Heat bloomed in my belly and I wanted nothing more than to have this moment with him, for the two of us to forget the world, forget our problems and just be here, with each other.

"Please, Astrid." His lips pressed just below my ear. "Just let me be close to you."

I shook my head. This wasn't real. This wasn't him. He was under a spell and I couldn't give into it, no matter how much I wanted to. "No."

I pushed him back and he let me. "We can't."

He turned from me and paced back and forth. "Was it something I did? I'm sorry, Astrid. I'm sorry."

"No, you didn't do anything wrong." I moved away from the tree and grabbed his hand. "We just have to get back."

I couldn't do this. It felt like taking advantage of him. Sure, we kissed twice, now three times, but still he was under the influence of a potion and I wasn't. I had to take care of him the way he took care of me.

Beckett shoved his hands into his hair and tugged at the strands. "Astrid, please." He dropped to his knees in front of me. "I just need to love you."

Ugh, he needs to love me? If only . . . wait, no . . . we're just friends. I grabbed his arms and pulled him to his feet. "Come on."

His face crumpled in pain and a deep whimper escaped his lips. I didn't know what brought me to do it, but I pulled him down to me and pressed a kiss on his cheek.

"It's going to be okay, I promise."

He threw his arm around my shoulders, pulling me close into his side. "I'm with you, always."

I rolled my eyes. "Yeah, okay, let's go, Casanova."

Though Beckett had dragged me in here, I was going to stumble our way out. I guided him through the forest, over fallen trees, and under low-hanging branches. All the while he never let me go, his warm hands pressed into my sides, his scent surrounded me. By the time we returned to the path, he was back to sniffing my hair. Like nothing happened. *So like every other day between us.*

I got him up the stairs and across the porch. As I reached for the door, it swung wide-open. Maze filled the doorway. He leaned up against the doorjamb, holding a bowl of ice cream and spoon most people would use for a huge pot of spaghetti.

"Sup?"

I shoved past him and stopped in the foyer. "Beckett's been bespelled."

Maze snorted. "Oh, I know."

"You know?" I ducked out from under Beckett's arm and stormed up to Maze. "What do you mean you know?"

He tapped his finger against his temple. "Psychic."

I snapped my hand across his cheek. The spoon flew across the foyer and the bowl of ice cream clattered to the floor. Vanilla ice cream pooled on the hardwood floor at his feet.

He shook his head. "Woooo, what the hell was that for?"

"You're the psychic. Did you see that one coming?"

I put my hands on my hips. "A little warning next time."

He rubbed his hand over his jaw. "I might have deserved that."

"You think?"

Logan walked down the stairs and stopped on the last step. "Did I miss something?"

Where Maze was all dark, in his trench coat and black army pants, Logan was suave in his black dress pants and button-down burnt orange shirt. Even his blond hair was trimmed close to his head and laid perfectly. When Cross walked in through the front door, I was surrounded by all the heirs.

I sighed. "Beckett has been bespelled with a love potion and you all need to help me cure him of it."

Cross took a step back. "Hold up a second, did you give him the potion?"

"No!" I wanted to throat punch him, but Beckett was behind me, rubbing my shoulders. "Kitty gave it to him."

Logan took the last few steps down and cleared his throat. "Did he pick an object of his obsession? I just want to be prepared, you know, just in case."

"Yeah, he picked me."

A burst of laughter exploded from Cross. "This just gets better."

"Guys, this isn't funny." I swatted Beckett's hands away. "He can't be like this. We have to cure it or give him an anti-spell or something."

Maze picked his bowl up off the floor along with his spoon and continued eating whatever was left. "Anti-spell, how cute. There's no such thing."

"Well, then what the hell am I going to do with him?" There had to be a way for Beckett to get back to normal.

Beckett leaned down and whispered in my ear, "I can think of a few things you should do with me."

Even Logan had a stupid smirk across his face. "There's only one thing to do. Well, if you agree to it."

For some reason I had a bad feeling in the pit of my stomach. "What's that?"

Logan shrugged. "Just give into him, let him go as far as you want to let him until the potion wears off."

"You can't be serious." How would this even be okay? "He's under a spell and I am not taking advantage of that."

Maze lifted the bowl to his face and licked it. "If you want, I can chain him up in the basement and keep him there until it wears off . . ."

"Yes, good, finally someone who makes sense."

"But he'll be in extreme pain if I do. I heard it's a lot like what humans go through when they hit withdrawal. You know, shakes, sweating, stomach cramps. I even heard it could feel like your bones are being broken." He sighed and looked down into his bowl. "I hate it when the ice cream is gone."

I snapped my fingers. "Maze, focus."

"Right, yeah. I mean, we can tie him to his bed. I'm sure it won't be that bad." His gaze flickered up to mine. "Unless . . ."

"Unless what?"

"Unless you want to be there to help him." He arched his eyebrow at me.

When I looked around, all of them were staring at me. I shifted from one foot to the other. "Oh, come on, guys. This isn't right. He can't even choose for himself. I say we tie him to the bed."

"Very well." Cross made his way to Beckett. He stopped in front of me. "Just so you know, a person under the influence of a love spell who picks an object of obsession is giving consent. It means they trust you."

Like I was going to believe that. "Says who?"

Logan grabbed onto one of Beckett's arms. "Warlock bylaws, Astrid. He could be running around the school kissing trees and obsessing over every little thing. Instead he chose you."

Cross grabbed Beckett's other arm. "So now it's up to you."

He and Logan yanked Beckett away from me. Beckett instantly grew hostile. He kicked his legs out and reached for me, trying to fight them both off.

Cross gritted his teeth as he shoved him toward the stairs. "Just think about it. We aren't saying you should sleep with him. But if you're near him, it could ease him."

Dark orange smoke seeped from Logan's hands. "Sleep."

Beckett slumped in their hands and his head lulled to the side. I sighed. "There, we can just keep him asleep until it wears off."

Logan dragged him farther up the stairs. "He's an heir, Astrid. It's not going to last long. Hopefully long enough for us to get him restrained. But he'll do best with you."

Maze whispered in my ear as he passed, "Decisions, decisions."

CHAPTER 21

ASTRID

*A*n hour later I sat on the floor in the hallway outside of Beckett's room. I pulled my knees up and rested my arms across them. I leaned my head against the wall, softly banging it. Beckett had been screaming for the past hour and I wanted nothing more than to go in there.

Through the door Cross snapped at Logan. "For shit's sake, put him back to sleep."

"If I could, don't you think I would?"

I'd never heard Logan snap before, but his voice was low and cutting. "He's too strong!"

"Astriddddd!" Beckett screamed at the top of his lungs. The bed creaked and groaned like he was thrashing around on it.

I pressed my hands to the sides of my head. *One*

hour, three minutes, and thirty-five . . . thirty-six . . . thirty-seven seconds. "He's going to be fine. One day, it's only going to last one day."

"Maze! Hold his legs down." Cross grunted and his voice squeaked out. "He kicked me in the balls."

"No way am I getting my balls next to his legs." Maze gave one bark of laughter. "My future soul mate wouldn't like it. I know. I've seen it."

"Shut up about your stupid visions. No one gives a shit about your soul mate!" Cross barked at him.

"Jealous I'll get mine and you won't get yours?" Maze taunted him.

"Shut up or I'm gonna throat punch you!"

"Both of you are screwed. Because my—" Beckett's words were cut off immediately.

"Astrid! Help me, please! Astrid!" he pleaded, while all the wild sounds of fighting and struggling came from the room.

One hour, three minutes and forty-five . . . forty-six . . . forty-seven seconds . . . Screw this!

I jumped to my feet and turned for the door. *What am I doing?* He bellowed again and I couldn't stop myself. Something drew me to him, and I was tired of fighting it. I shoved the door open and walked into a war zone. Maze and Logan stood opposite each other by the head of the bed. Maze's hair fell across his face.

He'd thrown his trench coat into the corner of the room and stood there in only a black tank and his black cargo pants. For a guy who only ate junk, he was ripped, and by ripped I meant shockingly hot.

He nodded. "I know, surprise. Right?"

"Shut up." I turned to Logan. "Why aren't your powers working on him?"

Logan stood there breathless and the front pocket of his button-down shirt was ripped clean off and his sleeves were rolled up to his elbows. "The more I use my charm speak on him, the more immune he becomes."

Beckett thrashed on the bed and the sound of rustling chains filled the room. When my eyes met his, he smiled at me like I was his savior. "They want to keep me from you. But nothing will ever keep me from you."

"Yeah, that's not creepy at all, dude." Cross shook his head and ran his fingers through his hair, pushing back only to let it fall right back in his face.

Beckett's eyes bugged out of his head. "They're trying to kill me, I know it."

I whispered, "Get out."

Maze walked over to the corner of the room and grabbed his jacket. He slid his arms down the sleeves as he walked by me. "Don't have to tell me twice."

Cross quickly followed behind him. "Good luck."

Logan stopped beside me. "He's already starting to feel the withdrawals, but it will be easier if you're touching him. The more skin to skin contact, the better."

"You're not suggesting I-I sleep with him?"

"I'm not suggesting anything. I'm simply telling you the facts of the potion. The rest is up to you." He walked out the door, leaving me completely alone with Beckett.

"Astrid, pssstttt." Beckett let his head roll back on the bed. He squeezed his eyes shut and his body shuddered. His hair was sweat soaked and falling back from his face, splaying over his pillowcase. His sun-kissed skin looked paler than usual. "I don't feel so good."

If our places were reversed, what would Beckett do? He'd do anything to help me, I knew it, and I would do anything to help him. And now he needed me.

"As much skin as possible," I squared my shoulders.

Beckett's hands curled into fists and the chains rattled once more. He grunted and his face contorted in pain.

I marched over to the bed and pressed my hand to his forehead. "You're burning up."

When he looked up at me, his eyes were filled with pain. "Everything hurts."

"I know. I'm going to make it better." *Screw this.* I yanked my sweater up over my head, exposing myself to him. I stood there in my skirt, tights, and black cotton bra. I fought the urge to cover myself when his eyes locked on me.

"What are you doing?"

I climbed onto the bed and threw my leg over his hips, straddling him. I reached up to the headboard and unhooked the cuffs holding him. He didn't hesitate to wrap his arms around my waist. His touch was scorching, yet he didn't move, didn't let his hands go.

"You're so soft."

My heart rate skyrocketed, and I sucked in a breath, waiting to see what he would do next. But he didn't move, didn't breathe, just stared. I looked from his hands on my hips down to the hem of his shirt. "Just let me."

I curled my fingers in the material and slid it up his torso. His muscles rippled with every inch I raised it. When I got to his chest, he licked his lips.

"What now?"

"Off."

He sat up and came nose to nose with me. The muscle in his jaw flexed and the tension between us simmered. "You don't have to do this. T-the potion." Every word he uttered was a struggle.

I pressed my finger to his lips. "Shh. You took care of me. Now I'm going to take care of you. Arms up."

He lifted his arms over his head, and I pulled his shirt up over his chest. I paused for a second, admiring the way his muscles twitched in the cool room, and how his skin was sun-kissed all over. I pushed it up over his elbows and then free from him. When I cupped his cheeks in my hands, I leaned in slowly, savoring the closeness I felt with him. This wasn't our heated kisses, this was slow, deliberate, and exactly what we both needed.

"Astrid?"

"Just this, okay?" I wrapped my arms around him and pressed my body flush up against his.

He let go a deep sigh of relief. "Okay."

He leaned back and I followed him down with our skin pressed together. And it was kind of . . . *perfect.*

CHAPTER 22

BECKETT

The smell of strawberries filled my nose and I sucked in a deep breath, relishing it. Strands of silky hair fell over my arm and tickled low in my stomach. A small leg was intertwined with mine and my blankets covered me from the waist down. Delicate fingers splayed across my chest and warm, even breaths drifted over my skin. She felt so damn good pressed against the side of my body wrapped in my arms.

I grabbed a lock of her hair and ran it over my cheek. I didn't want this moment to end, didn't want her to leave. This was the way fate meant for it to be. I ran that lock of hair down her tiny, pert nose. She wrinkled it and her eyes blinked open. A lazy smile spread across her face. "Hi."

"Hey." I brushed my fingers through her hair, lifting the silky strands and letting them fall back into place.

Astrid sat up on her elbow. "How do you feel?"

"Surprisingly good."

"Good." She climbed up my body and lay across my chest. She leaned in and brushed her nose against mine. "Then you won't mind if I do this."

When she pressed her lips against mine, my pulse went wild. I wound my arms tight against her body and pulled her to me. Her fingers tangled into the hair on the back of my head and she deepened our kiss. My tongue danced with hers and I sighed with how right it felt. She swung her leg over my hip and straddled my waist. "I want you, Beckett."

She reached behind her and unfastened her bra, then slowly let it slide down her arms until she was completely bare to me from the waist up. I swallowed around the nervous ball in my throat and reached for her.

"Are you sure?"

My heart beat so hard I thought it might explode from my chest. She nuzzled my cheek, then whispered in my ear, "I'm sure."

A jolt went through me and I wrapped my arm around her waist and flipped her onto her back. I rested my elbows on either side of her head and let my chest brush against hers. Though she still had her skirt and tights on and I had my jeans in place, I never felt closer to her. I let my lips drift down to her neck. Her taste invaded my mouth and I shuddered as I kissed up her neck, across her cheek, and finally melded my mouth to hers.

She pulled back and gazed up at me with those hypnotic eyes. "J-just be gentle with me, okay?"

"Always."

I trailed my hand down her stomach, over her pale silky skin, so warm and soft. Lower to the top of her skirt. I hesitated . . .

"Beckett!" My shoulder jerked back.

Wha . . .

"Beckett!" Again my shoulder jerked.

This time I felt myself being pulled away. Like fighting to the surface of water. I shot up straight in my bed and sucked in heaving breaths. *What the hell?*

I pulled my knees up to my chest and brushed my sweat soaked hair from my face. *It was a dream? A freaking dream!*

"Are you okay?" Her voice was warm and soft.

I startled and nearly fell out of the bed. "You're here?"

"Yeah, I'm here." She arched her eyebrow at me.

"You're being kind of weird."

I climbed out of the bed and grabbed my sweater off the floor. "What happened last night?"

"You don't remember?" She let the blanket fall to her waist and my eyes locked on her bra clad chest. The chest she'd bared to me in my dreams and damned if I didn't want to know if my dreams of her were accurate.

I shook my head. "No, not really. Not sure I want to. Did something happen?"

"Nothing happened. God, you don't have to look so . . . so appalled." Astrid threw the blanket the rest of the way off and jumped out of the bed. "You were the one who got me involved in all of this."

"I didn't mean it like that. I just meant, that . . ." I pulled my shirt over my head and tugged it into place. "It would be bad if something did."

She crossed her arms over her chest and my eyes were drawn back down. What was wrong with me? I'd been in the same room with her naked before and kept it in check. Now my eyes were locked on all that milky white flesh and I couldn't look away.

"You know I really hate it when my boobs keep staring at your eyes!" She snagged her shirt off the floor.

I shook my head. *You idiot! Stop!* But I couldn't stop.

I just kept picturing her lying beneath me with those trusting eyes, that sweet strawberry scent, and her silky soft skin. I wanted to be that close to her. But I couldn't have her and here she was my own living torture. Her eyes drifted down to my waistband to where I knew that traitor stood at attention. I pulled my shirt up and over, covering myself. "Now who's staring?"

"You know what, I don't need this." She plunged her arms into her sleeves and yanked her shirt on. "After what I did for you last night . . ."

She stormed toward the door and I didn't want her to go. "Astrid, wait."

"What?" She hesitated with her hand on the door-knob, a second away from leaving me.

"For what it's worth. Thanks."

She made a disgusted sound in the back of her throat and stormed out of the room. She left the door wide-open and I stuck my head out. Maze stood against the wall across from my room, just shaking his head.

That could not have gone worse.

I narrowed my eyes at Maze. "Shut up!"

"I didn't say anything."

"You didn't have to." I slammed the door shut in his face.

CHAPTER 23

ASTRID

He sucks so bad! I walked into my room and slammed the door behind me. "Ugh! The nerve."

Odin lounged in the middle of my bed, his tail flicking back and forth. A box of chicken nuggets sat in front of him and he eyed me closely. "Chicken nugget?"

I paced back and forth at the foot of my bed. His head turned from side to side as he followed my move. Anger, the kind of anger only Beckett could fuel in me, simmered just beneath my skin. "You know what?"

"What?" Oden pulled a chicken out of the box and took a bite.

"I don't need this shit from him." I threw my arms up and let them slam back down on my legs. "I spent the whole night in his room, in his bed, making sure *he* was okay. All because of one crappy love potion!"

"Kind of like he did when you ascended." He finished off the chicken nugget he'd been working on then pulled out another.

I stopped and spun to face the bed. "What did you say?"

"You know, he helped you, you helped him. It's almost like you two care about each other."

I put my hands on my hips. "Who asked you to be the voice of reason here? And where the hell did you get chicken nuggets from?"

He gave me a deadpan look. "Maze. Dude has so much food."

From just outside my door I heard Maze in the hall. "Here kitty kitty."

Odin took another bite. "Like I'm going to answer to that. Psh, I had dinner with demons in hell!"

I began to rub little circles in my temples. "Please don't remind me you're a hell demon."

"But I'm your hell demon."

And then it hit me. I was standing in the middle of my room, in the middle of the day, bitching about boys to a demon cat who was making too much sense. I grabbed my phone. "I gotta get out of here. I'm surrounded by boys."

Odin curled his body to look between his legs. "Oh yeah, would you look at that. No wonder why I like lic—"

"Don't finish that sentence." I was suspended for another day and I wasn't going to spend it locked in this room. Not in the house and not near Beckett for one more minute. I needed a break. I opened my phone and brought up a text thread to the only person I knew wouldn't mind company right now.

Hey, are you up for visitors?

Those three little dots appeared and a quick answer. *Yes, bring pizza. I miss pizza.*

What kind? She'd have whatever kind of pizza she wanted and then some.

Why do I have to choose again?

I typed quickly. *I knew we were friends for a reason. Be there soon.*

KK

I hesitated a moment wanting to contact Tilly, wanting to bring up our epic text thread and send her a shit ton of gifs explaining exactly how I felt right now. But I couldn't open up that can of worms, even though she was the only person who would truly understand. There were two hundred and twenty-six unread texts in my phone and all of them were from her. My voicemail box was completely full, so were all my social media messages. Something was going to have to give and soon. I missed her. Her absence was a hole in my chest no one else could fill. I tossed my phone onto my bed next to Odin.

He looked down at it and pulled another nugget out. "That thing doesn't stop buzzing."

"I know." I reached across the bed spread. "Stop eating in my bed. I hate crumbs."

"Something for later?" He continued to chew and didn't move.

"You really are a cat."

"You say that like it's a bad thing." He chuckled.

CHAPTER 24

I stood outside of Astrid's bedroom door for an hour. Okay, maybe two. I didn't know what to say to her to smooth this all over. Before I'd taken the potion, we'd reached some kind of truce. But now all I could think about was that dream and I wanted it. Four problems stood in my way: My own stupid mouth, the fact I couldn't have her, the fact it was illegal, she had no idea we were soul mates, and she probably hated me. *Fine five things.*

"Don't forget that you basically kidnapped her and keep her locked up here like some kind of fairy princess when Astrid is the furthest thing from it," Maze whispered from right beside my head.

I jumped back. "Don't do that shit!"

"Do what? Tell you when things aren't going well?"

He held one hand up. "First, you want me to give you more of a heads-up. Then you take it back. No wonder why she finds you so frustrating."

"What are you doing here?" I hissed under my breath so Astrid wouldn't hear me outside her bedroom door and think I was spying on her.

He leaned his nose up against the door and sucked in a deep breath. "Found them! Looking for my nuggets. That damn cat is sneaky as hell. Oh and to give you a heads-up that Astrid will be leaving the premises in . . . three . . . two . . . one."

The sound of her opening her window came through the door. I took off like a shot and headed toward the stairs, pumping my arms every step of the way. When I reached the top of the stairs, I vaulted off the top step and hoped I didn't break my legs when I landed.

My stomach went up into my throat as I dropped. When my feet smacked into the hardwood floors in the foyer, I rolled onto my side and slid toward the front door. When I popped up, Logan stood over me with raised eyebrows. "Something I can help with?"

A sharp pain shot through my side and I was pretty sure I twisted my ankle, but it didn't matter. "Gotta go out . . . door."

Logan reached for the door and held it open. "Perhaps next time use the actual stairs."

I scrambled to my feet and my boots slipped on the floor. I was like a cartoon character trying to run but stuck in place. "Yeah, I didn't think of that."

Traction and I ran across the threshold out into the late afternoon air. It was crisp and the wind whipped down the path. The sound of creaking branches came from the side of the house where Astrid's bedroom windows were. I jogged over there only to see her standing on top of a tree limb with another thick branch acting as a railing. She tapped her foot, waiting as though she was going down an elevator and not making a hulking plant bend to her will. Golden smoke flowed from her hands all around the tree. The moment her feet hit the ground, she patted it like it was an old friend. "Thanks, Guy."

She dusted her hands off and began to walk out toward the path at the front of the house. Where was she going in her ripped up black jeans, black turtleneck, and gray leather jacket? Her hair was long and flowing in big curls down her back. She held her hand out facing up. A little puff of gold smoke and a set of keys appeared in the palm of her hand.

Are those Cross' keys?

She spun them around her finger. I pressed myself

up against the wall just around the corner of the house and waited for her to walk past with her hips swaying.

"Going somewhere?" I snapped a little louder than I meant to.

Astrid jumped. Her arms flailed and the keys went flying off into the woods. Magic shot from her hands as she spun around to face me. "Stalker much?"

I moved in closer. "Where are you planning on going?"

"I'm going out."

"Astrid." I followed behind her. "You know it's not safe. You should stay here."

She stopped dead in her tracks and slowly turned to face me. Her body quivered from head to toe. "You want to keep me locked up here like a princess in a tower and despite what you thought when we first met, I am not a princess!"

"That is not the point. It's dangerous out there and you're not ready."

"Not ready? Ugh." She held her hands up and let her magic seep from her palms. "You think I can't."

She summoned a knife, then let it disappear, then a sword, then a set of ninja stars. Each one flashed in her hand then was gone. "I can summon whatever I want. And use it however I want."

Magic seeped from her hands onto the ground around her feet.

Frustrating girl! "If you don't know how to use any of those weapons, then it doesn't matter."

"Ugh." She spun back around and marched on. "Before this I had the freedom to roam all of New York and I survived without you hovering over me. And now you want me to sit in a locked room like some kind of porcelain doll. Go to school, Astrid, come home, Astrid, stay locked up, Astrid. No more!"

I ran my hands through my hair. "Why do you have to be so damn difficult?"

"I NEED a break from being surrounded by dudes." She glanced over her shoulder. "I'm going to hang out with Medusa."

Three students who were passing by all froze and looked at her like she was crazy. Because legend said no one survived Medusa and now my soul mate was just going to "hang out" with her. *Right because that's normal.* "Ugh, fine, let me take you at least."

"I hate your portals! If I puke, I swear I will aim for your shoes."

*I*t was crazy to think the last time I was in this cave I was terrified. Now I was looking forward to it. Even as I passed statue after statue of her victims. A stag stood frozen on its hind legs. Its antlers were so huge they spanned nearly the whole ceiling of the tunnel like cave. I moved around it then stepped over a man frozen as he fell back on one hand while he held the other out pleading. I was going to have to ask Medusa about that one. "Helloooooooo."

"EEEkkkkk, I can't believe you're here!" Medusa's voice carried on an echo to me.

"I told you I would come over." I stepped out into a large room onto black and white checkered tiles. The transition from hard packed dirt to tile was surprisingly smooth. Black gothic columns rose up from the floor toward the ceiling. They arched up like a church. At one end was a circular stained-glass window with a large snake depicted in. At the other end was a statue of a cyclops. Its head nearly brushed the top of the ceiling. I pointed to the statue. "You really have to get rid of that creepy thing."

Medusa skipped out from her den at the back of the cave and ran toward me. This time I braced for impact. When she was three feet away, she leapt and threw her arms around my shoulders. I staggered back but didn't go down like I did the last time we met. She was smaller than me, standing at only a few inches over five feet. Her features were delicate and elf-like, with a small pert nose, pink rosy cheeks, and full bow-shaped lips. Her eyes were huge and hypnotic. She had the body of a complete bombshell, which was why I suspected most of these men died smiling. Her flowing black and purple snakes placed little kisses all over my cheeks and this time I wasn't shy about batting them away. "Your snakes are tonguing my face."

Medusa swatted them to the sides. "Down, boys, down."

Once they fell down to her elbows in submission, she clapped her hands together. "Oh my God, you're here!"

"I am. I needed some serious girl time." I took a step back. "What are you wearing?"

She held her arms out and the sweatshirt blanket thing covered her from neck to knee. It was huge and swallowed her body completely. Her little legs popped out of the bottom and were clad in black leggings. Thick fur lined boots covered her feet up to her knees. "It's called a blanket sweatshirt."

"You look like that big purple cartoon dinosaur." I giggled then a chill ran up my spine. "But I get it."

"Oh come over by the fire." She grabbed my hand and her fingers were ice cubes. She tugged me across the gallery down two steps. In front of us was a huge flat screen TV with a cushy purple crushed velvet sectional sprawled in front of it. Under the TV was a fireplace complete with a roaring fire. To the left of that up against the wall was a four-poster king-sized bed with a bedspread that matched the couch. To my right was a full chef's kitchen with stainless steel appliances, marble countertops, and shaker cabinets.

I walked down and stood in front of the fire, letting the heat seep into me. "I can't believe how cold it is in here."

"It's a cave in the mountains with twenty-foot ceilings. This isn't even bad. Wait till you get to the shit months like February and March. I mean February is so bad they take days off it to make it go faster. Where's the pizza?"

"What kind do you want?"

"Pepperoni. Wait no, cheese. No, veggie." She bit her bottom lip. "I have no idea."

"I got you covered." I held my hands out in front of me and smoke covered my palms as I pictured my favorite pizza in the city. Three boxes appeared and I dropped them onto the countertop.

"Now that's cool." She opened the top box and steam wafted up toward her. She sucked in a deep breath. "It's been so long since I had good pizza."

"Well, next time call for delivery." I pointed to myself.

She grabbed the box and walked over to the couch and plopped down. No plates, no napkins necessary. *Reasons why we are friends.* She pulled her feet under her and shoved a bite into her mouth. "So do tell, what's the deal? How's Beckett? Things progressing with you guys?"

"Ugh." I leaned back on the couch. "It's so complicated."

"Well, uncomplicate it for me." The flickering fire light cast shadows over her skin.

This was why I was here, why I needed her. I had no one else to turn to and above all else Medusa was my friend. "Okay, first I ascend, right? And nearly freaking die from it . . ."

"Yeah, Gregor almost died too." She waved me on. "Keep going."

"My great-great-great-grandfather? He almost died during his ascension too?" For some reason I found that comforting. Like maybe I wasn't the only Lockwood who suffered from their powers.

"Yeah, but we'll talk about it later. I want to hear more about sexy Beckett." Her eyes flashed. "That boy is fine!"

"Right, okay. So then I'm dying and he's there day and night taking care of me." I lowered my voice. "I even took a bath in front of him."

She raised her eyebrows. "Oh my God!" She dropped her pizza on the couch and clapped her hands together. "How was it? Super amazing? Did it hurt? Was he all aggressive or sweet and gent—"

"Okay, stop." I waved my hand back and forth. "No, nothing happened."

She rolled her eyes. "Lameeeee."

"No, it was kind of . . . sweet. He was a perfect gentleman."

"I hate it when they do that." She grabbed her pizza off the couch, blew on it, then took another bite.

"Oh, come on, it was actually pretty great."

"Aww you totally love him."

I shook my head. "Okay, no, stop."

"I'm sorry, but come on, you two are fire." She finished off her slice then grabbed another. "Oh, yeah. Coke, please."

I held my hand out, summoned one, then gave it to her. "Do you want me to keep going? Or not?"

She popped the top and took a sip. "Yeah, but like, is there a hot part and are we getting to it?"

I hesitated. "Yes and yes."

Her smile broadened and she waved me on.

"Okay, first he kissed me twice, then he's all we're just friends. Then I almost die, and he takes care of me for *days*. Then the warlock council shows up and he turns back into bossy Beckett. Then when I think I can't take any more, he arranges this whole awesome sleepover with the witch queens. And right after that shoves me back into classes, where this horrible bitch doses him with a love potion and he chooses me as the object of his obsession. The guy has so many mood swings I'm getting whiplash from the roller coaster he has me on. Then we spent this incredible night together, which he doesn't remember and turns back into a bigger jerk than before. To top it all off, I can't call my bestie Tilly and it's slowly killing me inside."

Medusa froze with a new slice of pizza in front of her open mouth. "Wow, that's a lot."

"Tell me about it." I let my head fall back on the couch. "And when he was under that potion I was only suspended. Luckily I wasn't expelled for good. But still this horrible council guy was there along with the headmaster and they said it was good this was just a spell because anything between the heir lines was strictly forbidden."

Medusa wrinkled her nose. "What do you guys care? You're trying to take over them anyways."

"That was my thought too at first, but then I realized something. If we are going to take over the council, then we're also going to need the support of the warlock world, which means we have to respect their laws."

She waved that away. "At least until you can change them yourself."

"Do you think?"

I didn't want to sound hopeful, but I knew I did. There was a part of me that deeply wanted Beckett, more than I'd like to admit to Medusa or myself. I felt connected to him in a way I couldn't explain or fathom. Being close to him was both agony and bliss.

Medusa nodded. "First you gotta breathe. These kinds of things can't be forced. If it's meant to be, it will be. In the meantime we can drive him crazy, just for fun."

"I don't even have to try at that, I just do it. He wants me to control my magic all the time and I literally just got it. And not all of it, mind you." I walked over and grabbed the box of cheese pizza and brought it with me to the couch.

"Here, give me your phone." She motioned for me to hand it over. I pulled it from my pocket and gave it to her.

"Wait, what are you doing on my phone?"

"I'm setting up a catfish profile for Beckett. It works wonders on Athena. I mean, she is royally pissed and I think it's perfect to drive him insane too." She scrolled up and up an up. "Do you have a picture of him in your phone?"

"No." I grabbed my phone and pulled it out of her hand. "You're so bad."

"Oh come on." She pointed to her snake hair. "Athena deserves this and so much more. You should see the hate messages she gets on Facebook and I'm a hundred percent sure her Snapchat is full of random"—she coughed and gestured toward her hips with a wink—"*snake pics*, all thanks to me. We can send snake pics to Beckett too."

"Somehow I don't think that will help." I slid my

phone back into my pocket. "Now maybe you can help me with some magic?" *Because the Beckett situation is hopeless.*

My grimoire dropped into my hands and I laid it out between the pizza boxes. Medusa reached for it and opened the book. She thumbed through the pages. "Ohhhh let's make him sound like a frog every time he opens his mouth, or how about random weight gain? That would piss me off so much."

My jaw dropped. "How can you see my book? No one can see it."

"Same way you can look me in the eye and not turn to stone." She shrugged. "Gregor's magic."

She held the book close to her chest and a wistful smile played on her lips and her voice softened. "We were friends. He was the only friend I had until you."

I glanced around the cave and sighed. She was so lonely here, yet she sat here listening to me talk out my problems. I wanted to do something for her, something she needed. "What is something that you want?"

She snorted. "I'd love to be warm."

I flipped through the pages and found a spell all the way at the back, one I knew would be hard to do, but I wanted to try. I jumped to my feet and rubbed my hands together. I called upon my magic and let it rise up inside me.

"Four corners of the Earth I call you near,
See my mind then make it here.

By strength in soil, mind, and heart,
Feel tides awash and fires restart.

I seek to move this place of mine,
Through the abyss thy space entwine."

Smoke flooded from my hands, covering the floor like a tidal wave. The cave rumbled and shook, rocks fell from above our heads, and dust rained down. Medusa jumped to her feet and moved to my side. "What did you do?"

"I'm not sure." More power and suddenly my stomach shot to my toes.

A huge crack fractured the floor and Medusa screamed. "Dude, I didn't want you to break my house." She pulled out her phone. "I'm going to put it on YouTube if you do."

I batted it away. "You can't . . . magic . . . remember."

"Right, good point." The floor dropped out from beneath us and we threw our arms around each other. The hair blew back from my face and her snakes looked cartoon like as they too flew straight up.

"I am seriously regretting those five slices I just ate." She squeezed her eyes shut.

The floor rose up beneath us and I braced for

impact. At the last second I spotted the bed and used my powers to summon it right beneath us. We landed in a heap and the wood frame split under the drop.

When I looked up, the entire cave was covered in dust. Some of her statues had broken. I glanced at the cyclops. *Nope, still there.* Medusa sucked in a deep breath. "What happened?"

"Why don't you take a peek outside and look?" I smirked. I didn't know if it worked, but if it did, magic was freaking awesome.

Medusa planted her feet and shook her head. "I can't go out there. W-what if I hurt someone?"

Rays of sunshine crept in through the entrance of the cave. Medusa's eyes widened and she sucked in a deep breath through her nose. "Is that the ocean? I haven't seen the ocean in years."

A warm breeze swept in through the opening and she let go of my hand. "No, Astrid, take me back. I don't want this."

"Come on. I just used my powers to move you to Magen's Bay. Closer to your sister." I wanted her to be happy, to be warm, but most of all to be free.

"Just hold on a sec." I held my hand out. If I could summon pizza and Coke, these should be a breeze. I pictured reflective aviator glasses. The glass was a one-way mirror that only Medusa could see out of, yet no one could see into them. I gave them silver blinders on each side, so her peripheral vision wouldn't accidentally catch someone. I handed them over to her.

She held them up, examining them. "Are you serious?"

"Oh and this too." I handed her a long piece of purple cloth. "That way you can wrap up the boys and no one will see them. Oh and I made it so once it's on, it'll stay in place. We wouldn't want any accidents, would we?"

Her mouth dropped open. "Astrid, I don't know what to say."

"Don't say anything. Just go have fun and say hi to your sister for me." I took a small step back and leaned up against the wall.

She pulled her sweater blanket from over her head and threw on the ground at her feet, then kicked off her boots. A wide smile spread across her lips. "No one has ever done something like this for me . . . you gave me *freedom*."

CHAPTER 26

*T*he blue portal exploded open in front of me. Wind whipped through it and the magic swirled as he prowled through the tunnel. His hair whipped around and his face was a mask of anger. His brows were drawn low over his eyes, and his lips were pressed into a hard line. The muscle in jaw ticked and he didn't utter a single word. He stopped just inside of the portal and reached his hand through. He crooked his finger at me then turned and walked back.

Nervous butterflies filled my stomach. *Crap, crap, crap.* I stepped into the portal after him and was dragged into a tornado. I thought I knew how violent it could get . . . I didn't. My body whipped from side to side. I twisted like a corkscrew and I was sure my stomach just fell out of my butt. My face smacked into something fuzzy yet hard underneath. *Did I stop moving?*

I placed my hands down and shoved myself up to a stand. My stomach was definitely not in my body anymore, otherwise I would have hurled. *Nope, nope, there it is.* I swallowed, trying not to lose all the pizza I'd eaten with Medusa. I hadn't thought about it before I stepped into the portal, but it was the most turbulent of all the portals I'd ever been in. Which made me believe two things: One, his portal's level of comfort was based on his mood or two, he liked making them turbulent . . . just to torture me. I turned for my bed on shaky legs and plopped down. Odin tiptoed across the bed and made himself comfortable on my lap.

Beckett paced back and forth. Step, step, step, turn and repeat. Odin looked up at me with that one eye of his, then subtly nodded toward Beckett almost asking, "How did you break it?"

I shrugged and turned my attention back to Beck. "Beckett, I—"

He held his index finger up, cutting me off. When he opened his mouth to speak, he just shook his head and turned to pace. Then finally he stopped with his hands on his hips. "Do you have any idea what you've done?" His voice was low and menacing.

"She's my friend."

"It doesn't matter, Astrid." He threw his hands up. "What you did was—"

"Was what? She's been trapped there for centuries, freezing in the winter. Lonely, with no friends and not a person to talk to." I placed Odin on the bed next to me and rose to my feet to face him. "You'd go crazy like that."

"At this point I really don't think I would." He stopped right in front of me, so close I could smell his clean, fresh scent. Heat radiated off his body. His eyes flashed with anger as he looked down his prefect nose at me. "The seclusion might be nice."

Ouch.

I was seriously reconsidering Medusa's offer to fill his inbox with inappropriate pictures from strangers. "She was going stir-crazy."

"Medusa is crazy!" He pointed to his head. "You think she's got all her marbles in place? I can assure you a monster does not!"

"She's not a monster!" Anger flared in my chest. "I'm sorry, but so not sorry!"

"Clearly not!" He towered over me, with his face red with anger. "But did you think for one second what it would mean to move an entire cave halfway around the world?" His body quaked from head to toe. "The exposure alone."

"What do you mean exposure?" My voice rose with anger.

"You think magic gives you the right to do anything you want, and it doesn't." He held his hands out in front of him like he wanted to strangle something.

Adrenaline flooded my veins. "You can't just leave her there. It's not right."

"I didn't say it was right. But you can't expose magic like that. There are consequences. And your biggest problem is you don't think about them. It's always what you want to do and nothing else matters."

I took a step toward him. "This wasn't about me! It was about her and the freedom she deserves."

The tension between us was palpable, sizzling in the air around us. It brushed over my skin like a scorching touch. He growled low in the back of his throat and tugged on his hair then threw his arms out wide.

"You need to learn that there are bigger things to be afraid of than just the council. If you expose magic, then this could all be gone like that." He snapped his fingers to emphasize the point.

"She's not exposed. She's in the forest surrounding the Bay, and the glasses I gave her will keep her safe."

"Astrid! Those glasses could get knocked off. What

about all the innocent people around her? What about the developers who want to build those mansions? Did you think of any of that? What if they walk into that cave while she's just relaxing? Don't tell me you didn't see all those statues she collects." We were so close his breath fanned across my face. I couldn't decide if I wanted to kiss him or kill him. "*You* need to stop being so impulsive, otherwise we are going to be in more trouble than we can handle."

I didn't mean to expose magic. I thought I was just helping a friend and I definitely didn't want to get him in trouble. I was hearing him and he sure as shit wasn't hearing me! If he would just listen! "Maybe you were okay with leaving her there, to freeze and rot for eternity, but I wasn't."

"You know what your biggest problem is? You always think the worst of me! And I haven't given you a reason to." He curled his hands into fists at his sides. "If you had just asked me to help you, I could've done it easily. When are you going to trust me? When is what I do for you going to be enough?"

His words stung. Was I too impulsive? Had I done the wrong thing? The burning fire I felt running through my body turned cold as ice even though my heart was racing. "Trust needs to be earned."

He threw his hands up, then smacked them down

on his thighs with a loud slap. "Then you tell me how everything I've been doing the past few weeks hasn't all been for *you*? I try to be nice. I try to get you into classes I think you'll like. I look the other way when you sneak out of the house in the middle of the night to go hang out with your friends. All I've asked is for you to take this seriously and you just can't." He reached for the door and wrapped his hand around the knob. "You know what, I'm not mad. I'm just disappointed."

Everyone knows that's so much worse than mad!

"Beck."

He hesitated and glanced at me over his shoulder.

I swallowed down my nerves. "I'm sorry."

"Like you said before, you're really not." He turned and walked away. I glanced out the door to watch after him. He threw his fist out and punched the wall beside his face, splintering the hard wood there.

When I turned back, Maze stood there staring at me. I startled and jumped back. "Ew, what are you doing here?"

His dark hair hung in his eyes and a dangerous smile passed over his lips. "The cat has my marshmallows . . . I know it."

I glanced over my shoulder at Odin then back at

Maze. "There aren't any marshmallows in my room, Maze."

He pointed a finger at my face. "If I catch him stealing my food . . . I'll skin him."

"Okay, gross." I closed the door in his face and turned to the bed.

I dropped down on it and let my arms and legs flop.

Odin curled on his side next to me. "I think you broke the pretty blond one." His voice was low and hissing.

"Yeah, well, you broke the dark twisted one."

Odin chuckled. "I know. Isn't it great?"

No, no, it's not . . .

CHAPTER 27

"*A*nd then he said I'm really not sorry. I've never seen him so mad before." I crossed my arms on the table in front of me and laid my head on them.

"Well, you did kind of move a mountain. So I can see his frustration." Leo rubbed one of his hands in small circles over my back. With the other hand he held his cell phone up as he texted fast and furious messages.

"I mean, it's pretty awesome if you ask me." Cassidy leaned back in her chair and glanced over her shoulder at where the rest of her house was sitting.

I nudged Leo. "Are you even listening to me?"

A small smile played on his lips and he bit his bottom lip. "I'm listening."

"You so are not, and that smile says boy . . . cute boy." Just because I was having problems with Beckett didn't mean I wasn't happy for Leo. He needed to move on from Kyle and whoever could make him smile like that was good in my book. "So what's his name?"

Leo glanced over his shoulder at the wave of students sitting around us. Then leaned in closer to me. "I mean, he's kind of a famous witch and I don't want to make a big thing of it because we're just chatting, you know?"

"You're dating a witch?" I hissed under my breath. "Isn't that taboo in the warlock world?"

Leo snickered. "Yeah, it is, but I don't care."

"Good, me neither." I reached out and snagged his phone from his hand. I glanced down at the name. "Ohhhhh Poison Roycy. I kind of love it. But why poison?"

He grabbed his phone back and shoved it into his pocket. "Because he's a badass. But it's really not my story to tell. Especially not here."

The cafeteria around me buzzed with activity and I could see why he wouldn't want any of that to get out. It was both crazy yet somehow controlled with all the other students. We sat in the middle of it all and anyone would be able to hear us if they got close enough.

The students sectioned themselves off according to what house they each belonged in. The Malback House took up one corner of the cafeteria. It was a sea of black jackets with the hydras on the back. Shouts and cheers filled their side of the room. Some of them arm wrestled while others fought over who could eat the most chocolate pudding in one sitting. Plastic pudding cups littered the tables and some of the floor. A boy who was the size of a bear squeezed two cups into his mouth at the same time. While his competition, a stealthy-looking girl with short black hair scooped pudding into her mouth with blinding speed. As she took the last bite, she leapt to her feet and chucked the empty plastic cup in the guy's face. She threw her arms up and a chorus of cheers broke out.

Cassidy gave a halfhearted, "Whoo."

In the other corner of the cafeteria sat the students of Whitmore House. They reminded me of the preppy students I used to go to school with in New York. Their shirts were either polo or pressed button-downs. The boys' haircuts were short and girls wore high ponytails. Under their bomber jackets their clothes were every color of the rainbow. If it was a competition to see which group was the loudest, they

were a close second. To my right over by the entrance
sets of booths lined the wall and only a few of the
students of the psychic house sat there, each one
looking more fragile than the next. With barely a
morsel of food on their plates.

It all seemed so normal, well, if Dustwick House
wasn't floating tables and chairs over my head. The
clattering and clanking over my head wasn't helping
the splitting headache I was rocking.

"Look, guys, I know I messed up, but I couldn't just
leave her there, you know?"

Leo nodded. "Oh I get why you did it, but he was
right."

"Ugh, I know he was right." I lifted my head and
pressed my hand over my face. "How is it possible to
feel like I messed up but didn't all at the same time?"

Two chairs dropped down right behind me and a
smaller warlock with dark black shaggy hair waved
his hand at the table. "My bad."

"Ugh." I waved my hand and let magic go. Golden
smoke grabbed every piece of furniture over our heads
and placed it all back where it came from, the way I
visualized it. Dozens and dozens of tables and chairs
all perfectly back in place.

The cafeteria went silent and all eyes swung
toward me. I glanced around. "What?"

Cassidy leaned across the table. "Um, Astrid, no one has seen power like that before. We all kind of, you know, have an average amount. Not move an entire cafeteria full of furniture that a dozen other warlocks are messing with."

"Um, well, they were giving me a headache and I really didn't want a table dropped on my head." I ran my hand through my hair. "But really, guys, what am I going to do?"

Leo sat back and crossed his legs. "You could send flowers, candy, perhaps even a love note?"

I rolled my eyes. "Be serious."

"Oh I am, use your feminine wiles." He bumped me with his elbow.

"I don't have feminine wiles."

Leo pursed his lips. "You know nothing. Of course you do."

Just as the noise of the cafeteria rose back to its thunderous level, the doors busted wide-open, smacking into the walls. "Astrid!"

My head snapped up. "Maze?"

He quickened his pace toward me as he wound his way through the chairs and tables of people. The noise died once more, and he charged forward, unaware that everyone stared at him. His eyes were wide and round with panic. I sat up straight, butterflies fluttering in my stomach. I too glanced toward the door, looking for someone . . . Beckett. If something went wrong, he came for me, but this time he was nowhere to be found. Which made my nervous flutters turn to full-blown worried tremors. As he got closer to our table, I rose to my feet.

"What's happened?"

"Y-you had better come quick." He wrapped his hand around my wrist and pulled me toward the door.

I called back to Leo and Cassidy. "I'll text you later."

Everyone watched us and it only made me more uncomfortable. I hated being the center of attention and now I was the lead role in today's dramatic enter-tainment. Maze pulled me through the door and down a long hall flooded with students. When he walked, they jumped out of his way and didn't even try to make eye contact. When I was with Beckett it was the complete opposite. They always wanted to see Beck, talk to him, or get his attention in some way. For Maze they couldn't move fast enough.

"Maze, where are we going?"

"Home."

I tried to slow him down, but he wouldn't stop. "Is everything okay?"

"No."

My heart skyrocketed and panic over came me. "Did something happen?"

"Yes."

These one-word answers were killing me. Why couldn't he just be a normal person instead of acting like some cryptic magic eight ball? He marched me through a set of double doors and we were out in the middle of the circle path that connected all the buildings of the school. It was late morning, nearly noon, and the air held that crisp cool feel I might've enjoyed if he wasn't completely freaking out. What the hell could've gotten him like this? And why wasn't Beckett the one to come get me? Was he really that mad or did something worse happen to him?

If something happened to him, I'd kill whoever did it. *Where'd that come from?* "Did something happen to Beckett?"

I held my breath, waiting as he dragged me around the corner toward our house. His long legs ate up the distance and I had to practically jog to keep up with him. The muscles in my legs burned. When he didn't answer, I planted my heels and forced him to stop. When he whirled around, I pulled my arm from his grip. "Maze, what the hell happened?"

"Just come on, you have to see this." He grabbed my

arm once more and pulled me up the stairs and onto our front porch.

It wasn't an answer, but it was more than one word. I'll take it. I followed him through the foyer, past a wide-eyed Cross, and up the stairs. Logan stood on the top step. "Where are you two off to?"

Maze didn't stop. "Move."

He shoved past Logan and turned to go down the hall toward my room. I glanced over my shoulder at Logan.

"I'll let you know as soon as I find out."

When I turned to look at Beckett's office door, which usually stood open, now it was closed up tight. The sound of him moving around traveled into the hall, yet he didn't come out. I didn't have time to think about it as Maze shoved my door wide-open and dragged me in. He pulled me around in front of him and pushed me forward.

I stumbled and caught myself on my desk just in time to spot that unmistakable short blond hair full of curls.

"What's up, bitches?"

My jaw dropped open. "Tilly?"

She clapped her hands together and squealed. "The one and only."

I glanced from Maze to her and back again. "What did you do?"

"I didn't do anything. She just showed up here." He rubbed his hand over the back of his neck and took a small step back from her. "I saw her coming."

Tilly sauntered over to him and looked up at him with those big brown eyes of hers. "You certainly did." She held her hands out. "And now here I am, thanks to you."

Maze swallowed and his eyes went wide. "I, um, I, um..."

My emotions warred within me. Elation flowed through my body so hard I could barely contain myself. I missed her so much it was a constant ache in my chest. Now she was here with me, in the flesh. I wanted to both hug her and send her away. It wasn't safe here and if anyone deserved my protection it was my bestie sister. I rounded on Maze. "What were you thinking bringing her here?" I marched past him and slammed my door shut.

"Um, ouch much." Tilly's face fell into a deep scowl. "You could at least pretend to be happy to see me after you ghosted my ass for the past few weeks."

Her voice was laced with hurt and for a moment I'd forgotten the infallible Tilly could be deeply hurt sometimes. I didn't want to see her upset. If she was hurt, I was hurt too. That was the way we worked and though I was different, nothing could change that for us.

I walked across my room and threw my arms around her shoulder and hugged her tight. "I missed you so much."

She stiffened for a moment then hugged me back. "Not enough to tell me where you were."

I pulled back and looked her dead in the eye. "You can't stay here. It's not safe."

"Bullshit. If you're here, then I am too." She shrugged and turned away to walk around my room. "It's not that big, but we'll make do. I didn't bring that many clothes. I figured I'd borrow yours and we can bunk together until I get a hold of the manager of this place and get my own room, or is it the headmaster?"

"Till, you're not listening to me." Footsteps sounded in the hall. I lowered my voice. "Seriously, you cannot stay."

"Oh no you don't." She shook her head. You don't get to transfer to a fancy new private school without me. What were you thinking? Honestly, Astrid, if I wasn't so confident in our awesome bestieness, I would be hurt, truly hurt."

Her eyes glistened for a second and I saw it all, how upset she truly was. We were family and I messed it up, but what could I have done? She wasn't a person of Evermore and my secrets were forbidden to show to mortals. I glanced up at Maze for some help here. How was I going to make her leave without devastating her?

Maze crossed his arms over his chest. "And now you see why I had no choice but to bring her here."

"Yeah, you did, big guy." She beamed at him and he took another step back.

Maze, the badass psychic who ate like a pig, predicted the future, saw worlds no one else could understand and would kill just as easily as he would make a sandwich, was thrown by little Tilly Astoria. "Astrid, this is all you."

"Wait, what? You brought her here and you're bailing?" I marched over to him, grabbed his arm, and pulled him into the center of the room. My magic began to rise with each passing moment. I had no idea what I was going to do and he was going to help me. "You are staying."

"Okay, I'm staying." His brows furrowed in confusion. "I don't want to, but I am. Why am I?"

"I have no idea, but I'll take it." I shook my head at him. "I can't believe you did this."

"Hey! Don't blame him. He stopped me from knocking on the front door." Tilly moved to stand in front of him and face me. Like she was going to protect him from me.

I threw my arms up. "Then how the hell did you get here?"

"You know, you could act kind of happy to see me." She put her hands on her hips and arched her eyebrow the way she always did when we were about to argue.

"I am happy to see you. But this place is hidden." *For your protection.* "For good reason." *So I don't accidently kill you.* "And we have to follow those rules."

"Well, I got this text from some girl named Medusa. I mean, who names their kid Medusa nowadays? I'm all for that girl power and naming your kid after a woman who could turn people to stone, but so weird."

Maze locked eyes with me and glared. I'd done Medusa a favor and now she was doing me one. I gave her, her sister and now she was giving me mine. *Damn my good intentions.*

"So she gave you the address and here you are?"

"Here I am." She held her arms to her sides, presenting herself like a present.

I ran my hands through my hair and tugged on the strands. How could one good intention backfire so bad? "Till—"

A firm knock sounded on my door. "Astrid."

Shit, Beckett. If he didn't hate me for what I did last night, he'd for sure hate me for this. "Yeah?"

"What's going on? I heard voices." His voice was so smooth, yet goose bumps covered my skin every time he spoke.

The toilet in my bathroom flushed and Odin strolled out. When he spotted the three of us, he stopped dead in his tracks. "Meow?"

I turned to Tilly and lowered my voice. "You have to hide."

"Where? Why?" She began looking for a place to hide, but there weren't many options. My bed was too low to the floor and the bathroom was always an obvious hiding place.

"Help me." I hissed at Maze.

"What am I going to do?" he snapped back.

"If he sees her here and knows Medusa sent her then this is even more my fault." I turned and paced back and forth.

"Astrid, open the door," Beckett demanded.

Smoke poured from my hands and panic overcame me. *Shit, shit, shit.* After last night I was in so deep with him I didn't want him to be even more pissed at me. I shook my hands, trying to calm down, but no matter what I did smoke poured from me.

"Um, dude, you're on fire." Tilly pointed to my hand.

Odin looked up at me. "Meow."

I turned to Tilly. "Do you trust me?"

She nodded. "Yeah, totes."

"Okay." I opened my hand over her face and a puff of gold smoke smacked her in the nose and Tilly crumbled at my feet.

CHAPTER 28

"*A*strid, you can invite me in, or I'll invite myself in, your choice." I stood outside her door, not so patiently waiting. The hair on the back of my neck stood at attention, like a sixth sense it told me when magic was being used.

"Just a sec." Her sweet voice carried to me and I wanted to be patient to give her the benefit of the doubt. I wanted to, but I couldn't. I let my magic seep from my hand under the door and the lock clicked open.

"Ready or not." I turned the knob. "Here I come."

Astrid stood before me. Beads of sweat dotted her forehead and cheeks. Her hair was a tangled mess and fell in tatters back from her face. Her eyes darted toward the floor. I followed her gaze down toward a white fluffy cat.

"Another cat, really?"

"I practiced. She's pretty, isn't she?" Her words were rushed, and she shifted her weight back and forth like she wanted to pace but couldn't.

"Yes, very." Maze's deep voice came from just behind the door. I hadn't seen him when I walked in. I yanked it back, giving him space to move out from where he hid.

Why would he be in Astrid's room and why would he be hiding it? "What are you doing in here?"

"Just hanging out?" It sounded more like a question than a statement. Why was he so unsure of himself? The only thing Maze gave a shit about was food and fun. Now he was all cozy with Astrid. When did they even become friends? Maze didn't have friends. I was barely his friend and we'd known each other all our lives.

He moved to stand next to Astrid and the two of them faced me. I glanced from one to the other and back again. I stared, they stared. I bent down in front of the cat and met its bright brown-eyed gaze. "Why's it so still? Did you break it?"

"I didn't break it."

"She didn't break it."

They spoke at the same time. I reached out to pet the cat and it darted between my legs then out the door. They both dove forward, trying to catch it at the same time. They smacked together and fell to the floor in a tangle of limbs and legs. Astrid was sprawled across his chest. Her hair fell over his face and her legs were wrapped around his.

She groaned and pushed up from him. "Sorry."

"You're crushing things you shouldn't be." His voice was a pained rasp. "Move your knee."

"Shit." She rolled to the side, scrambling off of him.

"Whoaaaa." Maze groaned as he cupped himself and rolled to the side, curling into the fetal position. "Next time you're on top be a little gentler, okay?"

"There damn well better not be a next time she's on top," I snapped and they both froze. I rose to my feet, towering over the two of them. Something inside of me shifted and I hated the way they lay next to each other, the way she didn't stiffen, the way they seemed to share a secret I wasn't in on. "You guys are hiding something."

Astrid scrambled to her feet and tossed her hair over her shoulder. She tugged down on the hem of her sweater and smoothed her hands over her ripped up black jeans. Her bomber jacket hung off her shoulders at her elbows. "What do you mean hiding something?"

"Exactly what I said."

Maze came up to his knees and sucked in a deep breath. "Don't look at me. I'm just waiting for my boys to drop back into place."

Astrid wrinkled her nose. "Ew." She shoved him toward the door. "Go look for my cat and when you find her, don't let her out of your sight."

With his hand draped across his midsection, he limped toward the door. "Yeah, I'll find the fluffy white thing."

"So worried about the cat?" There was a presence here, something unfamiliar I felt it in my bones. *But where is it?*

"I made her. She's my responsibility." Astrid glanced toward the door like she wanted to follow Maze out, yet she stood there facing me.

"So now you're taking responsibilities?" My voice came out harsher than I expected.

Astrid flinched away from me. "I told you I was sorry."

"I would've helped you if you only asked me, Astrid." If she found out how powerful her asking me would be then I'd be screwed. I'd do anything for her, make anything happen for her. But I wanted her trust, which she seemed to have in everyone else but me. It hurt like a cut deep in my stomach that just wouldn't heal.

"Sure you would have. Right after you lectured me worse than a parent. Which I've never had."

She and I were too similar for words. I wanted to tell her about everything about how both of us didn't have the families we needed, how I understood her more than everyone else could because she was mine and I was hers. "I get it."

"Do you?"

Maze ran back into the room. He hunched over in front of Astrid and sucked in deep breaths. "Can't find the cat." He stood up straight. "But the front door was open."

"Shit." She dashed for the door. "Beck, I gotta go."

I reached out and wrapped my hand around her upper arm, stopping her from leaving me. "You can trust me, you know."

She placed her hand over mine and gazed up at me. "I want to."

"All you have to do is try." I pressed my fingers into her skin and flashes of the dream I'd had flew through my mind. My fingers on her stomach running lower, her hair spread over my pillow, and the way her breaths came in little puffs.

Astrid pulled her arm free of my grip. "I gotta go."

Without another word, she ran after Maze and the two of them together went to look for her fluffy cat. How could she trust Maze over me? I glanced around her room once more then stormed out. There was nothing there for me but fresh torture. How the hell was I supposed to fix any of this? I marched down the hall toward my room. There was only one thing I could think of that could help me ease this frustration. The second I got to my room I quickly closed the door behind me and ripped my shirt over my head. I threw it on the bed and swung my arms across my body to stretch them out.

When I turned, I froze. That damn fluffy cat sat perched on my dresser, staring at me. "Astrid!"

I waited for a response, but there was only silence. She had to have left the house looking for this cat. Without me...

CHAPTER 29

"*H*ow could this happen?" I chided Maze as we hurried down the path toward the school. It was late afternoon and this time of year the sun began to set at 4:00 p.m. Cool air seeped in through my sweater and I pulled my bomber jacket higher on my shoulders to fight the wind.

"Your crazy friend showed up," he snapped back.

"You didn't have to let her in!" Classes were over for the day and the other students were all heading back to their houses or hanging out laughing in groups of friends. Their lives all seems so carefree. I almost missed the days when all I had to worry about was classes and Tilly.

Maze tapped his temple. "She's important. I've seen it."

I stopped in my tracks. "Important to what? What's going to happen to her?"

"Nothing, if I can help it." He turned from me and kept walking.

I quickened my pace to catch up. "What the hell does that mean? If you can help it?"

"We're going to need her. That's all I can say."

I grabbed his jacket and jerked him to a stop. He arched his eyebrow at me and pointedly looked at my hand.

"Ballsy."

"I don't give a shit how ballsy you think I am. You need to start talking and you need to start talking now." I shook him. Some of the students openly gaped at me, but I didn't care. "Tilly is freaking lost in this magical hell she has no clue about. She's a cat and is probably losing her shit. So if you know something, spill it now."

Gold magic poured from my hand and surrounded him.

He looked down at my hand once more. "You're gonna want to let me go."

"Or what?" I wasn't scared of him the way everyone else was. This was Maze and after living with him for weeks, the only thing I was worried about around him were my goldfish snacks.

Green smoke poured from his hands and the lapels of his jacket opened wide. Tarot cards flew from his pockets and surrounded me like a tornado. They glowed and the images blurred together as they moved faster and faster. Students ran and ducked for cover as I stood in the middle of this. My own magic rose to meet his and I didn't stop it. His cards glowed to a blinding color and I dropped my grip and shielded my eyes. Green smoke blasted me and my body flew up and back. I twisted in the air and dropped toward the ground.

I held my hands out and let my magic go. I pictured myself floating down to the ground and my fall slowed to a float and I righted myself. I dropped down a few feet away from him and stepped from the air like I was walking off the bottom step. I straightened my jacket and stomped up to Maze. "What was that for?"

The cards drifted back down into his pockets and his smoke dissipated as quickly as it came on. He cracked his neck and locks of his midnight hair fell asleep. His eyes darted around to the crowds watching us. When he didn't turn to look at me, I snapped my fingers in front of his face.

"Maze, what happened?"

He leaned in closer. "You aren't the only one who

can't control yourself sometimes. I don't like being touched, okay?"

Any kind of annoyance I had at him vanished. "Okay." I didn't know what happened to him, but whatever it was I wasn't going to push a boundary he had.

"I-I mean it's not always. Just when I'm nervous." He shifted from one foot to the other.

In all the time I'd known Maze not once did his feathers get ruffled. "Are you nervous?"

"We have a *human* lost. She's going to be important. And yeah, I might be a little nervous about that."

"Astrid!"

I spun around toward my name only to see Leo running to me. "Hey, I got your text. What do you mean have I seen a white fluffy cat?"

He stopped and looked over my head at Maze. His eyes widened behind the thick rims of his glasses. "Mazerial." He whispered his name like a curse. "Your reputation is . . . are you sure you should be out?"

The longer we stood still, the more the students began to encroach on us. Each of them giving Maze sideways glances.

Maze spun in a circle. "I'll be fine."

"Why are you both out here looking for a cat? Is it

cursed or something?" Leo lowered his voice. "Because if it is, I know a place we can hide it."

"No, it's Tilly." I hooked my arm with his and turned him so we could continue walking.

"Tilly your friend, Tilly?" He glanced from me to Maze and back. "She's not the—"

"Cat, yup." I sighed. "It was a bad idea and now she's running around here somewhere doing God knows what and probably terrified."

My cell buzzed in my pocket and I pulled it out to show Maze the screen. "Beckett."

I slid my finger across the screen. "Hey."

"Hey." His voice was warm and sultry, and goose bumps broke out over my skin at the sound of it. "I got something you want."

So many things. "Oh yeah?"

"Give you a hint. It purrs when I touch it." He chuckled.

She better not be freaking purring. "You found my cat."

Leo's eyebrows rose nearly to his hairline and he mouthed the words *oh shit*. Maze pointed back toward the house and we all began walking in that direction.

"Yeah, you better come and get her. She likes to knock things off my dresser." He sounded out of breath.

"I'll be right there." I paused. "And, Beckett, thank you."

"No problem." The line went dead and my heart rate skyrocketed.

"Guys, I can't believe he has her. I mean, what if she changes back in front of him?" I quickened my pace and we all began to jog back. "We need to get her out of here and back to New York. She doesn't belong here."

Maze shook his head. "It's too late now."

"I honestly don't care what you say. I don't care how important you think she is. This can't happen, Maze. She's a human in a warlock world." *How could I protect her from myself?*

The three of us hustled up the steps to the house and into the foyer. Becket stood in the middle of it, waiting for us. He was shirtless and grains of sand clung to his skin. Within his arms he cradled Tilly to his bare chest. His hair flew out in all different directions and my eyes couldn't decide where they wanted to look first.

"Damn," Leo muttered.

You have no idea. I held my hands out. "Thank you for finding her."

"No problem." As he handed her over to me, my

fingers brushed over his bare skin. He was warm to the touch and looked like he'd been working out.

I wrapped her up in my arms and held her tight. Though she squirmed in my grip, I didn't let go. I just held on tighter. I pressed my face to her ear. "Keep squirming and I'll turn you into a spider."

She froze. Tilly hated spiders. I ran my fingers over the top of her head. "I hope she wasn't too much trouble."

Beckett gave her a sideways look. "She's oddly smart but nah. It was all good. But if you guys are okay here, then I'm going to take a shower."

"Can I watch?" Leo whispered low enough for only me to hear. I stifled a giggle and jabbed him with my elbow.

"Okay." I held Tilly close to me as I walked by Beckett. "I'm just going to take her back to my room."

"Okay." He began to follow me up the stairs.

I froze. "Are you coming?"

"Um, no, but I'm going to shower . . . like I just said. Are you okay? You're acting weird." He looked at me like I'd sprouted eight heads.

"Right, yes. No, I'm fine." *Why was my voice so weird? You're a shit liar, Astrid.* I moved up the stairs quicker.

Logan paused at the top of the steps to let me pass. "Where are we all going?"

"To the shower." I blurted out then shook my head. "No, I'm going to my room. Beckett is going to take a shower."

He glanced past me toward Leo and Maze. "And them? Is there some kind of meeting I don't know about?"

"I mean, is the shower an option?" Leo teased and Beckett's cheeks flamed bright red.

Funny, I didn't think I'd ever seen him blush before. I reached back and tugged Leo with me. "No, it's not an option."

Leo hiked his thumb at me. "Then to her room it is."

Maze didn't say anything. He simply followed me farther down the hall and I was glad to get some distance between Logan and Beckett.

I waved over my shoulder. "Catch you guys later."

Before either of them said anything to stop us. I waved Maze and Leo into my room and slammed the door behind them. I dropped Tilly on the floor. "Bad, Tilly, bad."

"Can she understand you?" Leo bent down low and examined her.

Tilly swiped her paw at him, and he fell back onto his hands.

"Yeah, she gets you."

I held my hand out and pictured her changing back into her normal form. Gold smoke poured from my hand and surrounded her. It curled around her body as she grew in size. She turned from house cat, to the size of a jaguar. Her lips pulled back from her teeth and she hissed at me.

"Just another second." I held her there with my power. Until she contorted up on her hind legs and slowly the fur receded back into her skin. Her face changed from feline back to Tilly's soft elven features. Her bright blond hair popped from the top of her head and fell down past her shoulder in wild ringlets. A golden glow that matched my magic clung to her skin, making her shine like a star. She was back in her fuzzy cream sweater and dark blue jeans she'd been wearing when she arrived.

I dropped my hand and Tilly hunched over and coughed. "Ugh."

"Just take a deep breath. I know it's a lot to take in." I stepped to her side and ran small circles over her back.

"Ew, yuck, blah." She stuck her tongue out and pulled pieces of hair off it. "That was . . ."

"I know and I'm sor—"

"Awesome." She stood up straight and met my eye. "This place is amazing. Sign me up."

"Seriously?" When I'd first arrived, I was terrified and wanted nothing more than to be normal. To go home. Leave it to Tilly to be ready to jump in with both feet.

"When we were eleven, did you get a letter of acceptance here and not tell me? Because if I had known, I would have kept an eye out for my owl." She sauntered up to Maze. "What about you, big guy, you got some kind of freaky power going on too?"

He took a small step back from her. "You could say that."

"I'm into it." She winked and he swallowed.

"Till." I snapped my fingers to get her attention. "What are you doing here?"

"Isn't it obvious? I'm here for you." She shrugged.

I hated every second of not being able to tell her. I dropped down to sit on the foot of my bed. "I didn't want to keep any of this from you. But I had to. At least that's what Beckett said was necessary."

"Oh him, dude is intense but in like a I-can't-get-enough-of-Astrid kind of way. He's got it bad for you. My recommendation is you just give *it* to him. Whatever *it* is."

Heat flooded my cheeks. "Tilly!"

"What? It's true." She pressed her hand to Maze's chest and closed his eyes and sucked in a breath.

"Till, don't touch him." I rose to my feet to grab her.

Maze held his hand up. "No, it's okay. I can handle it." He went motionless and his eyes locked on hers. "Be gentle."

"Oh, big guy, for some reason gentle is the last thing I think you need." She bit her bottom lip and smiled up at him. I'd never seen Tilly be so forward with a guy before. What had gotten into her?

I reached out and yanked her back. "I think my magic has gone to your head."

"I've never felt better." She didn't take her eyes off him.

Don't poke a sleeping bear. "Till." I shook her arm to get her attention. "You can't stay."

A flash of hurt colored her features. "You don't want me around?"

"No, that's not it." I shook my head. "It's not safe here for you. You've only seen a fraction of what I can do."

"I don't care. Give me a wand and sign me up, Harry. I'm freaking staying." She crossed her arms over her chest.

"If Beckett finds out you are here, he's going to kill me." I glanced at Leo, who was nodding in agreement.

Tilly glanced at Maze. "What about you, do you want to see me go?"

"No, you're staying." He crossed his arms over his chest. "She's not going anywhere."

"Maze! You can't decide that!" This was a freaking mess.

"I already did," he simply stated, then marched over to my desk and pulled the chair out. He dropped his big body down into it and made himself comfortable. "She stays."

"Ha! There you have it. My happy ass is moving in." She threw her arm over my shoulders. "Roomie."

I sighed. "Tilly, I love you."

"I love you too."

"I don't want anything to happen to you, okay? This world is dangerous." I lowered my voice. "I'm dangerous."

"And that's exactly why I know you won't." She dropped her arm then turned to face me. "You've got this. I know why you kept me in the dark. But now that I've seen what's up, I'm in. Plus, you need me."

She wasn't lying. I felt lost in this world most of the time and in New York she was my anchor. Could she be here? "Beckett would never allow it and you can't just walk around in cat form all the time." I already had a demon cat in disguise. I couldn't have a bestie like that too.

The door flew open and Beckett stood before me

in nothing but a towel wrapped around his hips. Drops of water clung to his skin and his hair fell in damp tatters around his face. He held a small blanket in his hands. "Hey, Astrid, I was thinking, your cat really liked this blanket. Do you wan—" His words dropped off and his face changed from soft and warm to pissed off in an instant. "What is going on here?"

I motioned to Tilly. "Beckett, you remember Tilly from the club."

"I remember her. What is she doing here?" He spoke through gritted teeth.

"Well, um, she kind of just showed up here." I pulled her back behind me.

"Humans don't just simply show up at Warwick, Astrid. How did she know where you were? Did you tell her?" He seethed, his words low and menacing. His grip tightened on the blanket in his hand. The blanket he was going to give to me for a new pet. Another pet he was going to tolerate . . . just for me.

"I swear I didn't tell her."

"Again, humans just don't randomly show up." He threw the blanket on the floor just inside the door.

"It's not her fault," Tilly snapped and stepped out beside me. "I got a text with an address and I followed it."

Beckett arched his eyebrows. "A text? That just

so happened to have the address of a place that remained hidden for centuries?" He rounded on Maze. "And what do you have to do with all of this?"

Maze lazed in my chair with one arm draped over the back of it and his legs spread before him. "I'm here to make sure she stays."

"Damn it, Maze!" Beckett growled. "There is no way in this burning hell that she's created"—he pointed his finger at me—"that Tilly is staying."

Maze shrugged. "I've seen it."

Beckett froze. "What do you mean you've seen it?"

"Our fates are now tied. She stays."

Beckett dropped a vile curse and shoved his hands in his hair. When he dropped his arms, he looked at me and all the fire left his eyes. "I can't win with you ever, can I?"

"I didn't mean—"

"You never mean, Astrid." He pointed to everyone in the room. "You give a shit about everyone else around you but me, the one freaking person who is trying to protect you. The one person who has done so from day one."

"Beck—"

"I'm not finished. Maze, Leo, get out, now." He narrowed his eyes at the two of them.

Leo nodded. "As much as I love the show . . . Astrid, text me later." He darted out past Beckett.

Maze slowly rose to his feet. "So she stays?"

"Oh yeah, she stays." The muscles in Beckett's arms and torso flexed and twitched with aggression. "You got what you wanted. She's tied to us, you've seen it. Now my hands are tied."

"She won't be." Maze ran his eyes over Tilly. "I'll make sure of it."

Without another word, he walked out, leaving the three of us alone.

Beckett looked at me then ground his teeth together. "Are you happy now?"

"Look, dude, don't blame her," Tilly snapped.

Beckett held his hand up, silencing her. "You have no idea what you've done." He spun to walk out the door but then turned back. "You know what, enough is enough. You think I've kept you locked away, you think you have no freedom. Did you ever stop for one second and wonder why I did any of that?"

"Beck, I—"

"I did it so you would have time to adjust to this world, so you could learn your powers without hurting yourself or anyone else. Now what are we going to do, Astrid? When the council finds out about her, what are we going to do? A freaking human in

Warwick. When are you going to learn the world doesn't revolve around you?"

"Come on, don't be so hard on her." Tilly stepped between me and him. The way she always did when trying to protect me.

"Screw this! You're grounded!" Beckett motioned to the two of us. "Both of you can't leave until I figure out what the hell to do with you."

"Grounded?" He had to be out of his mind. "You can't ground me!" He wasn't my father. He had no right. I was here to help him. Sure, he was mad, but grounding me? There was no way in hell that was going to fly.

He gave a dark snicker. "I just did." He slammed the door behind him.

Jackass!

CHAPTER 30

"Grounded! He *grounded me.*" I turned my back to the door and faced Tilly. "Can you believe him?"

"Well, yeah, kind of." She shrugged. "I'm not sure who the council is, but dude wants to destroy them. And I'm guessing me being here throws a wrench in that."

"Why are you being so calm?" The door swung open and Odin strolled in and jumped up on the bed.

Tilly's brow furrowed. "Your cat can open doors?"

I turned back and slammed the door shut once more. "You have no idea."

"Just relax. Give him a day or two to calm down. You know, then just go in there and tell him to suck it."

Tilly flopped down on the bed and ran her fingers over Odin's ears and under his chin.

"You don't know. Beckett rules them all and everyone around here bows to him like he's freaking royalty."

"I mean, I can see why. Have you looked at the guy? He's gorgeous. Why wouldn't they follow?" Tilly rolled on her back and scooted up toward my headboard. She snuggled down into my pillows.

"It's more than that. In this world the warlocks revere him because of his bloodline." The bed dipped under my weight when I sat down on the edge.

"And apparently your bloodline as well. Otherwise you wouldn't be living in this house and not one of the other houses." She pulled a pillow into her lap and held it tight.

"How did you know that?"

"It's amazing what animals can hear from a far distance." She chuckled. "You're important to their cause and for some reason I trust these guys you're with. But really, though, why are they all so hot? Is there something in the water?"

I giggled. "I know, right?"

"Especially Maze. There's something about him. He's sexy in a dirty hot kind of way."

I wrinkled my nose. "That's poking a bear you do not want to poke."

"I wasn't trying to poke the bear. I was trying to get the bear to poke me." She tossed the pillow at me.

I caught it and threw it back at her. "Ew."

"Some like it hot and some like it dirty hot. I don't begrudge you your hottie. You don't begrudge me my dirty hottie. He's like Lucky Charms sinfully delicious." Tilly reached down and picked up Odin and brought him to her lap.

"Oh my God, just stop while you're ahead."

"But seriously, though, your guy. He's got it bad for you. I spent some time with him when I was a cat. You just need to figure out how to get along with him and not let him ground you like he's your daddy." She sat up straight. "Unless you want him to be."

I gagged. "Don't ever say that to me again."

Her eyes lit up. "What? Who's your daddy? Tall surfer boy with attitude, tan skin, and muscles for days."

"Stop. He doesn't respect me, you know? He treats me like a child. One moment he's so kind to me, taking care of me. And the next he's bossing me around like the parent I never had. I can't figure him out."

"Sounds like you just gotta get out from under his

thumb, prove that you're good without him. That always does it for headstrong guys. They need someone just as strong as they are. And if anyone is stronger than that dude, it's you."

I glanced down at Odin and back up at her. "Oh come on, back at our school you ruled everyone."

"And yet they all steered clear of you." She winked at me. "Now what are we gonna do about giving you some freedom?"

I bit my bottom lip. "You know, I have an idea about that."

CHAPTER 31

ASTRID

"What are you doing here?" Kitty leaned up against the doorframe of Lockwood House, blocking us from entering. She crossed her legs at her ankle and held her arm over the opening. "And who is that?"

"It's Lockwood House. I don't need an excuse to be here." I put my hands on my hips. The sun had set, and it'd been a long day. I was tired, fed up, and nervous as hell.

"Just because you're a Lockwood doesn't give you the right to be here."

The temperature already dropped so low I could see my breath. "Yeah, that's exactly what it means."

Tilly stepped up next to me. "Oh I see what you mean about this one. Two words: move, bitch."

"Look at your little parakeet squawking away." Kitty eyed Tilly. "Does that work in the human world?"

A wicked smile curved Tilly's lips. "Why don't you let us in and find out."

Odin trotted up and didn't stop when he got to Kitty. He simply jumped through what little space she had left open. Kitty looked after him. "Where does he think he's going?"

"Haven't you heard? We're moving in." I needed to get out from under Beckett's thumb. But I had to stay at the school for the fight to come. The freaking fight no one would tell me about. But I knew I wasn't ready for it. As my powers grew, I felt something ominous in the air.

"You're not moving in." Kitty shook her head. "I'll call my father and he will—"

"Do absolutely nothing." I let my smoke flow from my palms.

Kitty dropped her arm and moved back into the foyer. "You wouldn't dare."

"Wouldn't I?" I took a step into the foyer. Black and white checkered tiles lined the floors. Two opulent staircases ran up from the center of the floor, one twisted from the left and one from the right. They met in the middle where they opened up to the second floor. A small balcony overlooked the foyer. The last time I'd been here it was in the middle of the night. Now it was barely past dinner time. Though it was dark outside, the chandelier in the center of the ceiling illuminated the room in soft lighting. It reflected off the golden railings inlayed with a snake skin print.

Tilly walked around the foyer, looking up at the ceiling and down the hallways going in all different directions. I knew if she walked straight back down the hall she'd find the kitchen. On the second floor there was a hall of portraits of all the Lockwood heirs who'd come before me and one of them would lead to a secret room. My smoke drifted over the floor, crawling along.

Kitty backed away from it. "This isn't your house, it's ours."

Tilly scoffed. "Looks like you just got two new roommates." Odin meowed from the second floor and Tilly corrected herself, "Sorry, three."

Kyle stopped halfway down the stairs. "What is going on here?"

The two of them were so similar in looks. Both with that brownish red hair, both with those green half-moon-shaped eyes. Their cheekbones were too high and their lips too thin. Kitty climbed up the steps to stand next to him. They intertwined their fingers, and each of them held out their free hands. Faded yellow smoke seeped from their hands. It was nothing like the fog I wielded. This was a drop of rain against a flooding tide.

Tilly chuckled. "Guys, come on, I've seen way more than that. Is it really worth challenging her?"

Kitty fired a shot of magic at Tilly. I held my hand out and my smoke rose over Tilly, shielding her from the strike.

I narrowed my eyes at Kitty. "Big mistake."

A wave of magic rose from me. My smoke rolled toward them like a wave on the ocean. Just like that wave, it knocked into Kyle and Kitty. Their feet flew up and over their heads and they tumbled through the air. I froze them in midair, letting them hang there suspended ten feet off the ground. "Look, guys, I've had a very long night and this would go a lot easier if you would just relax."

Kitty's hair hung into her face and she squirmed against my hold. "Never."

"Oh for the love of Pete." I glanced over my shoulder at Tilly. "What am I going to do with this?"

"Just leave them there until morning." She yawned. "I'm exhausted."

"You can't leave us here like this." Red seeped into Kyle's face as I spun him upside down to face me.

"I honestly don't want to, but you guys aren't leaving me with much of a choice." I slugged my way up the steps with Tilly following close behind me. When I laid my fingers on the banister, the feel of the snake scale imprint felt like home against my skin and my powers vibrated in my body.

"You could always put them away." Tilly walked around them and up the rest of the stairs. She sauntered over to the balcony overhanging the first floor.

"They're not toys." Though the warlock powers inside me said otherwise. When the darkness rose up, it was tempting to tease them. Instead I moved up the stairs to stand next to Tilly.

"I don't know, they could be." She glanced around the house. "This place is pretty nice. Which wing do we want?"

Suddenly moving in didn't seem like such a bad idea. I glanced down the hall of portraits and knew exactly where I wanted to go. I waved my hand and sent Kitty and Kyle back to their rooms. They each flew off in different directions, spinning like mini tornados down the hall. Their hair blurred into one solid stream of color as they twisted within my magic. Their doors slammed at the same time. Behind me Kitty banged on her door over and over again, but I wasn't about to turn around and let her out.

Tilly chuckled. "Sometimes school bullies really deserve what they get."

"Tell me about it." I walked down the long hallway lined with portrait after portrait of the Lockwood line. Each of them was dressed in historical clothing sitting unsmiling as they posed. Even now I still felt connected to all of them. Their pictures were evidence of the ties I shared with them. I stopped just in front of the portrait of my ancestor Gregor Lockwood. The man who made sure I would be here someday, the man who wanted me to carry on our family line.

He was so young and yet he sat ramrod straight. His dark red hair was cut close to his head and fanned back from his face in soft waves. He had on a black three-piece suit, complete with pinstriped vest and tie. His high-collared shirt looked stiff against his skin. I ran my fingers over the thick frame. At the corners were those depictions of the face of Medusa and those swirling snakes.

Tilly stood beside me and bumped me with her hip. "You have the same coloring as this guy. Pale skin, dark auburn hair, sparkling green eyes."

"This is my ancestor Gregor Lockwood. I wish I knew him. He stood up against this evil warlock who wanted to take over the world and sacrificed himself so I could be here. So the world would be a safer place."

"Sounds kind of badass, like someone else I know." She wagged her eyebrows at me. "This is an amazing world, Astrid. You belong here."

"I have to admit it's overwhelming but pretty amazing at the same time." I reached behind the bottom corner of the painting and pressed the button. The painting slid to the side in a pocket in the wall, revealing a set of stairs. The last time I'd been here Beckett was beside me clearing a path through a sea of spider webs for me.

Tilly craned her neck. "Are we going to sleep in a dungeon? Because I might be okay with that."

"I'm thinking we'll remodel."

"Oh my God, we're going to sleep in a chamber of secrets. This gets better and better." Tilly motioned for me to go first.

I held my hands up and imagined what would make this hidden place so much better. My power flowed through me and I pictured candles flickering all the way down the stairs. One by one they appeared. Lining the walls each of them flickering and giving off warm light. A plush crimson carpet rose up beneath my feet and ran all the way down the stone steps. I began walking downstairs with Tilly hot on my heels.

When we reached the bottom of the steps, we stood side by side in a cold damp basement. The room itself wasn't very big and the only light coming in was from the candles I created on the stairs.

Tilly wrapped her arms around herself. "Not what I had in mind. But some carpets and space heaters and this place would be good."

I shook my head. If I had all this power then we were going to live like gothic rock stars. I forced the room to expand to twice its size. The house groaned yet complied and moved the way I wanted it. On the back wall an oversized fireplace sprang up. It was surrounded by a black mantel with carvings of all the things I'd seen, black-winged angels, Medusa and her sisters, magical vines, and wild animals. The fire sparked to life and crackled as the logs popped.

Two queen-sized beds sat across from each other. One on the right side of the room and one on the left. They mirrored each other. Both were four-poster beds with gauzy black material hanging from them. At the center of the room I made a chandelier hang between the beds. Wrought iron vines wound around each other and the flickering lights gave the room a warm glow. Two doors appeared next to each bed where our walk-in closets would be. Another door appeared next to the fireplace and that would be our restroom.

I pictured dark marble tiles, double sinks, and a huge walk-in shower. Tilly ran across the room and jumped on one of the beds. "I love magic. Can you make me taller?"

I shook my head. "Nah, not permanently."

"Pity." She motioned to the rest of the room. "I love it."

"Yeah, me too." I sat back on my own bed and faced Tilly. "Roomies?"

"Finally."

I lay back on my pillows. Exhaustion ate at me and perhaps a bit of sadness. I summoned the last two things I needed from Beckett's house. My grimoire dropped onto the foot of my bed and the ball of magic Zinnia had given me now sat in that locked cage beside my bed.

Tilly sat up straighter. "I thought I saw that thing in one of the living rooms at Beckett's house. Is it yours?"

I didn't want to tell her that I'd nearly died and left her in this world alone. "Yeah, when I got my powers, they were a bit too much. But this powerful witch took some out so I could learn to use them a little at a time."

"She gave it back to you just like that?" Tilly snapped her fingers.

"Yeah, she was pretty terrifying but also cool. I

think you'd like her." My gaze locked on my golden magic mixed with her silver as it swirled within that ball. I still hadn't learned enough to feel comfortable to take the rest of it.

"I say we go meet this chick and start our own house and rule the school." Tilly giggled.

I chuckled. "We can't."

"Why not?"

"Because she kind of rules every witch in Evermore." I kicked my blankets up and over my legs.

"What's Evermore?" She lay back on her pillows.

"Pretty much every magic thing on the earth belongs to the world of Evermore. It's what humans can't see." I curled on my side to face the fire. The flames danced and I felt myself relaxing for the first time in a long time.

"Wow, magic is so cool."

"It really is."

CHAPTER 32

BECKETT

"What do you mean she's gone?" I drove my shoulder into Astrid's door. It flew open and smacked into the wall with a bang.

Maze followed behind me. "Maybe next time you won't be such an ass, *dad*."

I glanced around the darkened room. Her clothes were missing. Her ball of magic was gone as well. I marched over to the bathroom. Empty. "For the love of all that is holy. Why does she do this every freaking time?"

"Because you're an idiot." Maze walked into the room and sat on the edge of her bed.

"Watch it. You might be psychic, but I doubt you'll see my fist connecting with your face coming." I shoved my hands in my hair and tugged at the strands. "Zinnia never gave Tucker this much trouble."

"You're forgetting one major fact about that situation." Maze grabbed a pillow and tossed it toward the door.

Cross walked in and caught it, then threw it back at him. "Ah she moved out." He said it so matter-of-fact. Like it was inevitable.

"What? What am I missing?" I put my hands on my hips.

"Astrid is not Zinnia." Maze pulled a flask from his back pocket.

"Are you drinking?" I arched my eyebrow at him. All my life he pledged never to go down the self-medication route. Now here he was openly drinking in front of us.

"Dude, no, it's perfect for pineapple cranberry juice. Stops my fingers from getting sticky when I gotta eat." He opened it up and took a deep sip.

I met Cross' eye. "Seriously? With this guy."

"What?" Maze took another sip.

I shook my head. "I can't deal with this right now. How do we get Astrid back here under our roof?"

"You could stop being so overbearing for starters." Logan strolled into the room. He was so calm, so put together.

Cross scoffed. "And I was there. I saw what Zinnia did to Tuck and it was no picnic either. When are you all going to learn?"

I crossed my arms over my chest. "Right, like you're such a Casanova with Ophelia. That girl has got you tangled in knots."

"We have our own set of rules to play by and a deal I have to hold up my end of. Once that's done, we'll see if you know what you're talking about." He walked farther into the room and pulled the chair at Astrid's desk out then dropped himself down into it.

"You guys forget one simple fact." Logan leaned against the doorframe.

"Yes, let's take advice from the one who lives like a monk." I pinched the bridge of my nose. We were like a bunch a hens in a coop clucking away about girls.

Logan arched his eyebrow at me. "Speak for yourself. I'm the only one here who has a date tonight while the three of you sit here and wonder where things went wrong. Here's some free advice. I'm sorry goes a long way. But not only that, maybe back it up with your actions."

"I wasn't wrong." I huffed.

"According to who?" Logan countered then started to back away. "I'm done standing here. I'm not leaving my Angel waiting. Later, guys, and good luck."

Cross rubbed his hand over his chin. "She is a warlock, Beck. Perhaps it's time to start letting her in on things. The war to come, the fallen, the plans for Evermore, just all of it."

"She freaked out just learning that she was a warlock and trying to control her powers. I don't know how she'll handle the rest of it. I'm trying to take it one step at a time, but it's not working."

"If we're going to take over the council then she needs to know this stuff." Maze grabbed up one of her pillows and held it to his nose and took a deep breath. "Chicken nuggets."

"What?"

He shook his head. "Never mind."

I paced. "We can't take over the council until she completes what's expected of her in the warlock world."

Cross slouched farther down in the chair. "It might not be as difficult as you think. There are those who aren't happy with the council and how oppressive they are."

"Your father is a big supporter of the council and he's got a lot of backing." I shook my head. "The fact she's gone doesn't help that."

"Don't you worry about my father." Cross curled his hands into fists. "I'll handle him."

"Still doesn't change the fact he's still out there and has Alataris' supporters rallying around him. And now I have to figure out how to convince Astrid to move back in here." I spun to Maze. "Any way she might be coming back any time soon?"

Maze sat up straight and his eyes went milky white. His head jerked to the right then to the left then straight back as he stared blindly at the ceiling.

I glanced at Cross and whispered, "I've never gotten a vision on demand."

Cross sat forward with his elbows on his knees. "Possible game changer?"

Maze sucked in a deep breath and shot to his feet. He glanced from the door to the window and back again. "Tilly!"

He sprinted from the room without another word. Cross jumped to his feet. "What was that?"

"Not a vision on demand. Follow him and make sure Tilly is okay. The last thing we need is for something to go wrong with her."

"Shit, I might need a strait jacket for this." He dashed out the door, leaving me alone in Astrid's room.

I pulled my phone from my pocket and opened up a text to the only person I knew who could understand what I was going through. Tucker.

Hey, man, I got a problem.

Three little bubbles popped up. *What's going on? Send me a portal. I can be there in seconds.*

Not that kind of problem. I hit send.

Oh?

I ran my fingers over the buttons in quick succession. *Astrid moved out and didn't tell me.*

Good to see that whole soul mate thing is working for you LOL.

I sighed and sat back on the bed. *Come on, man, what do I do here?*

I'm pretty sure I told you to tell her.

That's not going to help. I rose to my feet and walked out of her room, letting the door fall shut behind me.

My phone vibrated in my hand. *In my experience partnerships work better.*

I paused in the middle of the hallway. *Cross said the same thing.*

LOL surprised he has any good advice.

I continued down the hall and turned into my room. I kicked the door shut behind me. I held my phone over my face. It was the only thing illuminating the room in the darkness. *Me too, but I think you might be right. Time to take a different approach.*

Astrid has all the makings of a queen. Even though she's not, don't forget that.

Yeah, you're right.

GL bro.

I closed my phone and tossed it on the bed beside me. I pulled my shirt off and tossed it into the corner. Tomorrow I would settle this. Tomorrow we'd start fresh. My phone buzzed and I picked it up. A message from Cross appeared. *He's in the basement and I don't think he's coming out. Dude took ALL the snacks and locked the door.*

Fine.

One letter popped up. *K*

And the convo was over. I tossed my phone away again and slid farther back on my bed. I pulled a pillow behind my head and sucked in a deep breath. *Tomorrow will be a better day.* As my eyes drifted shut, a sense of calm hope overcame me and I let myself find the peace that could only come from a deathlike sleep.

CHAPTER 33

BECKETT

How did I get here? I sat up in Astrid's bed. Her strawberry scent flooded my senses and her pillows cushioned my head. I glanced down to the foot of the bed where Astrid stood looking down at me. My heart hammered in my chest and every muscle in my body tightened with awareness. She was beautiful, with her hair curling around her shoulders and down her back. My hands ached to touch her.

Her bright emerald eyes sparked with life. "What am I doing here, Beck?"

I sat up and reached for her. When her fingers slipped in my grasp, I pulled her closer to me. "I don't know."

She swung her leg up and rested her knee next to my hip. When I dropped her fingers, I let my hand wander down her side to the back of her other leg. My hands shook as I ran them down her legs. I gripped them harder and pulled her knee up and over to my other side. She straddled my hips then did a little hop and landed in my lap.

I felt so free with her, like nothing could keep us apart. "I'm so sorry."

"Me too." She titled her head to the side and pressed a kiss to my neck. Goose bumps broke out over every inch of my skin.

I closed my eyes and leaned my head back to give her more space. "I don't want to fight with you anymore." Her kiss scorched my skin. I gripped her harder, pulling her closer.

"Me neither." Another kiss and she grazed her teeth against my skin. I fought the urge to throw her down on the bed. This would be slow, deliberate. I might not be able to tell her we were soul mates, but I could make her feel it.

I cupped the back of her legs and pulled her tighter to me. We were nose to nose. Her breath was mine and mine was hers. I bit her bottom lip before sucking it into my mouth. "Let's not anymore."

She kissed the tip of my nose and let her lips drift lower down to meet mine. Our mouths melded together, and heat fired deep in my chest. As her tongue danced with mine, she reached down and grabbed the bottom of my shirt. She pulled back for a bare second to rip it over my head. We smashed back together in a tangle of lips and limbs. Electricity sizzled between us as we tumbled back on the bed. Her touch scorched my skin and I wanted everything she had to give.

When I reached down for the hem of her shirt, I hesitated. "Is this okay?"

Her eyes danced with mischief. "Off now."

She raised her hands over her head, and I pulled her shirt free and tossed it to the side of the bed. I twisted my body and rolled her onto her back. Her hands ran down my stomach and my muscles contracted to her touch.

"Let's just be good from now on, deal?"

"Deal." She wrapped her hand around my belt buckle and yanked at it. My hips jerked forward and the sound of clicking metal filled my ears. Excitement and nervousness warred within me.

I snapped the button on her jeans clean off and rolled that zipper down ever so slowly. She lifted her hips and let me peel her pants down her creamy legs. When I ran the tips of my fingers over her thighs, goose bumps broke out over her skin. I smiled down at her. "You're so beautiful."

She brushed her fingers down my cheek and over my collarbone. "You're not so bad yourself."

There was no one else I wanted to spend this moment with but my beautiful Astrid. I pulled the blankets up and over us and we were surrounded by warmth and all I could see was her. I rolled my body to rest against hers.

She cradled me within her hips and all I knew was her. I cupped her cheeks and met her gaze. "Are you good with this?"

She reached her hands up and wound her fingers into my hair, then pulled me down toward her. "More than good."

I ran my fingers down her bare body and hooked my thumb into the waistband of her panties. My hand shook as I slid them down her legs and unhooked them from her ankle. Her body quivered under my touch and I felt each tremble in her thighs as they brushed mine. As I pressed forward, joining our bodies, I locked eyes with her. "Astrid, you are everything."

Her fingers intertwined with mine and there it was, the connection I craved with her. This was us at our core. I wanted her and she wanted me. Every responsibility I had faded away to nothing. It was the two of us tangled in these bed sheets, moving as one. I didn't know where she started and I ended. I didn't want to know. We were one for this stolen moment and it was all I could ask for.

"Astrid, I lo—"

I shot straight up in my bed. My breaths came in ragged huffs. Sweat covered my body from head to toe. My hair clung to my head in soaking locks. I pressed my hand to my chest, trying to slow my racing heart. In the darkness of my own room I glanced around for her and ran my fingers over the top of my sheets, looking for her touch to meet mine. Yet there was nothing. I was utterly alone. I fell back onto my bed and let the cool air seep into my damp skin. As my breaths started to slow, my mind was a whirl with how real it was. I still smelled her scent, felt her on my lips and my skin sizzled from her touch.

I sucked in a deep breath. "What in the actual hell?"

CHAPTER 34

ASTRID

*M*y eyes flashed wide-open and I rolled onto my back. I sucked in a deep breath and stared at the ceiling. I was more exhausted than I was when I fell asleep.

I gradually sat up and glanced around at my new room. "Tilly?"

No answer. I threw my blankets off my legs and scooted to the edge of the bed. I searched for the rest and found none. Instead I woke up feeling more drained than before. My body ached and my mood was slowly declining with every passing moment. Everything was wrong. Beckett was pissed at me, I was living with Kitty Kalarook, and my bestie was loose in this house. I placed my feet on the cold stone and a chill shot up my body.

My shirt was soaked and clung to me in all the wrong places. I ripped it off and threw it onto the floor where it fell with a wet sopping sound. *Gross.* I hurried to my closet and dug into the piles of clothes there to find a baggy black turtleneck sweater and leggings. Today was a day to stay in bed and do nothing but wallow. I felt rotten down to my core about fighting with Beckett. Everything was off and I had no idea how to get back to where we were a few days ago. Whatever this was it was putting me into a funk of epic proportions. I padded over to the stairs and took them two at a time.

"Tilly? Where are you?" I pressed my finger to the back of the painting, and it slid to the side like a door. I stepped out onto the second floor and covered my eyes from the light shining in from the foyer. Did I have some kind of magic hangover?

When I came to the end of the hall, I glanced over the balcony into the foyer . . . empty. I moved to the set of stairs closest to me. I froze when Kitty stopped on the top step of the other set of stairs.

She looked down her nose at me. "You look like hell."

"Spare me the compliments." I rolled my eyes.

"I don't want you in our house."

"I think you made that perfectly clear last night

and I think I made my position perfectly clear." I placed my hand on the golden railing and began to walk down.

She ran her hand through her silky hair. Kitty was impeccably dressed, in her pressed khaki pants, tight polo shirt, and neutral makeup. When we both reached the foyer, she crossed her arms over her chest and narrowed her eyes at me. I really wasn't in the mood for this.

She huffed. "What's it going to take to make you leave?"

"Ugh, what's it going to take to shut you up?" I tried to run my fingers through my hair and ended up getting them tangled. I yanked them free and walked past her.

"I've already called my father and he will have words about this with the headmaster."

Back when I was in private school in New York, there were so many girls like this. Girls who wanted all their problems solved for them, girls who had daddy's money to back them up. It made me want to dig my heels in and stay longer. "Much good may it do you."

I headed straight toward the kitchen. It was similar to Beckett's house in that there was so much space, yet the foyer was bigger with the double staircases and open second floor. The kitchen had to be three times bigger than Beckett's.

Black cabinets lined the walls from floor to ceiling. The top set had glass fronts and the bottom were solid black. The countertops were a bright white marble with dark veins of black running through it, bringing it all together. At the back of the kitchen Tilly stood before a six-burner stainless steel stove with her back to me. Steam rose up around her and she held a spatula in her hand. The smell of bacon and pancakes filled the air and my mouth began to water. I couldn't remember the last time I had a fully cooked meal that wasn't prepared by me.

Tilly turned and faced the sink in the island. Her head snapped up and a smile crossed her face when she spotted me. "Hey."

"Hi." I shuffled my way over to the island and pulled a stool out.

"That bad of a night?" She walked over to a cabinet next to the stove and pulled two plates out. She glanced over her shoulder at where Kitty stood in the doorway. "You staying for breakfast?"

"Ugh, it's probably poison. Don't make yourselves comfortable. My father will have you out in no time."

Tilly rolled her eyes and turned to face me. "She's one of those?"

"Oh yeah." I pressed my hands to my temples and rubbed little circles as hard as I could.

"Whatever." Kitty whirled on her heels and left us alone.

I stretched my arms out in front of me and laid my head on the cold marble countertop. Hangover didn't even begin to describe what was going on in my head. I groaned and let the cool seep into my skin.

"Dude, what is going on with you?" Tilly scooped three pancakes out of the pan on the stove and placed them on the plate in her hand. She slid it across the island toward me.

I held my hand out and caught it. "So I had this dream and it felt so real."

Tilly walked over to the fridge and pulled the door open. Cool air drifted from it and it hummed as she examined everything. "How do these people not have syrup and butter?"

I waved my hand and a bottle of syrup along with a butter dish appeared in front of me. "Fork, knife?"

Tilly pulled open three sets of drawers before she found the right one. "Here you go."

I stacked the pancakes with butter and syrup. Enough to give me the sugar high I desperately needed. I shoved a warm bite into my mouth and let them melt. "Hmmmm."

"So based on the little noises you were making last night I'd say that dream was . . ."

"Not something I'm going to talk about in detail." But it was burned into my mind, every second of it.

"I'm thinking you're going to need two aspirin, lots of pancakes, possibly real cake, and ice cream." Tilly flipped three more pancakes on the skillet. "I don't know what's going on with you and Beckett, but you all need to figure some shit out."

I cut a piece of pancake and pushed it around the plate, gathering up as much syrup as I could. "Ugh, I know. I hate the tension between us."

A loud banging came from the front of the house. She snickered. "Here he comes now."

"I doubt it." I shook my head and shoved another piece down my throat.

"Someone to see you!" Kitty's smug shrill voice carried down the hallway toward us.

I pushed back from the counter. "What now?"

Tilly flicked the knobs of the stove top off then dusted her hands off. "Let's go see who it is."

I paused. "Maybe you should wait here."

Here we stood both of us barefoot, both in big comfy sweaters and leggings. Neither of us looking like we slept at all. Her curls were flattened, and my hair was a tangled mess. I wasn't even sure what time it was. All I knew was that if someone was here to see me, it couldn't be good.

Tilly moved to stand beside me. "It's like you forgot who I am just by being away from me for a little while."

She headed down the hall. I chuckled to myself and followed behind her. Cold air drifted toward me and I knew the front door would be wide-open. When I walked into the foyer, I nearly bumped into Tilly, who stood frozen staring. I moved around and took up a stance in front of her.

There before me was Headmaster Ridge with two council members flanking him. Cora Ferguson stood still as a statue looking more frogish than ever. Her gray hair was pulled into a tight bun that stood up from the top of her head. Dark purple robes hung from her body but did nothing to hide her short, stout stature.

Her lips turned down into a deep frown. "Miss Lockwood."

"Mrs. Ferguson, I wasn't expecting to see you so soon." Adrenaline pumped through my veins. "And you, Mr. Archer. How good of you to visit."

Behind the three of them stood Beckett, Logan, Cross, and Maze. Beckett spared me only one glance. But I could tell from here that he hadn't gotten any sleep either. Dark circles hung below his eyes, his hair was a tangled mess that fell into his face, and his normally pressed clothes were as disheveled as mine.

I forced the ball of nerves back down into the pit of my stomach. If they were here something bad was about to go down. "To what do I owe the pleasure?"

Ridge snickered, his hook nose wrinkled, and his eyes danced with excitement. "As if you don't know the offense you bring upon this school."

I shook my head. "I didn't offend the school in any way. I only want to go to class and learn how to harness my powers fully."

He pointed his long, boney finger at Tilly. "And what do you call that?"

Tilly put her hands on her hips. "*It* is called a Tilly."

I placed my hand on her arm, silencing her. "She found her own way here and only arrived last night."

Ridge's polished shoes clicked on the tile floor as he took slow steps around us. He looked Tilly up and down then me. Kitty stood by the front door with a beaming smile on her face. She took two steps closer to Beckett and stood right in front of him, with her ass practically pressed to his crotch. I ground my teeth together. What I wouldn't give to cement her to the floor one . . . more . . . time.

When Ridge walked by Kitty, he tucked her under

the chin and winked. She preened and fluffed her hair like she was something important. He spun on his heel to face me. "There is nothing left to do but expel you and send her back to the human world, with not a memory of you."

"What?" Panic flooded my body.

"You heard me." He clapped his hands together and rubbed them back and forth like he was savoring the moment.

"The council wholeheartedly agrees. I've already received permission from Damiel as the head council member to send you packing." He waved his hand to the door. "Out you go."

My jaw dropped open and I stood motionless. I knew this was a possibility. I knew everything could go wrong. I had no defense for this and no way of talking myself out of it. Maze stepped around them all and moved next to me, blocking Tilly from their view. He looked like a nervous twitching warlock. Twists of his dark hair fell over his face, covering his eyes. His trench coat was wrinkled and hanging sideways off his shoulder.

He raised his thumb to his lips and bit at his nails while he shifted from one foot to the other. "No, that won't happen."

Jiovanni Archer stepped forward. He clasped his

hands behind his back. Though he was smaller and worm like with a bald head and plenty of wrinkles. His robes matched Cora's and he too seemed delighted at the prospect of being rid of me. "And why is that, young psychic?"

"Tilly is laced with the future of all warlock kind and so we need her. I have seen it." Maze glanced over his shoulder at her, but when she smiled at him, he flinched.

Jiovanni chucked an ear-piercing laugh. "And we are supposed to believe the ramblings of a crazed psychic?"

"You forget yourself. I am not my father," Maze snapped. "And if you don't believe me, send her on her way . . . and watch all of the warlock world fall."

The smile dropped from his face and he turned to face Ridge. He leaned in and whispered something to Ridge then took his place back beside Cora.

Ridge narrowed his eyes at Maze. "This is to your advantage. How do we know you're not lying?"

Maze shrugged. "You don't."

I gazed past Ridge and the council at Beckett. He stood so still, so silent. "Are you even paying attention here?"

Everyone in the room turned to look at him and he held up his phone. "Be with you in a minute."

Seriously? "Don't just stand there. Do something."

Beckett was the one to handle them when they came for my magic. He was the one to stop them from getting rid of me and now he did nothing. No, not nothing. He stood there *texting.*

He took a step into the room and held his phone out then hit the speaker phone button. "We're all here."

"She stays." The voice was deep and full of authority.

Ridge paled and glanced from Cora to Jiovanni. An ugly green color flowed over his skin and he pulled at the tie around his neck.

Beckett took his call off speaker phone then pressed it to his ear. "Yeah, it's done. Thanks."

When he ended the call and slid it back into his pocket, he turned to Ridge without so much as a look at me. "We good here?"

Ridge shook himself and straightened the cuffs of his shirt, then ran his hands over the lapels of his jacket. "No, they both will remain confined here. She will go to classes and nothing more."

"And what of Tilly?" Beckett spoke about her like he was talking about the weather.

"She can attend classes and observe Astrid. Besides that I don't want to see her." Ridge glared at Tilly. "Humans at Warwick. Your father would—"

"Run," Beckett snapped. "My father would run like the coward that he is."

The council exchanged looks and Ridge glared down his nose at Beckett. "Such disrespect."

"Again, respect must be earned." Beckett motioned for Maze to join him and the others. Cross stood chuckling and shaking his head like he found the whole thing entertaining.

Logan punched him in the arm. "Shut up, you're not helping."

"I don't care." Cross turned and walked away. Logan shook his head and followed behind him.

Ridge pulled his jacket in closer to his chest and motioned to the door.

Cora glared at me. "There are only so many times you will slip through our grasp and when your time is up, we will gladly extinguish you."

I sucked in a sharp breath and squared my shoulders. This woman, this warlock, was terrifying. But showing weakness wouldn't help me or any of the others. I held my chin up and sucked in a breath. "You can try, crone."

She took a step toward me and Jiovanni held his arm out, blocking her from moving closer. "Not yet."

He looked at me and hissed low in his throat before he escorted Cora out the door. Ridge followed behind them, leaving me, Tilly, Kitty, and Beckett alone in the foyer. I sagged and sucked in a deep breath. My toes were frozen, my headache was back in full force, and I was completely exhausted. All I wanted was to make things right with Beckett and here he was standing in front of me looking anywhere but directly at me.

Kitty marched past him to get in my face. "I hate you."

"If you must." I waved for her to pass. When she stood frozen in front of me, I let my magic seep from my hands in warning. "Do you really want to?"

"Ugh." She stormed up the stairs, pounding her feet with every step she took.

"That's what I thought." I ran my hand through my hair, trying to untangle some of the knots before I faced Beckett. But he turned toward the door without a word. After the dream I had last night, him being so cold to me stung. "Hey, Beck."

He spun to face me. "Yeah?"

"Thanks." I motioned toward Tilly. "For your help."

He gave me a mock salute. "Hope you're happy now." He marched out the door without looking back. I'd gone from one jail to the other and he didn't even care.

Tilly moved up beside me. "Boy, he is pissed."

"Ugghhhhh, yeah." Now I felt even worse. I wanted the connection I'd felt in my dream.

"This sucks." She headed toward the kitchen.

But I couldn't take my eyes off Beckett's back as he walked away from me, away from Lockwood House, and away from the dream I had last night.

CHAPTER 35

"Three days locked in this basement is driving me crazy." Tilly sat on the foot of her bed, flipping through fashion magazines.

"We got out for classes."

Odin lay across my lap and I ran my fingers over the top of his head.

"Yeah, but I couldn't do anything in those classes and people didn't even talk to me. Well, except Leo. He was cool. But this was supposed to be magic school. There were no talking paintings, no moving staircases, and no werewolves. How disappointing is that?" She threw aside the magazine.

I lifted my hand and let my smoke drift to the wall where I pictured a portrait of the two of us hanging out. We both smiled, waved, and giggled. "I give you a moving portrait."

"Okay, that's not as cool as I thought it would be."

Tilly jumped to her feet. "You know what we should do?"

"Stay here and not piss anyone off?"

"No, how many times have we said we'd love to just teach our parents a lesson? You know for being so shitty?" She stood in front of my bed.

"Yeahhhh." I sat up a little more.

"Well, if ever there was a time, now would be it." She spun in a circle. "I mean, come on. Look at this place. A little redecorating New York style wouldn't hurt anyone."

"Till, it's such a bad idea. Like a super bad idea. I'm not even powerful enough to do this yet." I placed Odin on the bed next to me and pointed to the orb. "My magic is still in there."

Tilly moved toward the orb to stand in front of it, the glowing light reflected in her eyes. "Then touch it and take some more. You've been doing awesome. I've been watching."

I wanted to touch the orb, to take some more of my magic into me. It was important to get stronger to help Beckett and the rest of the warlocks. I hadn't heard from him in three days, hadn't seen him around the school, and it felt awful to try and stop by the house. Part of me wanted to apologize to him. The other part of me didn't want to apologize because it felt like admitting I was wrong, and I wasn't.

"I don't know. We're supposed to be staying in here."

Tilly clasped her hands to her chest. "Please, I just want to go get some tacos from that place near Columbus circle and maybe some fro-yo from that other place we like. And maybe just maybe rearrange some furniture. It's been a long time since I did something fun and guess what, it's getting to be about that time, or this Tilly is going to go boom."

"Ugh, fine, but we have to keep a low profile." I reached out for the orb. "And maybe just a little more juice."

CHAPTER 36

*T*illy sauntered across my father's penthouse with a taco in hand. She tilted her head to the side and took a bite. "What should we do first?"

"I honestly have no idea why he keeps this place. He's never here." I moved to the center of the room and stood staring at all the plain white things. I'd only been here a short while ago yet nothing changed. It was the middle of the night and not a single light was on. Only the glow from the streets below illuminated the floor-to-ceiling windows. Gauzy white curtains hung in front of them, dimming the lights of the street. I walked over to the lamp on the table and pulled the cord, flicking it on. The room lit up and the stark whiteness of it all made me cringe away from it.

Tilly walked over to the couch and plopped down

on the pristine cream-colored cushion. "We have to do enough to make a statement."

"I don't think we've ever acted out in all the years we've been alone. We just simply . . ."

"Carried on." Tilly sighed and took another bite of her taco. "Hey! I know. Let's make this look like we're in Mexico. Remember that time when your dad got so sick down there? He'd hate it."

"No, he hates Paris even more. Because of"—I held two fingers up—"wife number two."

Tilly's curls bounced as she popped up off the couch. She finished off the last of her taco and wiped her hand down her jeans. "I envision a bridge over there." She pointed to the far side of the room. "Perhaps a river. Ohhhh, how about a mini Eiffel Tower?"

I clapped my hands together and rubbed them back and forth. The small hit of power I took from my orb sizzled through my veins. It rose up around me, filling the room. "Okay, but after this we're going back to school, promise?"

"Promise." A wide smile spread across Tilly's face. "Oh, how I've missed Paris. Once we're not grounded we should go."

"Right, because grounding has always worked on us. As evidence of us being out right now." I held my arms up and let my magic flow. The room was large and airy, and I had a shit ton of space to fill.

The floor dropped down into a serpentine shape that zig-zagged all the way from one side of the room to another. Drops of water fell from the ceiling in perfectly straight lines to fill my makeshift river. The beige walls turned from plain sheet rock to stone that crumbled in some places, giving it that old world look. Tilly kicked her shoes off and sat down at the edge of my river.

She dipped the tips of her toes in. "I love it." She pointed toward the corner of the room. "Okay, Eiffel Tower now."

Before I struggled with my powers. Now the more I used them, the more confident I got. I felt them flex like a muscle I'd only begun to use. The room shook and I envisioned the Eiffel Tower rising up in the corner of the apartment. It rose from the ground inch by inch. First the point then every steel beam seeped from the floor. Cracks forked out over the ceiling and down the walls. Dust rained down on me and I wanted to end it where it was. I pulled my powers back into myself.

Tilly jumped to her feet and ran to my side. "Okay, dude, time to stop."

"I thought I did!" The room tremored beneath my

feet, yet the tower continued to rise. I grabbed Tilly's hand and yanked her as far away as I could. "You need to get out of here!"

"No, you stay, I stay."

The point of the tower pierced the ceiling and shot straight through to the roof. I shoved Tilly to the ground and threw myself over her. Pieces of the ceiling dropped to the floor like meteors. The white tile exploded up around each one.

The beams above us bowed down. I grabbed Tilly and yanked her back to her feet. "Move!"

We ran toward the door only to have a big chunk of sheet rock fall in front of it, blocking us in. Tilly turned and backed up against it, her eyes wide and her mouth dropped open. "You have to stop this."

"I thought I did." The river rose up over the ruined floor. It dipped and flowed over everything, rising so fast I didn't know what to do. I held my hand out, trying to envision it stopping, but all that came out was a small puff of smoke then nothing.

I shook my hands, trying to get my magic to work, but I was too panicked. My heart raced as the water rose up to my knees. I grabbed ahold of Tilly and dragged her behind me as I trudged through it toward the stairs leading up to the second floor. One step, then two, then five and only the bottoms of my shoes were in it.

"Um, Astrid? What is that sound?" Tilly turned to face the destroyed apartment.

Over the sound of falling water, cracking walls, and plunges of pieces of the apartment came a noise I didn't want to hear. The cracking of glass. On the far side of the apartment those floor-to-ceiling windows barely held on. Fissures forked out across them like spider webs. Streams of water poured out of them into the night sky.

"Please hold, oh God, please hold." My eyes locked on them and I willed them to hold the water in.

"Astrid." Tilly tugged at my arm. "Move up."

"No, no, no." I hunched over, staring at the windows. A piece of the roof flew over the side of the building down toward the street below. Screams sounded and the sound of a boulder hitting the ground shook the entire building. The windows exploded outward, shards of glass raining down on the street. Horns blared, screams filled my ears, and cars crashed together. The water rushed from the apartment and it too fell toward the street. The ceiling was nearly gone and what was left of it was on the floor. Puddles of water remained in the dented tiles. The sound of chaos from below echoed in all directions.

I fell back on the stairs and wrapped my arms around my knees. Tears threatened to spill over and I bit the inside of my cheek to stop them. "Till, I messed up . . . bad."

The wind kicked up around me and my hair flew back from my face. Tilly scrambled back, pointing toward the sky. "What the hell is that?"

Wings, hulking big black wings filled my vision. My blood froze in my veins and my sopping wet pants only deepened the chill in my bones. I shook from head to toe as I rose to my feet. "Stay behind me."

Like a shot he dropped down in front of me, a tower of an angel I'd never seen before. His hair was cut short and fanned back from his chiseled face. He was only an inch bigger than Aidenuli, but I felt the power rolling off of him and smacking into me. His sapphire eyes glowed with fury and the muscle in his jaw ticked. If I thought Aidenuli was scary, this guy had him beat by miles. Sword handles poked out from the holsters on his back and weapons dripped from his hips. He wore a tight black tank top that matched his black combat pants and boots perfectly. He put his hands on his hips and glared at me.

Then one by one other black winged angels dropped down to flank his sides in a perfect V shape. Aidenuli was the last to land at his side. His long midnight hair fell into his face, covering his hypnotic eyes and that scar in his eyebrow. He pulled one of his earbuds out and let it fall down across his chest. I was screwed . . . so screwed.

Each of the angels was beautiful in their own way. There were eight of them, all with big black wings, all dripping in weapons, all looking thoroughly pissed off at me. *Fu—*

Aidenuli arched his eyebrow at me and suddenly I was hit with the fact he could hear every damn word I thought. Heat licked at my face and I gazed at the sky once more only to be blinded by flaming wings. Zinnia's wild hair flew around her face and Tucker dropped her down next to the head angel. Her crown was firmly perched on her head. Those sharp points gleamed in what was left of the lights in my apartment. She wore black leather leggings and combat boots that matched her black ripped up sweater perfectly. Silver sparks of magic lingered down her arms and in her hair.

I froze. *I might die. They're going to strip my magic and kill me.* Probably throw me into a jail for the magically insane criminals. Where I'd grow old without ever getting past second base with Beckett. *Damn it!* Aidenuli snapped his fingers to get my attention. Heat flooded my cheeks and I knew he heard every word.

Tucker pulled his wings in behind him and glanced around the apartment. He let a low whistle go as he shook his head. The lead angel stepped toward Zinnia without ever breaking eye contact with me. He leaned down and whispered something in her ear and she nodded up at him.

Zinnia stepped toward me and a wave of magic smacked into me, knocking me back a step. She threw her arms up. "What the hell is this, Astrid?"

"I—"

She rushed forward and jabbed her finger in my face. "You've exposed magic for all the world to see."

"I didn't mean to." A ball formed in my throat and I wanted to cry. I was wrong and I knew it. This was a huge mistake and deep in my bones I knew it was going to cost me.

"You didn't mean to? You destroyed the building and the street below." She crossed her arms over her chest.

"Hey, it wasn't her fault," Tilly snapped.

I glanced over my shoulder. "Yeah, it was." I turned back to Zinnia. "I can fix it."

"Fix it? This should've never happened in the first place!" Fury rolled off of her. Her magic wound down her arms and legs. "Oh no, you've done enough."

I glanced down at the floor and blinked away the

tears gathering in my eyes. I wrapped my arms around my midsection. I knew better and things just got out of hand. "I'm so sorry."

"You were supposed to be at school where crap like this can happen because there are people there to help you. But no, instead you took it upon yourself to redecorate the city." Zinnia marched toward the door and stopped in front of the boulder blocking it.

The lead angel held his hand up and it crumbled to dust on the floor at Zinnia's feet. My eyes widened and I leaned away from him. If he could do that to a boulder, what could he do to my bones? Zinnia yanked the door open then turned to look back at me. "Now I have to go clean up *your* mess."

She marched out of sight. Tilly leaned into me and whispered, "Man, she is a bitch."

"No, Till. She's right." I wanted to cry and throw up all at once.

Tucker pulled his phone from his pocket and pressed it to his ear. "Hey, man, got your girl. You better get here . . . fast."

Ugh, not Beckett. I didn't know if I could stand to see the disappointment in his eyes. But there was no way it'd be worse than the disappointment I felt in myself. I dropped down onto the stairs and sat there with all their eyes locked on me. The angels began to walk around the apartment, examining all the damage I'd done, yet none of them spoke a word to me. A blue light glowed in the corner of the room and I wanted to crawl under a piece of the roof and die. At first his form was a shadow walking toward us. As he came closer, he became clearer, his broad shoulders, narrow hips, and tousled blond hair. When he stepped through the portal, his eyes flared wide.

He narrowed them at me. "What have you done?"

I let my head slump forward into my hands. "I don't know."

Cross walked through the portal behind Beckett. A chuckle burst from his lips. "Holy shit." He spun in a small circle. "This is pretty impressive."

Beckett grabbed Cross and shoved him behind him. "Shut up."

Logan strolled through next and pushed Cross to the side. "Crap, are we in New York?"

"Yeaaa." Every time someone spoke it just made things worse.

Beckett bowed his head slightly toward the lead angel. "Matteaus."

Matteaus? Shit, the Matteaus? The leader of the fallen, the guy everyone revered and answered to. He ruled Evermore with an iron fist and I'd just thoroughly pissed him off. *Crap, crap, crap.* Maze walked through the portal and trudged across the room toward Tilly and me. He didn't look at me or anyone else, only at her.

He extended his hand out for her. "Come on, let's go."

"What, no? I'm not leaving Astrid." Tilly placed her hand on my shoulder.

I slid out from under her touch and turned to face her. "He's right, you should go. I have to take care of this."

"O-oh okay." She glanced at the ground then back up toward me. "If you say so."

I threw my arms around her and pulled her close for a quick hug. Everything was so wrong. I was scared for my own fate and I didn't want her to be here to witness this. "It's going to be okay. Just go with him. He'll keep you safe until I get back."

She nodded and took Maze's hand. There was something off about him. He didn't smile, crack a joke, or even have a snack in his hand. He simply dragged her toward the portal, with her trailing behind him. Her clothes were sopping wet, her hair was a mess, and yet she tried to stand by me. None of this was her fault. We were just going to have some fun. Fun, I hadn't had fun in weeks. And the first chance I got at it I screwed it up, royally.

Matteaus crooked his finger at Beckett and moved to the other side of the room, out of earshot. Beckett glared at me over his shoulder then turned toward Matteaus. Matteaus jabbed a finger into his chest and Beckett bowed his head. Even though I couldn't hear the words, I knew Matteaus was tearing into Beckett. His motions were sharp, his eyes were like piercing lasers, and every muscle in his body shot tight with tension.

Logan strolled over to me. "This is something else."

"Ugh, I know. I didn't mean to." I shook my head and motioned to the falling ceiling.

"Whether or not you meant to, Astrid, isn't relevant at this point." He stepped in closer and lowered his voice. "You did all this. You exposed magic to the human world. It's bad enough that you have Tilly here but now this. Don't you think it's time you take a good hard look at things and decide if you're in or out?"

The fallen walked around the room, kicking pieces of the roof out of the way. Cross stood beside Aidenuli, chatting him up. And I'd never felt so alone, never felt so out of place like I did right this second.

I met Logan's gaze. "What do you mean?"

"I mean you've been fighting Beckett every step of the way since you've been here. Don't you think it's time to choose to stay and fall in line or leave and be what you want to be?"

I sucked in a sharp breath and flinched away from him. I didn't think I'd fought him so much. I went to the school he told me to, took the classes he told me to, did the missions he told me to. Was I really that bad?

"Logan," Aidenuli called out to get his attention. "I think you need to go downstairs and help Zinnia do some crowd control. Perhaps convince them it was a gas explosion or something?"

"I'm on it." Logan leaned in. "Think about it."

He turned for the door and walked away from me. I sank back onto the steps and plopped down there. A single tear streaked down my cheek. I swiped it away before anyone could see. Water seeped into my jeans, soaking me through to my skin, but I didn't care. I'd ruined my father's home, exposed magic, and messed things up with the others. Tucker shook his head and chuckled as he dropped down beside me.

I sniffled. "You think this is funny?"

"Well, it sure as shit isn't sad." He bumped me with his arm. "Astrid, we all mess up. It's just a matter of how you bounce back from this. Are you going to let it weaken you or are you going to face what you did?"

Stay or go? Cry or fight? "I honestly don't know."

Tucker patted my knee and embers sparked in his eyes. "I think you'll make the right decision. Whatever that might be."

I hung my head. "Yeah, I don't think this could get any worse."

"Well, well, well." The door creaked open and there stood Damiel Edwards. I shot to my feet. He looked more pristine than ever, with his hair pulled back with his leather strap. His clothing was pressed so much that the collar of his shirt stood stiff against his neck. He stepped into the room with his cane leading the way. Tap, step, step, tap, step, step.

His yellow eyes danced as he took in the destruction. "Ms. Lockwood, if this isn't grounds for expulsion, I don't know what is." A wide smile spread across his face and he held his hands out to his sides. "Impressive."

Beckett cleared his throat. "What the hell are you doing here, Damiel?"

"A show of this amount of warlock power, how could I not be here?" He used his cane to shove a piece of the roof out of his way as he walked into the middle of the room. "It was a ripple that any practiced warlock could feel. And I'm sure Ridge will be so pleased to know what you've been up to. Especially after I gave him strict orders to have you restricted to the school."

Aidenuli titled his head, studying him. "This is Fallen business and we will handle it as we see fit."

Damiel let out a deep, hearty laugh like this was the funniest thing he'd heard in years. "But in such a limited capacity. Isn't that right, angel?"

Aidenuli pursed his lips together but didn't say anything else. The others started to gather around him in a circle, each of them having their hands resting on a weapon of some sort. Even Aidenuli had his hand on the hilt of a knife at his hip. Tuck's flaming wings popped from his back and he held a ball of fire in the palm of his hand, tossing it up and catching it.

Beckett moved from the other side of the room to stand in front of me. He held his hand up and those blue orbs danced between his fingers. "You can't do anything if they can't find you."

"Are you threating me, boy?" The smile dropped from Damiel's face and he turned to face him fully.

Beckett shrugged. "Take it how you will."

"Beck, don't." I placed my hand on his back and he stiffened at my touch. I cleared my throat. "Don't do this for me."

He glanced at me over his shoulder. "Stay out of this, Astrid. You've done enough."

I dropped my hand and took a step back from him. He was right, I'd done more than enough already. All I wanted to do was go home, wherever that was, and stay there.

"I didn't think you had the guts, Dustwick. You'd do your father proud." Damiel gave Beckett a mock bow and his lips turned up in that snide smile.

Smoke erupted from Beckett's hands and his body shook from head to toe. "I hope you rot in hell beside him. Where you both belong."

Dead silence fell over the room and I didn't know what to say or do. Tension hung heavy in the air. Beckett's body quaked with power. His shoulders were stiff. He opened his stance like he was about to attack Damiel. What the hell happened between them? Between Beckett and his father? And what did Damiel have to do with it? Matteaus stomped into the middle of the circle and faced Damiel. Power rolled off of him and my heart sped at the feel of it.

He seethed from head to toe. Drops of water rose up from the ground like it was raining backward. Particles of dust rose in streams up toward the ceiling in slow motion. His eyes blazed bright blue and I stood frozen, unable to turn away from his power.

The muscles in his body thrummed and he came

nose to nose with Damiel. "Get"—his voice was a threating growl like a dog about to attack—"out."

Damiel took a step back, and another. "You forget yourself, angel. This isn't your fight and stepping in is against the rules."

Another angel, the one with piercing green hazel eyes and dirty blond hair, shook his head and gave a humorless chuckle. "Fallen for a reason, you idiot. We don't play by the rules."

"Not surprised to hear that from you, Mika. You always were obstinate." Damiel turned on his heels and headed for the door. He paused for a moment and pointed his finger in my direction. "This isn't over."

I wanted to say something cutting, to stand up to him the way the rest of them did, but fear and exhaustion held me silent. Beckett moved to the side.

He tossed his orb up and caught it. "Oh, I think it's over."

Without another word, Damiel stormed from the room, leaving the rest of them to stare at me.

Shit, this is bad, sooooo bad. How could I mess up like this?

Zinnia marched back into the room and stopped dead in her tracks to stare at the water and rising dirt. "What happened?"

Tucker sighed. "Damiel Edwards was here and he's

decided to try and expel Astrid from the school for good."

Matteaus locked gazes with me and marched in my direction. I shrank away from him and my heart raced. Black dots swarmed my vision and I fought how dizzy I was. *I'm gonna pass out and pee. Pee and pass out all at the same time.* This was the head of the freaking Fallen and he was coming for me.

He stopped only a few feet from me and held his hand up. Power gathered in his palm, at first just a faint glow. My eyes widened as the ball of swirling golden and silver magic formed in his hand. The orb! My orb! The one filled with my magic hovered just over the palm of his hand. He glanced at it then back at me. What was he going to do? *Please don't destroy it. It's a part of me and I need it.*

He narrowed those burning sapphire eyes at me. "Mine now."

His wings shot from his back and a gust of wind blew into my face. He pulled those black oily wings in and with a single pump shot straight up into the night sky.

Crap, crap, shit, damn it, no. What the hell am I going to do? Fu—

"Astrid." Aidenuli's voice snapped me to attention. "We'll be in touch."

Then one by one the Fallen took off through the roof of my father's apartment, leaving me alone with Beckett, Cross, Zinnia, and Tuck. An involuntary groan left me and my lips trembled. A ball formed in my throat and I felt an ugly cry coming on.

Magic seeped all around Zinnia and she held her hand out toward me then curled it into a fist and pressed her lips into a hard line. "Astrid, learn your freaking control!"

She turned and out the door she went with Tucker hot on her heels. There was no walking away from this, no forgiveness for this. I'd exposed magic to the world and the rulers of Evermore responded quickly and harshly. Beckett opened his mouth and I could tell he was about to give the tongue lashing I deserved, but I didn't have it in me to take any more.

I held my hand up, silencing him. "I know what you're about to say."

"No, you don't." He put his hands on his hips. "How could you do this, Astrid? How could you be so irresponsible? I get not wanting to live under my thumb but this?" He threw his hands up.

His voice dripped with disappointment and it broke the dam of emotions I'd been holding in. Tears streamed down my face and I didn't bother to hide them. "I know you expected more. Hell, I expected more." I sucked in a sobbing breath. "But can we just, can we just go? I can't handle seeing you look at me like that."

His brow furrowed. "Like what?"

"Like you wish I weren't me. Like you wish I didn't exist in your world. You know what the shitty part is?"

He hesitated. "What?"

"Sometimes I wish it weren't me either so it all could be easier for you too." I shook my head and let my tears fall down my cheeks and drip from my chin. The ball in my throat burned and I just let it. "Can, can I please go home? Wherever that is."

His eyes widened and he stepped to the side. He swept his arm toward the portal. I let my shoulders hunch over and the wracking sobs take me. I trudged toward the blue pool of magic all the while looking at the destruction I'd caused. All I really wanted in that moment was for him to hug me and tell me it would all be okay. Instead, I was completely and utterly alone . . .

CHAPTER 37

I fell back onto my bed and groaned. Astrid moved out and in the three days she'd been gone she managed to destroy a penthouse, expose magic, piss off the Fallen and Zinnia. I pressed my palms to my eyes and rubbed them so hard I'd explode an eyeball if I didn't stop. That was all nothing compared to how she'd looked at me. She thought I wished she weren't the Lockwood heir, that I didn't want her here. When the truth was she was the only one I wanted near me. She plagued my days and my dreams. But I didn't know what to do to fix any of this or how to help my soul mate. I curled on my side and let my eyes drift shut. *If there was just something I could do.*

I fell in blackness. I reached out yet felt nothing at

my fingertips. I summoned my magic to light the way .
. . nothing. The only sound in the room was my own
ragged breaths and something . . . faint. I took a
cautious step toward it. I held both my hands out,
hoping I wouldn't smash into something. There it was
again, a sob in the darkness. I didn't know who or
what it was, but the sound lashed me down to my
soul. I moved quicker now, taking one step at a time
toward the sound. A dim light shone and I hurried
toward it, running down a dark corridor. The closer I
came, the louder the sobs became and I knew it
was her.

I sprinted headlong into the darkness. That beacon
of dim light grew bigger until finally I walked into a
plain black room. A single bed sat in the middle of the
room and there on top of the thick comforter lay
Astrid. She was curled on her side with her back to
me. Shudders wracked her body and her little sobs
were like an arrow to my heart.

"Shhhh, Astrid, shhh." I didn't hesitate. I climbed
into the bed and curled my body around hers. She was
so small, so fragile. I pulled her closer so her back was
flush up against my chest. "Shhhh, my girl, it's okay."

"I-it's not okay." She cried harder. "You hate me."

Her words sent a sharp pain through me that
sucked the breath right from my lungs. I ran the back

of my fingers over her cheek. "How could I possibly hate you?"

"You do, don't lie to me about it." The more she sobbed, the more the bed shook beneath us.

I pressed a kiss to her temple and to the back of her neck. "No, my girl. I could never hate you."

She curled into a tighter ball like she was protecting her heart from me. "I am so sorry for everything."

Every tear that dropped from the corner of her eye was a slap to my face. "I know you are."

"Can you just . . . stay here with me for a moment longer?" Her voice was so small, pleading.

In that moment nothing could've dragged her away from me. I had to be there for her, to help her through this. I wrapped my arm around her and held her tighter to me. "For as long as you need."

Her small hand curled around mine and she threaded our fingers together. "Thank you." She pressed a kiss to the back of my fingers. "I just need you."

I lowered my lips over her ear and whispered, "I need you too."

CHAPTER 38

"One scoop of strawberry, a scoop of chocolate, and three scoops of vanilla." I grabbed the can of whipped cream from the fridge and headed back to my bowl of feelings. I turned the can upside down and filled that sucker to the brim with whipped goodness.

Tilly walked by and grabbed the spoon out of my hand. "You cannot drown your sorrows with whipped cream and layers of ice cream at ten o'clock in the morning."

"Hey! I was eating that." I wrapped my arm around the bowl and marched over to the drawer full of utensils. I yanked it out and they clanged and rattled against each other. I snatched up the biggest spoon I could find and walked out of the kitchen.

Tilly was hot on my heels. "Don't you dare get back in that bed."

I marched up the stairs toward the entrance of our room. "I'm just going to have a little nap."

"Dude, no, you can't just lie here. You have to go to class. I know I messed up both of us, but we have been through worse." She stomped along behind me as I turned down the hall of portraits.

I stopped in front of Gregor. "I don't plan on lying here forever. But I need another day, okay?"

"Fine!" Tilly hooked her finger in the back of the frame and flipped the button. "Go wallow then. But I am not going to sit here and watch you do it."

I shrugged. "Great, while you're out . . . goldfish. I'd really love some goldfish."

"Why don't you do yourself a favor and use your little powers to make some?"

I spun around to face her. "You know my powers and I are on a break."

"Riiigghhhttt, like Ross and Rachel." She rolled her eyes. "You can't avoid using them forever."

I spun back around and stepped into the hallway. "Not forever, just a bit."

"I can't even with you right now." The portrait slid shut behind me and I took the steps one at a time all the way down. The bowl was cool in my arms and I wanted nothing more than to dig into it. When I got to the bottom of my steps, I glanced up at my bed and my jaw dropped along with the bowl.

It clattered at my feet. Ice cream fell across my toes and whipped cream shot up into my face. I ran my hand over my cheek to brush some of it away. "Aidenuli?"

He didn't move, just sat on the foot of my bed staring at Tilly's bed. Odin sat as still as a statue, staring back at him. Neither of them moved or spoke. I picked up the hem of my T-shirt and ran it over my face to get the rest of the whipped cream. Though I was pretty sure there was some caked in the bun on top of my head.

I tiptoed forward. "Umm, Aidenuli? Hello?"

He jerked back and arched an eyebrow at Odin. "Interesting pets you keep."

"He's a good cat." Did he know what Odin was? *Crap, he can hear me. You can hear me lalalalalalalalalalalalalalalalalalalalalalala.*

He held his hand up. "Okay, stop. That is not what I'm here for."

"Then why are you here?" I suddenly felt so awkward talking to him while wearing my pajamas and not my cute pajamas. These were my wallowing, bad day pajamas. The ones that were fuzzy but ugly as sin. I turned my head to the side and took a quick sniff of my shirt. I didn't think I smelled.

Aidenuli snapped his fingers and Beckett stood in the middle of the room with nothing but a pair of jeans that hung so low on his narrow hips I could see every muscle in his stomach, including that delicious V shape. Sweat coated his body and ran down his muscles like he'd been standing in the rain. His hair fell in damp tatters into his eyes.

He spun in a circle. "What the hell was that?"

"I brought you here." Aidenuli rose to his feet to stand between us. "Things haven't been going well for the two of you."

"I can do better, I swear. I just—"

He held his hand up, silencing me. "You just like to be destructive and have a hard time following the rules. I can respect that. Rules in my opinion suck. Doesn't change the fact that a war is coming our way and you're not ready. And we need you to be ready."

Beckett looked me up and down and I knew he was seeing me at my worst. Hair in a knot at the top of my head, baggy dirty clothes, and makeup that'd been long since cried off.

He sighed. "I know she hasn't gotten off to a good start, but I have some ideas."

Aidenuli shook his head. "No offense but all of

your ideas lately have sucked too. Astrid isn't the type to be ruled over and we all know that. Which makes her a perfect warlock."

My jaw dropped. *Was that a compliment?*

Aidenuli continued on, "But also you guys need to figure out how to work together without killing each other."

"What did you have in mind?" Beckett rolled his shoulders and glanced at me. "Hi."

"Um, hi?" What was happening?

"Are you okay?" His eyes bore into mine and I didn't know if he was really concerned or if I looked that bad.

"I think so."

Aidenuli snapped his fingers. "Focus, teenagers." We both turned to face him and he pulled a rolled up piece of paper from his pocket and handed it to Beckett. "This is what Matteaus is calling a team building exercise."

Beckett took the paper from his hand. "A what?"

"Team building. You two are the strongest warlocks in Evermore and it's time for you to start acting like it. So this is your test. You pass and Astrid gets *all* of her power back, and, Beckett, you get to keep leading the heirs."

I wanted it bad. I wanted the power Matteaus took

from me. It was mine and I had to prove I deserved it Peter Parker style. "And if we fail?"

"Matteaus is prepared to take more of your power to make you an average warlock student here at Warwick where you will continue your education but not join with the heirs. And Beckett will return back to Evermore Academy to help Zinnia as best as he can without the help of the warlocks in the war to come." He shook his head. "I really hope you guys succeed because we need you."

Beckett unfurled the scroll and held it up. "Shit! The Greeks, really?"

Aidenuli chuckled. "It's what Matteaus wants. That scroll will help you get started. Astrid needs to learn control and Beckett needs to learn to be a better teacher."

I bit my bottom lip. "What do you mean the Greeks? Who are they? Why are you not happy about that?"

Beckett rolled the paper back up and shoved it into his back pocket. "Get dressed, Astrid, we've got work to do. Meet me at my house in thirty minutes."

Aidenuli chuckled. "Good luck. You're going to need it."

That did not sound good . . . none of this sounded good.

CHAPTER 39

ASTRID

took a deep breath and stepped up onto the porch. My hair was still damp from the quickie shower I took and I wasn't sure what kind of mission we were going on, but I decided on combat boots, ripped up jeans, and a black turtle neck. I lined my eyes with dark liner in hopes it'd just blend in with the bags. I was wracked with dreams I couldn't control, which wasn't making sleep any easier. It was like my subconscious was giving me my deepest desires the only way I could get them, through my dreams. I lifted my hand and knocked on the door in three quick raps.

Logan swung the door wide-open. "What happened? Why are you knocking?"

Beckett walked past the door, absently looking at the scroll in his hand. "Because she thinks she doesn't live here anymore."

"That's funny. I always thought she was welcome here." Logan stepped back from the door and held it open for me.

"She is," Beckett called from the sitting room. "She just thinks she's not."

I stepped over the threshold and walked into the sitting room where he was. "Maybe we could stop talking about me like I'm not here."

Logan swung the door shut. "Yeah, I've got a date to get ready for."

"You're not staying?" I hesitated in the foyer, waiting for the others to join us.

Another light knock came and this time a broad smile spread across Logan's face. "I am not."

He was more clean-cut than usual with his crisp white button-down shirt, and his black dress pants hanging perfectly from his hips. He smoothed his hand over his hair then grabbed the door and opened it once more. "Angel, hi."

A girl my age walked through the door and Logan beamed. I didn't realize the heirs had time to date, but here he was thrumming with excitement. She was pretty, with a willowy figure. She stood a few inches taller than me at five-foot-six and her hair held the color of a true redhead. It was shades lighter than my nearly black. Light freckles were sprinkled across her nose and cheeks. She was cute down to her delicate face and button nose.

She tucked a lock of hair behind her ear. "Hi."

"Astrid, this is Angel." He motioned between the two of us. "Angel, this is Astrid Lockwood."

Her baby blues went wide. "It's so nice to meet you. I've heard so much about you."

I extended my hand out toward her. "Don't believe everything you hear. I'm not as bad as people think."

A giggle escaped her lips. "Oh please, nobody believes what the Kalarooks have to say. But I think some of your feats are badass."

"Oh really?"

"For sure. The time you got a plant to eat them, the time you ascended, the time you told off the council, and my all-time favorite that time you were on the beach and took out all those rogue warlocks." She slapped her hand over her mouth. "I'm sorry. I just have this perfect recall thing and sometimes I can't stop myself."

"Perfect recall?"

"Yeah, I can remember everything that has ever happened around me. And if I read it, there's no forgetting it."

Logan wrapped his arm around her hip and pulled her closer into his side. "Angel is top of the class this year. She's brilliant."

Her cheeks turned a bright shade of pink and I smiled at her. "Now who's the impressive one?"

It was so sweet between the two of them, so simple. He liked her and she liked him. He asked her out and she accepted. *Is that so freaking hard?* They smiled at each other and in that moment the little green-eyed jealousy monster clawed its way into my stomach. Not everyone was as lucky to have what they had. The excitement of new love, not the torture of having a love they couldn't keep.

Angel blushed even deeper and Logan beamed down at her. "You ready to get going?"

"Yeah." She turned back to me. "It was really nice meeting you, Astrid."

"Nice meeting you too." I watched as they walked arm in arm out the door, laughing as they strolled down the sidewalk in the chilly sun. I grabbed the door and pushed it closed a little too hard.

Beckett's head snapped up. "Something wrong?"

You're an idiot. "Nope."

"Good, so I was looking at the scroll and I think I know where our first trip is." He rolled the scroll out onto the coffee table between the two couches. I walked over and sat down next to him.

The couch dipped beneath me and my shoulder brushed his. He stiffened but didn't move away. I leaned over the scroll and pointed to the writing and read out loud.

"If control is what you seek, face those named Greek.

Choices must be made, to earn the token to be paid.

A consort of death she won't be denied, flow her way by river side.

A crown you must claim, to face the brothers to be tamed.

Look not with eyes but with thy heart, for love tears the soul apart.

Face these challenges three, and present the prize on bent knee.

Say these lines with a spin, and your final fate will begin."

"So all I have to do is say these while I spin?" I rose to my feet.

Beckett slammed his hands down on my shoulders. "Don't do it unless you are ready to go right now."

"Aren't you ready to go?"

He shook his head. "We need to think about this and what we need to prep for."

"Pretty sure I can summon anything we will need. But if you want to wait . . ." I let my words trail off. I wanted to fix what I messed up and to earn my way back into this world.

"I can only think of one place we'd go if we were to court death." He pinched the bridge of his nose. "The underworld."

He turned away from me and began pacing in front of the fireplace. "I can't believe he turned to the Greeks. Everyone knows Matteaus can't stand most of them."

"Wait, like the Greek gods?" I'd seen a lot in Evermore over the past few weeks, but the Greek Gods . . . *no way.* But I supposed if Medusa and her sisters were real, then the bigger ones were too.

"Technically they're not gods, but they have power as if they were. They're the first supernaturals ever created. They were meant to help the Fallen in their own battle, but they're a handful for Matteaus and the others." He shook his head. "And after everything else that happened with them."

"What happened?" Worry bounced on my nerves. I thought this would be a test, something to teach me, but maybe this was a way to get rid of me for good.

"They were abysmal when it came to working with Zinnia. Hermes almost killed us all and don't even get me started on Poseidon. My lungs still hurt just thinking about it." I couldn't take my eyes off the predatory way he moved. Like a panther prowling a cage. "And then there are the rumors."

I sat on the edge of the couch. "What rumors?"

"Supposedly some of the Fallen"—he made air quotes with his fingers—"'dated' the Greeks, which is a hugely bad idea."

"Why is it a bad idea?" My voice came out a bit more salty than I wanted. I didn't understand why couples were such a bad thing. Why Beckett and I would be such a bad thing? My dreams were trying to tell me something. Yes, I was attracted to him. Of course I was. Who wouldn't be? He was gorgeous. But deep down it was more. I liked the way he fought for what he believed in, how he always tried to do the right thing and how loyal he was to those closest to him.

"Because dating can only make things more complicated. Especially for people like us."

"What do you mean people like us?"

"The heirs, the Greeks, hell, even the witch court. It

only complicates things." He pinched his bottom lip. "Can we focus here?"

I wasn't ready to talk about the mission yet. I wanted to know why he was so against relationships. "Logan doesn't seem to think they get in the way."

"Logan is dating a normal warlock with normal powers. She's not like the rest of us. There are rules for a reason. Powers and high emotions don't mix. That's why it's in the warlock bylaws." He pressed his lips together.

"What are you talking about?"

"It's like with Zinnia and Tuck. They weren't supposed to be together because a knight is not to be with a queen. When choices get difficult, which they always do, the couple will pick each other over the good of the many. The same goes for the heirs. They don't want two houses to align against the others." He put his hands on his hips. "Honestly, Astrid, we need to focus on the task at hand."

Message received, not interested. "Fine."

"If we have to go to the underworld, I think we should get Nova. It only makes sense."

Nova, again with Nova. Beautiful goth Nova. "I thought this challenge was ours to undertake not the whole cavalry."

"What do you have against Nova?"

You want her. And I wasn't jealous, not one little bit, not even for a second. Sure, Logan gets to have his cute date, but I have to live in the land of forbidden crushes. "I don't have anything against Nova. All I'm saying is I don't think we should break the rules from the get-go. I know we're warlocks and all that but still. I'd like to get *all* of my powers back."

"Fine," he snapped. "No Nova."

"Good."

"Good." He threw his hands up. "I think I know of a way to get in, but we'll have to leave at night."

"Great, nighttime it is." I rose to my feet. "Anything else?"

"You're leaving?"

"Well, yeah, unless there was something you wanted to discuss." Tension hung between us.

He shook his head. "Nope, nothing."

"Good."

"Good."

"Stop saying that," I snapped. "If you have something to say then say it."

I stood waiting for him to blow up at me for ruining the apartment, for not listening to him, yet he said nothing.

He shook his head. "I don't have anything to say."

"Fine then." Things were just awkward between us.

I didn't know what to say to him or do around him. I both wanted him and wanted to get away from him.

"Fine, good." He put his hands on his hips.

We stood glaring at each other for long moments. Neither of us saying anything, and neither of us moving. I didn't know if I wanted to kiss him or hit him. Maze walked in from the kitchen and stood between us. He glanced from Beckett to me and back again.

One by one he placed little cone-shaped snacks on the tips of his fingers. He pawed his hand through the air and hissed like a cat. "Damn, I thought you guys worked out this whole tension thing."

"What the hell are you babbling about? There is no tension." There was definitely tension. I just didn't want to admit to it.

"Um, yeah, there is. You guys should just stop doing that dream bang cuddle thing you've been doing and get to it in real life." He bit the snack off the tip of his finger.

"WHAT?" We both yelled at the same time.

"Oh come on, like you guys didn't know." He reached into the bag on his lap and placed another snack on his fingertip.

"Maze!" I gave two quick claps to get his attention. "What are you saying?"

He looked from Beckett to me then threw his head back laughing. "You guys honestly didn't know?"

"Didn't know what?" Beckett snatched the bag of snacks away from him.

"You all have been you know, bow chicka wow wowing in your dreams. You know, doing the dirty, hiding the trout, tickling the pickle, slap and cuddles, wetting the whistle, laying the pipe. Grinding metaphysical nasties." He laughed even harder.

I was going to throw up. Those dreams, they were so real, so close, so freaking intimate. I shook my head and whispered, "You don't even know what you're talking about."

"Bizzzzzzzz." Maze made that annoying game show sound. "Survey says the psychic is right. Ding ding ding."

"Holy shit, Astrid." Beckett took a step toward me.

I held my hand out, stopping him. "Nope." I had to run, to get the hell out of there before this got any more embarrassing. "So yeah, I'll meet you tomorrow night."

I ran toward the door.

Beckett leapt over the coffee table to chase after me. "Astrid, we should talk."

The cold air hit my face and I pumped my arms even harder. "Later," I called over my shoulder and ran headlong from the house. There was no way I was going to talk about this with him, not now, not ever. It was too embarrassing. I gave him the metaphysical booty and he knew it. *Shit shit shit.* I dared a single glance over my shoulder to see if he followed. But he stood still as a statue on the porch, staring after me.

CHAPTER 40

I slammed the door shut with all my strength. The walls and windows rattled and I turned to face Maze. I was in front of him in two strides. Before I knew what I was doing I wrapped my hand in his shirt and yanked him to his feet.

His snacks fell to the floor. "What the hell, man?"

"What is wrong with you? How could you just blurt out something like that?" I shook him. "How long have you known?"

Green smoke seeped from his hands and he looked down at my fists in his shirt. "Beck, you know I don't do well with the whole touching thing."

I shoved him away from me and he fell back on the couch. The leather creaked under his ass and the couch scraped against the hardwood floors. I moved to stand in front of the fireplace. Heat kicked out from it in waves against the back of my legs. I was dumbfounded. Did I go after her?

I cleared my throat. "Let me get this straight. She and I . . ."

"Yup." He nodded.

"But that's impossible." I shook my head, not wanting to believe it. We already had so much to overcome between the two of us and now this.

Maze bent over and scooped one of those little cone snacks off the floor. He blew on it then shoved it into his mouth. "Not if you're a dream walker."

"No warlock has had that gift in centuries. It's too dangerous."

Maze slid off the couch to sit next to the pile of snacks on the floor. He blew on each one before he put them into his mouth. "And yet you and your girl both have it."

I didn't know why, but it made me feel better that we both were participating in this little mess with our powers. "No, that's not possible. Powers don't work like that. Besides, I've had the same powers all my life."

"Well, I imagine that if you share a deep connection with someone, that might open up some avenues for other powers to manifest."

"I can only think of one other warlock who

supposedly had that power and it just can't be." I put my hands on my hips and bit my bottom lip.

"Or can it?" Maze arched his eyebrow.

"Is there something you're not telling me?"

"Is that a trick question?" He shrugged. "Of course there are things I'm not telling you, duh."

"I have a headache. *You* give me headaches." I wanted to swipe the food from his hand. "It's not like we don't have other snacks here. Why are you eating off the floor? The germs alone, man."

"Alas germs are not how I'm going to die. So you see, dirty won't actually hurty."

I rolled my eyes. "Come on."

"Where are we going?" Maze rose to his feet and looked down at the mess he was about to leave. "Where's the damn thieving cat when you need it."

"You can't feed a cat those things." I motioned for him to follow me up the stairs.

"You can feed a devil cat anything," Maze muttered.

"Devil cat?" I climbed the stairs two at a time.

He grabbed onto the railing and followed me up. "Stole my chicken nuggets . . . what kind of monster does that? A devil monster, I tell you."

I turned down the hall and marched toward my father's office. The moment I walked in the smell of old books filled my nose. A single desk sat in the middle of the room and to the right of it another door to a secret room stood wide-open. I'd discovered the room when I was a small child. It held all the secrets the warlocks of Evermore wanted to keep. I walked into the dust-covered room and gazed at the books lining the walls and stacked precariously around the floor.

Maze stopped just inside the doorway. "What exactly are we looking for here?"

There in the back corner of the room sat a book as thick as two Webster dictionaries. The cover was a hunter green with gold writing on the cover that read *A History of Warlocks.* I grabbed it with both of my hands and dragged it over to my father's desk, where it landed with a loud thud. Dust flew up at us. I waved it away and cleared my throat of the bits I inhaled.

Maze hunched over and sneezed. "Stupid dust bunnies."

"You know what this is, right?" I opened the book and flipped to the table of contents.

"Yeah, they made us read it when we were kids. It's the stuff of nightmares. The origins of the entire warlock race." He scoffed. "Hard pass on the history lesson."

"Just wait." I flipped the book to the page I was looking for. I pointed to the picture of a beautiful woman with long blond hair that ran from the top of her head down past her hips. The dress she wore was a deep green color straight out of King Henry the 8th's time period. The neckline fell across her shoulders. The corset cinched in at her waist and the dress puffed out at her hips. She was beautiful, with a straight regal nose, large round emerald eyes, and milky skin.

"Penndolyn Fairmont." Maze whistled. "She was a looker for sure. But oh the things she was capable of."

I sat back in my father's chair and read the text. "She was the first warlock ever. The one to walk away from the witches and join Alataris' side. She betrayed them all."

"Yeah, but think of it this way. If she hadn't then we wouldn't exist. Warwick wouldn't exist." Maze clapped me on the shoulder. "Ballsy, very ballsy of her."

I pointed to a line next to her name. "And the only one on record to have the dream walker ability. So how is it possible that I have it? And why Astrid?"

Maze pointed to the picture. "Beck, man, look at the mark."

I narrowed my eyes and leaned in closer to the book. "Is that . . ."

"The same one Astrid has . . . yeah."

I shoved away from the book. "Shit."

CHAPTER 41

ASTRID

This is going to be fine, totally fine. Just going on a mission to get my powers back. Nothing more, nothing less. So why did I feel like I had to puke and poop all at the same time? My insides were in knots and I wanted to turn around and walk away from the door. Instead, I sucked in a deep breath and knocked.

"I thought Beck told you not to knock." Maze pulled the door open and didn't even look up at me. The smell of cookies wafted down the hall and he held a spoon covered in batter in one hand and a bowl in the other.

I walked past him and paused in the foyer. The fires were lit in both sitting rooms yet no one was there. I glanced up the stairs, looking for Beckett. "It's awkward to just walk in now."

"Why?" He scooped some batter onto the spoon then shoved it into his mouth.

"Because, you know." I walked over to the hall leading back to the kitchen and glanced down. "Where is he?"

Maze moved past me and down the hall. "Wasn't my turn to watch him."

My boots clicked on the hardwood floors as I followed him. I walked into the kitchen behind him and froze. "What happened in here?"

Flour littered the island and floor. Cookie sheets were stacked in piles and laid out across all the available counter space, and scores of cookies were strewn about in various states of preparation. I walked over to a stack of chocolate chip and grabbed one. It was still warm in my hand. Maze stopped what he was doing and pointed the spatula at me like he was going to smack my hand with it.

I slowly brought the cookie to my lips and made a show of taking a bite of it. It was warm and gooey. The chocolate melted and stuck to my fingers. "Maze, these are delicious! But why so many?"

"Cookies are a huge part of life, Astrid." He gave me a deadpan look. "Do I have to teach you everything?"

"Really? I'm pretty sure you haven't taught me anything so far." I leaned back and looked down the hall. Still no Beckett. "We were supposed to leave tonight. It's not like him to not be where he says he's going to be."

"I'm sure you know exactly where he is *every* night." Maze chuckled to himself as he bent over and opened the oven. He reached in and pulled out a cookie sheet. When I didn't laugh, he glanced over his shoulder at me. "What? To soon?"

I pursed my lips. How could he blurt that crap out like it wouldn't be embarrassing? I sighed and sank down onto a stool next to the island. "Gee, you think?"

He pointed toward the door. "In three . . . two . . . one . . ."

"Astrid, hi." Beckett strolled into the room looking finer than ever in his dark blue jeans, combat boots, and his sun-kissed skin stood out against his crisp white V-neck shirt. He tugged his sleeves up to his elbows.

"Hey, you ready to go?" I didn't meet his gaze. I couldn't, not yet.

"Yeah." He lowered his voice. "Don't you think we should talk first?"

I wasn't ready to deal with this. I rose to my feet and walked back toward the hallway. "Nope."

Beckett followed behind me. "No?"

"No." I shook my head.

"Astrid, we have to talk about this." As we walked back into the foyer, he grabbed my arm and spun me around to face him. "Please."

Please? We had to talk about what happened, about the things we said to each other and where that left us now. I softened my voice. "We will, but can we just focus on one thing at a time? I've messed up a lot lately, and I want to prove to Matteaus that I belong here and I deserve to have my powers. Hell, I want to prove it to myself and to you."

"To me?" He slid his hand down my arm and wound his fingers with mine. "I always knew you belonged here."

Heat sizzled between us and for a moment I wanted to forget the task at hand and just lean on him. Let him take me in his arms and tell me everything was going to be okay. But I couldn't, not yet. I had so many questions. Why was he so open with me only in his dreams when I needed him to be open with me in real life?

I glanced down at our joined hands then back up at his deep ocean eyes. Something clicked inside of me. This was right between us, yet we kept on denying it.

"Okay, then let's get this over with so we can figure *us* out."

"Yeah, it's about time." He smiled down at me. "This isn't going to be easy."

"Us or the mission?"

He shrugged. "Both."

"Since when do we do anything easy?" I squeezed his hand and for the first time had the guts to do something I've wanted to do since the day I met him. I wound my other hand into his shirt and tugged him down toward me. When his lips met mine, my insides went wild and I pulled him closer to me. He lifted our joined hands up and held them over his chest, close to his heart. This kiss wasn't the frenzied ones we'd shared before. No, this was a slow burn. A melding of lips and tongues that made me feel things down to my toes. That burning connection we shared in our dreams, the need for each other and desire for so much more. I moaned into his mouth and he took my lips harder.

"Glad you two made up!" Maze bellowed from the kitchen.

We jumped apart and I glanced around the room, then lowered my voice to a whisper, "How did he know?"

Beckett sighed. "He's an insane psychic, that's how."

"I'd hate to know what else he sees." A shiver went down my spine at the thought. "Or how much."

"Don't worry, Astrid, it isn't much! Before you ask, no, I didn't hear you." The sound of clanking pans came from the kitchen. "Damn, that's hot."

"Just ignore him." Beckett pulled the scroll from his back pocket and handed it to me. "Before you start reading that and we leave, there's just one more thing."

It could've always been this easy between us, this playful. "What's that?"

"Now that we're more than friends, you can admit it."

"Admit what?"

His tongue darted over his lips, wetting them. "That you *like* the way I taste."

CHAPTER 42

ASTRID

*L*iked it? *Try loved it.* He was so minty and fresh like a winter party in my mouth. "Let's focus here."

"Suurreee." When he looked at me with that cocky smile in place, so playful, it made me want to kiss him all over again.

I held the scroll open. "So I have to read this and then spin around and then what?"

He stepped in closer to me and placed his hand on the small of my back. Electricity shot straight through me then centered low in my body. I leaned into him, letting my back rest against his chest. He reached over my shoulder and read the spell once more. "Yeah, that should be good."

Something brushed against my hair and Beckett

sucked in a deep breath. I glanced at him over my shoulder. "Did you just smell my hair?"

"Don't be silly. Who even likes strawberries anyways?" He walked around to face me then winked. "Okay, step back."

"Okay, here we go." I sucked in a deep breath and read the lines.

"If control is what you seek, face those named Greek.

Choices must be made, to earn the token to be paid.

A consort of death she won't be denied, flow her way by river side.

A crown you must claim, to face the brothers to be tamed.

Look not with eyes but with thy heart, for love tears the soul apart.

Face these challenges three, and present the prize on bent knee.

Say these lines with a spin, and your final fate will begin."

As I read the last line I spun around and let my powers flow through me. Smoke flooded the room and the walls shook so hard that even the windows rattled. Beckett grabbed onto my hand. "Hold on."

"What's happening?" I yelled over the earthquake.

"I don't know."

Two thick metal doors materialized from out of nowhere. They hovered in the air above our heads. Each of them appeared to be put together by extra pieces of scrap metal held together by thick bolts. Beckett grabbed my arms and dragged me back. We tumbled over the arm of the couch and fell back with me on top of him. I scrambled off of him in time to see the doors swing down from where they hovered. They slammed into the hardwood floors, sending planks splintering up from the impact. Dust filled the air and the space between the two doors shimmered.

I rose to my feet and shoved. "What was that?"

"Not what." A deep rough male voice came from the door.

"But who," another much smoother, younger voice added.

As the dust cleared, a man stood between the two doors. He was nearly the same height as the door and wore an old Greek soldier's uniform. A golden breast plate covered him from shoulder to hip, and deep red material covered his arms and legs. But that wasn't the most disturbing part of the man. No, this man was neither young nor old . . . because he had two freaking heads!

I looked from one face to the other, not knowing

who I was supposed to look in the eye. The one on the right side was an older man with a thick beard and shaggy gray hair that fell into dark brown eyes. Deep wrinkles fanned out around his eyes and down his cheeks. The one on the left was a young man with sandy brown hair that curled back from his face. His eyes were a crystal blue and when he smiled at me there wasn't a wrinkle in sight.

Beckett stood by my side. "Janus, it's . . . good to see you."

By the tone of his voice it didn't sound good. Young Janus chuckled and old Janus scowled. Old Janus cleared his throat. "We come at the command of Matteaus."

"He so rarely turns to us," young Janus added. "I'm not entirely sure this is necessary."

I leaned back and whispered to Beckett, "Remind me again who's Janus?"

"Dude gifted with power over doors, gates, beginnings, and endings," Beckett muttered.

Janus threw his arms out wide, holding one in front of each door. Young Janus smiled. "We come to present a choice. Pick a door, any door."

Old Janus cleared his throat. "Choose wisely. One will lead to most certain death."

"No, it won't." Young Janus shook his head.

"Indeed it will." Older one nodded. "Don't listen to the youngen. He's naïve in his ways."

"Right, like the crotchy grouchy old man knows. You forgot your name yesterday!"

Old Janus huffed. "I did not! Poppycock."

"Oh really? Then what is your name." All the while Janus gestured wildly with his arms while he? They? Fought themselves.

"Damn you. I know my name!" old Janus bellowed at the top of his lungs.

"Oh yeah," the younger one taunted. "What is it? Let's hear it."

"It's, um . . . ummm."

Young Janus threw his head back and laughed. "See, he's got no clue. You can only die if you open up the wrong door."

I pointed at the old dude. "He just said that!"

Young Janus' brows furrowed. "He did?"

"Bah, bah now who doesn't remember. Old, young, doesn't matter. Janus knows all." The older one snickered and I wanted to punch them both in the faces.

I held my hand up, silencing them. "How can the test be to choose a door when they both look the same? This is a test, right? Not a death match."

They both froze and put their hands on their hips. They gazed off in opposite directions as though looking out over the horizon instead of opposite sides of the ceiling. Young Janus was the first to speak. He muttered to his other half, "Were we supposed to not kill this one?"

"Yes, no," the other answered.

"That isn't an answer, you old fool." He swung his head back and smacked his cheek into his other half.

Older Janus huffed and the hand on his side of the body flew up and wacked the other one in the face. The smacking sound echoed around the room as his head snapped back. An angry red handprint rose on the young one's face. "That hurt, you old bastard!"

"I got more where that came from." The older one curled his hand into a fist and took a wild swing at his other half.

"Give it a rest, old man." He chuckled. "You're not fooling anyone."

"Ugh." I nudged Beckett. "We have got to get out of here before they kill themselves."

He nodded. "But which door? I'm pretty sure they messed up and one of them could kill us."

They abruptly stopped fighting and older Janus nodded. "Yes, one leads to death."

Young Janus chuckled. "It absolutely does."

I threw my hands up. "Well, which one? The right or the left?"

"Right," Young said.

"Left," Old said at the exact same time.

"Well, which is it?" Beckett snapped.

"Left."

"Right."

Again the two of them answered at the same time. I reached behind Beckett and shoved him toward Janus. "I think you have a few more questions, don't you?"

"I do?" He glanced over his shoulder at me. I gave him a single nod. His eyes flared for a second and he faced Janus. "That's right, I do."

Beckett motioned toward the doors. "Now, gentlemen, if it were you, which door would you choose?"

Again with the rights and lefts. They discussed the make of the doors, the way they smelled, who made them why they were made and yet we still came back to the left and right discussion. If the door opens from the right or from the left. What does it mean if they open the door from the right or left? Janus walked around each door like he was examining a car. Beckett followed along with him. He crossed one arm over his stomach and rested his elbow on it.

We'd stand here day and night debating things with a two-headed supernatural with two different minds. *Right? Left? Right? Left?* The three of them walked behind the door. If ever there was a time to pick a destiny, it was now.

I stepped up to the door on the right and wrapped my hand around the knob. "Beckett?"

"Yeah?" He peeked around the side of the frame.

I extended my hand out to him. "Time to go."

He took my. "But what if?"

As I turned the knob, my magic flared to life, my chest burned, and smoke poured from me. "This is the one."

I shoved the door wide-open. Beyond there was nothing, only darkness. Beckett squeezed my hand. "I'm ready."

Janus moved to stand behind us. Old Janus whispered, "I don't recall this, do you?"

"No, do you?" The younger one breathed on my neck.

"Enough." I took a step forward. "Here we go."

Beckett smiled down at me. "You jump, I jump."

And then we did . . .

CHAPTER 43

*M*y stomach dropped into my feet as we fell into the blackness. A scream ripped from my throat and Beckett yanked me to him. Blue orbs fired from his free hand right below us. They grew bigger and bigger as we fell toward them.

"Brace yourself!" he yelled over the wind whipping past us. Or were we whipping past it?

Terror flooded my body and smoke billowed from me. My body slowed from a free fall, to a slow drift. Beck chuckled beside me. "Whooooo, you did it."

"Not on purpose. It was like a sneeze pee, total accident." My arms flailed as we drifted down onto Beckett's platform. I landed flat on my stomach with a thud that sounded like a tennis ball hitting glass. Beckett stepped onto the platform like he was walking down the street. He bent down and grabbed my arm, helping me to my feet.

"Sneeze pee?"

"You don't want to know and we're going to forget I said anything." I sucked in a deep breath and glanced around at the nothingness. It was pitch-black all but for the faint blue glow of Beckett's platform. My stomach went from being in my feet right up to my throat. The wind blew my hair back from my face. If it wasn't for that, I would almost think we weren't moving at all.

Blue light illuminated Beckett's face. "Where do you think we are?"

"Black sink hole of death?"

"I'm not sure if this is the death one." He walked over to the edge of the platform and leaned to look over the edge.

"Are you crazy?" I waved for him to come back. "Don't do that."

"Worried I'll fall?" Why did he have to smile and flirt with me when we were falling into nothing? And be so damn cute while doing it.

"No."

"I think I see something." He leaned farther over the side and this time I grabbed his arm and pulled him back.

"Let's just chill with the jumping over the edge thing."

"I'm not kidding. I did see something." He pointed to a pin prick of light below us. It grew bigger and bigger as we drifted down to it.

Every time some extreme emotion hit me, my magic rose to the occasion. Was this mission part of teaching me not to do that either? I looked down at my smoking palms and shook them out. *Okay, stop now.*

Beckett reached over and intertwined his fingers with mine. "I like when they do that."

"You do?"

"Yep." He pressed a kiss to the top of my head.

"Beck, why the change in heart? Like why are you okay with us now?" His hand swallowed mine, warm and comforting in this moment of chaos.

He shrugged. "Tired of fighting it, I guess."

Yeah sure, that explains it all. I rolled my eyes. "You're right, we'll talk about it later."

"Here we go." The darkness slowly lifted like someone raised the dimmer switch. We dropped out of a hole in a cavern, a massive cavern. It was like flying over an entire universe deep within the earth.

In the distance a castle made entirely of onyx stood in the middle of it. Beyond that was a bright shining land with the fields looking like spun gold. Beautiful houses rose up all over and faint peaceful music carried on the wind along with the smell of the sea.

"Where are we?"

"The underworld." Beckett growled. "We have to stay together down here. Okay?"

"Yeah." I didn't turn to face him. Instead, I faced the other direction where the world grew dark. Pained wails drew up from the darkest part of the underworld. Glowing molten lava flowed through dark rocks and around a deep pit. The platform drifted to a stop and we bounced a little.

"Astrid, I'm serious." Beckett tugged me over to the edge. He stepped down off of it first. Then waited for me to follow.

"I know you are." The moment my feet hit the ground I had the overwhelming sense that everything was mundane. I wasn't scared or excited or happy. I just *was*. "Whoa."

"I know." All personality left his voice.

The field around us swayed with wildflowers and tall golden grass. It was beautiful, but everything felt so ordinary, like there was no magic in the world. Things were neither good nor bad. "What part of the underworld is this?"

"Asphodel meadows. Where souls who were

neither good nor bad come in the afterlife. Their lives were just unremarkable."

As I listened to his words, souls from all time periods sprang up around me. A civil war soldier walked by on my left. A man dressed in bellbottoms and white fringe shirt passed on my right. The field filled with people all walking around. Silence hung heavy in the air and I didn't know if I should move or not. "Beckett?"

"Come on, the dead don't interact with the living. We have to keep moving to find out why we're here." The blades of grass rustled with each step we took.

I felt we weren't getting anywhere, simply wandering. Until I looked out over the field of souls and spotted a single beacon of white among the mundane. "This way."

I moved through the meadow, walking around souls I could see through, stepping over rocks and twigs. Not even my footsteps on the gravel made a dent in the heavy silence.

Beckett followed close behind me as I came upon the small white flower. The petals were closed up tight and I reached out to touch it. When my finger brushed against the delicate petals, they unfurled one at a time, revealing a small trumpet-shaped center that was such a bright and cheery yellow even in this place.

"How beautiful." I bent down lower to examine it when the flower next to it opened up. Both of them equally beautiful, then another and another. When they spread across the meadow in a straight line heading toward the horizon. "I think this is a hint."

Beckett motioned for me go first. "Follow the yellow brick road."

"If that makes me Dorothy, then does that make you the Tin Man?" I bumped him with my hip.

"I think I could muster up something stiffer than tin for you." He chuckled.

Heat flooded my cheeks and I couldn't stop the laughter bursting from my lips. "Maybe I'll go with the scarecrow next time."

"Also a dude who works with a pole. You're making this too easy for me." He winked.

I smacked him in his arm playfully. "Okay, you win."

He started to chuckle then drew up short. I stopped and gazed off in the same direction he looked. The flowers continued to bloom all the way down to a river bed where they flowed out on top of the water in the shape of a raft.

"You don't think . . ."

"Oh, I do think." We walked in silence down to the

river and stood before the raft. Becket bent down and pressed his hand on the flowers. "Seems sturdy."

"How do we even know this is where we're supposed to go?" I looked up and down the river. There was nothing, yet the life seemed to be coming back the farther we got away from the meadow. A small wooden sign materialized just beside the raft. Words were carved into the single plank and I read it out loud. "Ride the tides and a crown will become your prize."

"Okay." I shrugged and took a step onto the raft. Beckett hesitated just off shore. "Are you coming?"

He gave me a single nod. "Astrid, no matter what's about to happen, you have to stay on the raft, okay?"

"Yeah, like I'm going to jump in. I've heard of the rivers in the underworld. I might not know as much as you, but yeah, I agree no jumping in." I plopped down in the center of the raft and crossed my legs.

"Good." He stepped up onto it and grabbed the pole at the back to push away from the shore. We slowly drifted away from the shoreline and Beckett guided the raft to the center of the river.

It was a slow methodic ride, where the only sound in my ears was the water tripping over the rocks. Then came the first whisper, a hissing voice low in my ear. "Did you hear that?"

"Hear what?" He looked farther down the river and his eyes widened. "Hold on."

They all assailed me at once. So many voices screaming at me. I hunched over and pressed my palms over my ears. I rocked back and forth. "No, no!"

He doesn't care about you, just to control you.

He wants you for the dreams.

He's just toying with you. He likes to play.

Toying with you.

Plaything, nothing more.

He'll leave you like everyone else does.

You're not important to him.

He's using you!

"Astrid? What's going on?" Beckett reached out and touched my shoulder.

I turned and only saw red. Rage rolled through me and I wanted to kill *everything*. I gathered my magic in my hand and leapt right at him with my fingers curled into claws, aiming for his face.

CHAPTER 44

*A*strid leapt at me, ready to scratch my eyes out. I dropped the pole and held my arm out, blocking her. She tore through my shirt with her nails. Her magic seeped from her and covered the top of the raft.

"Astrid, you don't want to do this."

She shook her head and her hair fell into her face. She hunched over and swiped out at me again. "You're only using me for my power."

"What?" The raft dipped as we slid into a set of rapidly moving water. I held my arms out the way I did anytime I surfed. It jostled up and down, bouncing us. Though I held my balance, Astrid dropped to her knees. She pressed her hands to the sides of her head. "Make them stop talking or I will kill you!"

What the hell was happening? And then it hit me. I dropped down to my knees beside her. I placed my hands on her cheeks. "Look at me."

She wound her hand back and let it crack across my cheek. "Hate you!"

My head snapped back and splitting pain shot up the side of my face. *Ouch!* I shook my head. "We're on the Styx! The river of hate."

"No! You're evil!" She shot her magic right at my face. I held my hand up and let my magic take most of the hit. I ducked to the side and some of her smoke streaked across my cheek. I pressed my hand over the stinging cut. The warmth of trickling blood coated my fingers.

My heart went into overdrive as she struggled toward me with murder in her eyes. "Hate you so much."

"Yeah, I got that." I gritted my teeth and used the bottom of my shirt to wipe my face. I grabbed her wrists and tossed her down onto the raft. Then held her there through every bump in the river.

She screamed in my face, "Using me!" She kicked out with her legs and tried to squirm away.

"Am not! Just rein it in until we get to the next river, Astrid. Come on! Control yourself!"

"Beckett?" She blinked up at me. "What happened? Why are you on top of me?"

"Is this really you or are you going to claw my eyes out?" I kept her pinned down.

"Scratch your eyes out?" When a drop of blood fell from my cheek, her eyes widened. "Did I . . . did I do that to you?"

I eased off her wrists and she sat up and pressed her hand to her head. "The voices, Beckett, they're telling me to do such bad things. Awful things."

"It'll be over soon." *I hope.* "Do you still hear them?"

She nodded and squeezed her eyes shut. "Yeah."

"But you're not acting on them, you've got control."

"Don't sound so pleased. They're screaming for me to kill you." She pressed her hands to the sides of her head and rocked back and forth.

"You've got this." This had to end soon. I looked out over the river and just as I thought things couldn't get worse. "Oh shit."

"What?" Her head snapped up. "Oh shit."

Mist covered the river where it fell off into a freaking waterfall. I grabbed at the flowers, searching for anything to hold on to. Astrid scrambled to her knees and held her hands over the flowers. Vine loops shot up from the raft like handles.

I pulled Astrid closer to me and we grabbed the handles. "Don't fall in the water."

"That's the plan." The raft shot off the waterfall and my stomach rose up into my throat.

We were airborne and the front flipped down. We dangled from the handles in midair with nothing but a flower parachute to hold on to.

A scream ripped from her mouth and I had to do something. I dropped my right hand and let my magic shoot from me. The raft snapped back around and I lost my grip. My body launched straight up into the air and I flipped over. My arms pinwheeled and I kicked my legs out. Dizziness overcame me as I spun.

"Beckett!"

I twisted in midair and fired my magic to propel myself down toward her. I dropped onto it just as the raft slammed onto the river. Water splashed up all around us and I fell onto my back, sucking in deep breaths.

My chest heaved as I tried to slow my racing pulse. "That was—"

"Beckett." She interrupted.

"Ye—" I glanced down at her and sucked in a sharp breath. *No! No!* My mind couldn't comprehend what my eyes were seeing. My hands shook so hard I couldn't control them. "Astrid. Oh God."

"It's not as bad as it feels, is it?" She swallowed hard and a tear leaked back from the corner of her eye.

"No, it's not," I lied. Two jagged thorns jutted from the raft and right through each of her shoulders. Blood coated the white flowers beneath her. I swallowed around the ball in my throat. "You're going to be just fine."

"Liar." She coughed and a mist of blood shot up from her lips. "On the plus side, we stopped moving."

I looked at the river and we hadn't stopped moving. The river went from white water rapids to smooth as glass. "No, we just smoothed out."

"What?" Her face was sickly pale and more blood seeped from her. "Where are we?"

I brushed my thumb over her cheek to smooth away the tears. She had to be okay. She was my love, my soulmate. If I lost her. Oh God, I couldn't even think about losing her. "Don't worry about it. We will get you out of here and back to Warwick. I'll call Niche. She will heal you just like she did before."

She shook her head. "No, Beck, what part of the river are we on?"

"Has to be . . ." My eyes widened. "The Acheron. The river of *pain*."

"Really lives up to the name." She gave me a weak smile.

"I can get us to the edge, get us home." I opened my hand, ready to use my magic to move us off the river.

"No, don't you see? This is a test." She struggled with every word. "I can't give up now. We have to continue on."

I shook my head. "How can this be . . . it?"

"Help me up." She reached for my hand.

"What? Are you crazy?" I wound my fingers with hers.

"Not crazy, I'm right." She started to pull herself up off the thorns. The raft rocked with her movements. The blood drained from her face and she turned a shade of green I didn't ever want to see on her.

I wanted to tell her to lie still, yet I found myself pulling her up off those thorns. The wet sticky sound of the thorns sliding out filled my ears. I wanted to trade places with her, to take that pain from her. As the last little bit slid free, she cried out and fell onto my lap. I pressed my hands over the gaping holes in her back. Her blood seeped between my fingers and dripped onto the raft. "Why did you do that?"

"Pain." She huffed and ran her finger over the blood coating her shirt, gathering it on her fingertips. She held it over the edge of the raft. "The river demands it and I refuse to give up."

Had the shock of her wounds gotten to her head?

Was she delirious like she was only moments ago? "I don't understand."

"Each one is a lesson, hate, pain. I needed to learn to control my temper and not give up when things get painful or hurt me." She let a drop of her blood hit the water and the raft surged forward as if I dropped an engine onto it.

She lay back and closed her eyes. Little by little the wounds on her shoulders knitted closed. Though her blood still stood stark against the white flower petals and her skin had only turned from green to ghostly white. I wrapped my arms around her and held her for long moments while we drifted. Music from Elysium mixed with the cries from Tartarus and the sound of trickling water, but all I could focus on was her even breaths.

"If I could take this for you, I would."

"I know." She sighed. "We're getting closer to the next one."

"How do you know?" Dread sat in the pit of my stomach. How much more could she take?

"I'm not sure, but you know what?" She sat up and cupped my cheek.

"Um, what?" I glanced down at her doe-eyed smile and knew something was up. The river changed from glassy clear to foggy mist. Just like Astrid had gone from writhing in pain to . . . this.

"You're right. Let's just go."

"Why would you want to go now? I think we've gotten past the worst of it . . ." Then it dawned on me. "Right, okay, so I think we're on the Lethe."

"What's a Lethe?" She smiled up at me with not a care in the world.

I met her eye and spoke slowly, "The river of forgetfulness."

"Riiiiggghhhtttt." She opened her palm and summoned the fog off the top of the river and made a little cloud shaped like a cat. "I'm sorry, were you talking?"

"The river of forgetfulness." I sat back and spread my arms out behind me. Something told me we were going to be here for a while.

"Right, okay, yeah." She poked her cloud cat in the nose and sent it drifting back onto the river. "Where are we again?"

"The Lethe." Her brows furrowed in confusion and I sighed. "The river of forgetfulness."

CHAPTER 45

BECKETT

n hour later...

"Okay, Astrid, say it with me." I was on my knees before her. The twigs from the raft dug into my skin and my patience was slowly slipping away. "The Lethe."

"The Lethe . . . which isssssssss . . ." She trailed off, waiting for me to finish.

"The river of . . ." I placed my hands on her cheeks, pulling her in. I pressed my lips against hers and let the heat between us take me. My hands drifted down her arms and around her back. I dragged her closer to me and opened my mouth to hers.

She yanked away from me. "Forgetfulness!"

Now of all times . . . now? "Finally."

The raft shot forward and I fell back on the flowers. Astrid looked ahead of us then back at me. "What happened?"

"No, not again." I groaned and threw my arm over my face.

She gave it a little tug. "Not what again?"

Her eyes were lucid this time, not that ditzy doe-eyed look she'd given me only moments ago. "Oh thank God it's over."

"I have no idea what you're talking about, but we're moving again, so that's a good thing." She rubbed at her shoulders.

"I have no idea what lesson was learned with that one, but it was a pain in the ass." The longer we were down here, the more I doubted what these rivers could teach us.

"Patience." She grabbed a flower and tossed it into my face. "Seems that one needs a bit more work on your part."

Sweat rolled down the sides of my face as I grabbed my own set of flowers and threw them back at her. For the first time there was a peace between us. Perhaps it wasn't so bad that Maze spilled the beans on our dream walking abilities. Perhaps things would get better between us. Maybe having the two of us aligned would be accepted by the warlock world. Hope sprang in my chest and this time I didn't want to put it out.

"Beckett!" Astrid jumped to her feet. "I'm not sure what kind of flowers these are, but fire doesn't seem like something they can withstand."

I jumped up next to her. "The Phlegethon! Astrid, wall, we need a wall of magic."

She threw her hands up and golden smoke exploded out of her, rising up in front of us like a brick wall. I turned and threw my magic out behind us. My blue smoke connected with her gold to form a barrier around the raft. Flames licked up the side of the dome and flew over our heads. She pressed her back to mine and we both held back the fire trying to consume us. Her body quaked against my back and I could feel her power fighting to hold against the magic of the river.

Flames exploded through our dome like a tube of death. I ducked down and dragged Astrid with me. All the while I held one side up while she held the other. The dome continued to weaken and I felt Astrid growing tired.

Sweat ran down my cheeks as the heat filled the dome. "This isn't working."

"Tell me about it. We need something more." I

could feel the press of her shoulder into my lower back and I wanted to shield her from this, from being burned alive. She ducked under my arm and spun around to face me. "Change of plans."

"What?"

"We need to combine our powers!" She held her arms up and wrapped her hands with mine. "Three, two, one . . . now!"

Power exploded out of us at the same time, her gold mixed with my blue. The dome pulsed outward, forcing the dancing flames back. The moment they hit the shoreline the flames extinguished.

"More, Astrid, more!"

Our eyes locked and I felt her power as if it were my own, washing over me. The flames slunk back toward the shore and I could see up ahead an end in sight. "Just a little bit longer."

The raft flowed forward and our dome held as if we were coming out of a tunnel. The flames peeled back over the dome until we shot out the other end. Astrid dropped my hands and fell into my chest. "Did you feel . . ."

"I felt you." I kissed the top of her head. "We've only got one more to go."

She fell back. Her hair fanned out around her in an array of deep burgundy that stood out among the white petals. Her chest rose and fell with each heaving breath she took. Her emerald eyes sparked, and she shook her head. "I don't think I have it in me to do another one. I'm exhausted."

I knew what she meant. I felt the exhaustion down to my bones. My eyelids dipped, and I dropped down next to her. We lay shoulder to shoulder, drifting along in a quiet sort of peace. "You know what comes next?"

She nodded. "Yeah, Cocytus, river of wailing."

"Yep." I curled on my side to face her.

"Yep." She mirrored my position and scooted in closer. "Will we hear all the cries of the damned?"

"Or the cries of people whose loved ones are down here." I reached out and drew her into my chest as the first faint scream broke the air.

"So far, we've learned anger management, determination, patience, teamwork. What could those cries possibly have to teach us?"

If there was one thing that I knew Matteaus wanted above all else, it was for us to be ready for the trouble to come. If the Fallen were worried, then I was too. Because there was only one thing I could think of that would force them to get all the races to work together . . . a worlds war. But with who or what I didn't know.

I'd lied to her about so many things, but this I wouldn't hide from her. And in time I would tell her the truth about everything. Even our shared soul mate connection. "What will happen to the world if the warlocks don't align with the witches?"

"Oh God, the end of the world?" Her eyes widened.

"I don't know, just hold on."

The cries grew louder as we drifted farther. I pressed her head to my chest and held my hands over her ears. I'd already been through enough of the bad in life that I could take this. I didn't want her to have to. I pressed my hands harder over hers to hold them tighter to her. The screams grew louder. Mothers wailing for their children, people crying out for spouses, screams of torture, all of it assailed me. It was deafening. I lost myself, forgot where I was and who I was with.

The raft jostled and bumped in all different directions, yet I didn't open my eyes. I just held on, listening to every voice. The raft hit a big bump and I curled my arms around Astrid tighter. "Hold on, just keep holding on." I didn't know if I was telling that to her or myself.

CHAPTER 46

The raft slammed into the shore and I flew up into a sitting position. Every muscle in my body ached. My shoulders still felt torn open even though they'd healed after we left that part of the river. Beckett lay in a heap beside me with his eyes squeezed shut while he rocked and mumbled to himself. The water lapped at the side of the raft and drifted over the riverbed. We were at the end of where we could travel. Beyond the small patch of land where we stopped there was nothing but water flowing out into a starry abyss. It was beautiful and mesmerizing as the water ran off into liquefied droplets.

I rested my hand on Beckett's shoulder and gave him a little shake. "Beckett."

He didn't move, just kept his eyes shut tight. I leaned in closer and ran my hand over his shoulder and upper arm. A heavy presence sat in the air. I felt it seeping toward us like a storm rolling across a field. The darkness of the underworld receded, and a bright ray of sunshine moved over the horizon. Light so bright it was nearly blinding. With one hand I shielded my eyes and with the other I began hitting Beckett harder.

"Beck, come on. You gotta wake up."

He rolled to his back and groaned. "Shut the light off."

"That's not a light."

He shot straight up. His eyes flashed wide. "The raft?"

"No more it's a small underworld ride for us. I think we reached the end." I rose to my feet as the ray of sun approached. No, not a ray, a woman. So beautiful, so bright in this world of darkness. She was only a shadow in the light, but I could tell she was statuesque. With curves for days and a saunter that rivaled supermodels on the runway during New York Fashion Week.

Beckett rose to stand beside me. A smile played on his lips like he was starstruck. His tongue darted over his bottom lip, wetting it. "Persephone."

I threw my elbow into his side. "You got a little bit of drool right here." I pointed to the corner of his lip.

"Never figured you for the jealous type." He chuckled.

"Oh yeah?"

He lowered his lips so close to my ear I could feel his breath against my skin. "I like it."

Heat flooded my cheeks and I turned my attention away from him and back on the task at hand. She was only ten feet away and I could make out her features. Long wavy chocolate locks fell from the top of her head all the way down to her knees. Flowers were wound in among the wild braids. A circular crown of Narcissus flowers, the same ones the raft was made of, sat perched on her head. Her face reminded me of one of those beautiful anime characters. Thick black eyelashes lined her huge seas of amber eyes that reminded me of golden fields of wheat. She had a small pert nose, heart-shaped face, and full light pink glossy lips. Her bohemian flowing white dress fell all the way down to the ground. The neck was a deep V cut that stopped below her belly button and tied on the back of her neck. The dress exposed her entire back and shoulders.

The light around her dimmed and she held a small crown of flowers in her hand. It was covered in wild flowers that were tucked in among winding twigs. She stopped just before us and waves of heat rolled off of her like the sun, and the smell of wild flowers drifted over us. "Warlocks, welcome."

I gave a small bow. "Persephone."

Beckett followed suit. "Persephone."

"You have traveled the many underworld rivers and mastered the lessons learned with each one. You must continue along this path to complete your journey." She pointed to a long winding road that led up a mountain in the distance. "There you will find the challenges set forth."

Her voice was calm and sweet like a song I knew but couldn't recall. "Will that lead us out?"

"Eventually yes." She held the crown out toward me. "You both have done well. I bestow this crown upon you. You must keep it and collect the tokens for accomplishing each challenge. Hook them into the crown for safekeeping."

I wanted to ask her so many things. Was Hades really mean? Did she like it down here? What was it like to be the queen of the underworld and if she didn't like it, was she taking volunteers to take her place? Nova would be the first choice, but damn if this place didn't capture my interest. *Well, after the torture and everything.*

I stepped in closer to her. "Thank you."

"You're very welcome."

When she placed the crown on my head, she held her hand out toward it and strands of vines ran down and braided themselves in among my hair, securing it in place. "There now, it's pretty."

"Thank you." I ran my fingers over the soft leaves in my hair.

"I must go. I only have so much time here." She turned and six white horses pulling a black chariot with golden flames stopped just behind her. She walked around the back and stepped up then took the reins. "It's not easy being queen."

She winked and spurred the horses forward. A second before they took off, her whole outfit completely changed from the bohemian flower child to femme fatale. A strapless black leather corset that matched her tight black leather pants covered her torso. Her hair still held the flowers, but they too turned black. She snapped the whip on the ground beside her and the chariot shot forward. The horses flew across the ground like a rocket and in an instant she was gone.

"I want to be just like her when I grow up." Both a bohemian princess and queen of death.

"God help me." Beckett chuckled and grabbed my

hand. "Come on, we have a long way to go before we reach the end of that path."

I turned to take a step, but my feet were cemented to the ground. I jerked against them. "I-I can't move."

Beckett too struggled to move. "What the hell?"

"Not hell, warlock. Justice." A low hissing voice filed the air.

My heart rate skyrocketed. "Is this part of the challenge?"

"I don't know." Every muscle in his body strained and his smoke poured from his hands. The ground exploded around his feet and leapt up into the air. Rocks and dirt flew in all different directions and he landed in a crouch next to me.

"Impressive, young warlock." A woman materialized right in front of us.

"Nemesis?" Beckett narrowed his eyes. "You can't be part of this."

"Oh no, why not?" She was deadly beautiful, with pin straight raven hair parted down the middle that fell to just above her shoulders. Her crimson red dress wrapped around her body and billowed in the wind. Long sleeves ran from her wrists down to the ground. Hulking gray wings jutted from her shoulders and she held a scale in one hand. But the most unsettling of it all was the crimson blindfold she wore over her eyes.

Beckett cleared his throat. "This is a challenge meant to teach control not dole out justice."

She tilted her head to the side like a hawk studying its prey. "Justice is met out in many different ways. It's all about balance." She held the scale up and it teeter-tottered on the tip of her finger. "You think you take a little ride on a pretty little boat and you pass the first test. How is that balance? How is that fair?"

I wiggled my legs, trying to break free. "What is she talking about?"

"What is she talking about?" Nemesis raised her voice and mimicked me in a mocking tone. "This is about balance. You think passing these trials is as easy as taking a math test and I will not allow it."

"That is not for you to decide." Beckett's whole body stiffened and he spread his legs as though preparing to attack.

I looked from her to him and back again. Her wings pulsed and she threw her head back laughing. "That's exactly what I'm here for."

He pulled the dagger from behind his back and leapt forward with it held high over his head. She threw her hand out and a cloud burst from her, covering him from head to toe. She cackled to the ceiling once more. The knife clattered to the ground and Beckett was gone.

"No!" I screamed and my magic exploded out of me in a shock wave. It knocked Nemesis off her feet long enough for me to kick the rocks holding me free. I ran at her and grabbed the sides of her dress and hauled her to her feet. "Where is he?"

She pressed a single finger to the center of my chest and I flew back. My feet kicked over my head and I landed in a heap of dust an inch away from the water, water I wasn't supposed to touch. I scrambled to stand then ran at her once more. I didn't hold back. I let my power roll within me and shot it out of my hands at her. At the last second she sucked in a deep breath and along with it all my power.

"Enough of these games." She lifted her hand and I floated in midair.

I pinwheeled my arms and kicked out my legs, yet I couldn't move. "Let me down."

"How about no." Again she turned her head in that birdlike manner as though she could see me through her blindfold. "You think this is to be easy? The Fallen pushed us to the breaking point and for what? Balance. It is all about balance. If the challenges are to be easy then what is there to learn?"

"You think that was easy? Ha!" My body twisted and turned like an astronaut in zero-g. "I nearly bled out."

"Too easy. You want him back, your man. Then good luck. I'll meet you at the end."

"The end of what?" She wasn't making any sense. She wasn't supposed to have anything to do with this. The Fallen were in charge and she was messing it all up. Beckett and I were supposed to be together, not split up and tossed around.

"Everything." She hissed and held her hand out. Clouds floated around me and I felt myself soaring through the air. To where, I didn't know. All I knew was I needed to get Beckett back and I needed him back now!

I shot out of Nemesis' cloud and rolled across the cold, damp ground. There was no stopping me. Rocks smacked into my back and sides yet the crown stayed on my head, but the vines holding it in place ripped at my hair. I came to a screeching halt when I smacked into a hard slab of stone. The wind whooshed from my lungs and I struggled to catch my breath. I let my arm fall across my rib cage and blinked against the spinning world. "That sucked."

As it slowly began to right itself, I sat up and leaned against the stone. "Oh crap."

Row after row of gravestones lined the small area. Each one was more dilapidated than the other. The night sky stretched out above me and the smell of damp moss filled my nose. The air was warm and sultry. A slow fog rolled over the ground, covering it completely and only letting the stones pop out of the top of it. I rose to my feet and pressed my hand to the bruises forming on my ribs. "Yeah, this isn't creepy at all."

Tall weeping willows stood like reaching shadows against the light of the full moon. A symphony of crickets and frogs filled the air as I spun around to figure out where the jerk of justice sent me. On one end of the field was an old little white church or what remained of it. The roof was caved in and the door hung off its hinges. "Yeah, not going in there."

I turned in the opposite direction to find a path running down the center of the graveyard, the only path without fog on it. "Does anyone else smell a trap here?"

I knew I was talking to myself, but I was freaked out and trying not to die horror movie style. A deep wolf-like howl pierced the night, silencing even the crickets. A chill crept up my spine and suddenly I wanted more than anything not to be completely alone out here. Smoke seeped from my hand down to my feet and I shook them out. "Come on, not now."

"What's up?"

I jumped ten feet into the air and threw up my heart out of my butt. I didn't know what happened, but it was not in my body anymore. I pressed my hand to my chest. "Am I dead?"

"Don't think so."

I looked down at the top of the gravestone next to me. "Odin, what are you doing here?"

His voice was low and scratchy. "You summoned, I here."

A brown paper bag sat on the stone next to him. "What's that?"

He hiss chuckled. "Chicken nuggets."

"Odin, Maze is going to skin you alive." I opened the bag and took a nugget out and handed it to him.

"He can try." He took a big bite and began to purr.

"Dude, now is not the time. We have to find Beckett." I gazed down the path leading into the woods. Something in me told me not to go there, not to venture into that darkness. But I couldn't portal or call anyone to come get me.

"Why don't you just ask her?" He pointed a paw behind me and I spun on my heels.

A woman wearing a long dark cloak walked toward me as if she'd just stepped out from the church.

Her white blond hair peeked out from under the hood. A floating torch hovered just above her palm as she took slow, methodical steps. On her one side was a dog the size of a small horse, its hair gray and wiry. It looked like part wolf, part greyhound. It threw its head back and that ear-piercing howl filled the air once more. On her other side a small creature resembling a ferret ran beside her. A perfect black line of fur covering its eyes, making it look like it was about to rob someone. Possibly me.

"She doesn't look like the type to give directions." I took a small step back.

She wound her way through the gravestones. Adrenaline ran through my system and I didn't know whether to stay put or run my ass off in the opposite direction. *Run, definitely run.* I was about to turn on my heels when the fog rose up in a dense wall behind me. *Stay it is.*

"Do you know who I am, child?" She stopped a few rows of dead people away from me.

I shook my head. "Should I?"

She rolled her icy eyes. "They never do." She mumbled as though speaking to her pets. Then she lifted her pointy chin. "I am Hecate, the original witch and the one who gave you that."

She pointed to my shoulder. I drew my sweater

down off my shoulder, exposing the half-moon scar I'd gotten from my house sorting ceremony. "This? But why?"

"Because I thought you might be worthy. Now I'm not so sure." She pursed her full lips and clasped her hands in front of her.

"What does it mean?" I ran my finger over the raised pinkened skin.

"Nothing, if you can't prove yourself," she snapped. "My disappointment is great."

I cast my eyes down toward the ground. "I am trying."

"Not good enough, Astrid. And this little quest Matteaus has you on . . . child's play. If you are worthy of your powers, I should at least be involved in that decision. But do you think I was? No, I was not."

"Wait, so you're not part of the mission he has me on?" I went from being embarrassed to annoyed in zero point two seconds.

She shook her head. "Nemesis and I, among others, are fed up with your lack of respect for the power bestowed upon you. And so we thought it was time to teach you a lesson."

"You're the ones who took Beckett." I took a step toward her and my power rose to the forefront, seeping from me onto the ground toward her. "Give him back."

"Earn him back." She held her hands up and flames erupted from her palms.

Her dog lowered its head and growled at Odin. Odin swiped at the air and hissed in his direction. I stepped in front of him. "Why don't you pick on something your own size, like the ferret?"

"It's not a ferret," Hecate snapped. "It's a polecat."

"Looks like a ferret!" I didn't know why I was goading her, but she was involved with taking Beckett and throwing me off my mission, so she would get all the New York sass I could muster.

Odin leapt down off the stone and walked to my side. A weird growl/tearing sound came from him and his body twitched. His bones pushed out against his black fur in a painful jutting manner. I turned to Hecate. "Stop it, you're killing him."

"'Tis not I!"

Odin jumped up, three times the size he was before. He opened his mouth and a feral growl escaped his lips. His fangs glistened in the night, his eye sparked, and he prowled away from me.

"A panther. You can turn into a freaking panther?"

"You said pick on my size. This my size."

Hecate's dog moved away from her side as well. The two animals faced off against each other.

Her eyes widened. "At least you're showing some promise."

"Eat magic, bitch." I threw my hand out and fired off a ball of golden energy at her.

She threw her hand up and blocked it with her flames. She threw a fireball at me and I dove behind a stone. "You can do better than that. Hell, baby warlocks can do better than that."

The impact exploded the top of the stone to rubble that rained down on me. Odin and the dog ran at each other full force. The dog leapt at him with its teeth bared and snarling. Odin swiped his paw across the dog's face as it tackled him to the ground. They twisted and turned in a tornado of teeth, growls, and hisses.

"No, Odin!" I wanted to protect him.

Odin rolled onto his back and shoved all four of his paws into the dog's gut, launching it up into the air toward the woods behind us. Trees bent and cracked and the dog yelped. Odin took off after it. "Got this, kill bitch witch."

Confident he could handle the devil dog, I shoved my hands into the ground and pictured the vines shooting up around her in a cage. The ground shook beneath my feet and the sound of cracking branches filled the air. I jumped up in time to see the vines shoot from the ground like poles. My magic rolled from me and the vines lashed out like whips, snaring her around her wrists and ankles. I threw my arms up and the vines lifted her off the ground and spread her limbs out like a starfish.

I took a step toward her. "Tell me where he is or I will have them rip your arm from your body."

"Better. But perhaps a little more creative." She opened her hands and flames singed the vines to ash and she dropped down before me. "My turn."

She sucked in a deep breath and blew it at me. The wind wound around me in a cyclone, sending my hair flying straight up around me. My feet lifted up off the ground and I started to spin like I was on the teacup ride at the state fair. The world blurred into one color and I couldn't tell up from down. I closed my eyes, fighting my own treacherous equilibrium. I fought against the wind holding my arms down and slowly brought them up. Picturing myself peeling this cyclone off the way I would take a dress off that was too tight.

Gold surrounded me and my feet slowly touched down onto the ground. I threw the cyclone back at her and dropped down onto one knee, fighting to catch my breath and not vomit at the same time. I'd done enough spinning for one night. I threw it at her, yet she caught it in the palm of her hand, holding it like she would a penny. She closed her fingers over it. "Eh, okay."

"Okay?" I called upon everything I had in. Thick black clouds rolled overhead, covering the stars from sight. Lightning forked out across the sky and I summoned it down to my hands. I held my arms out to my sides and let it strike, one then the other. It didn't burn. All I felt was pure power.

Hecate arched her perfectly sculpted eyebrow. "You wouldn't."

"Wouldn't I?" I shot a bolt at her, tagging her right in her hip. She lifted up off the ground and flew back. She smacked into the gravestone, rendering it to ash. As she struggled to her feet, I shot another, sending her flying again. And another. She flew back toward the church. I held both my hands overhead, summoning twice as much power to my hands. Bolts slammed down from the sky as if Zeus himself was handing them to me. Electricity sizzled in my hair and down my arms.

Hecate lurched to her feet and held her hands out in front of her. "Okay, Astrid, enough."

Too late. Darkness rolled in me and I let it go. I

screamed and shot those bolts right into her chest. Flames erupted from her arms as she soared through the sky and smacked into what was left of the little white church. The remains crumbled on top of her and I sucked in a deep breath. Bolts of lightning speared down to the ground around me and I had to release the power I used to summon it. I took slow deep breaths, holding back that dark tide I could only call my own. The lightning subsided and the clouds rolled back, letting the bright moon shine down on me once more.

I turned toward the woods. "Odin?"

The dog flew from the woods like a bat out of hell with its tail tucked between its legs. It yelped and ran in the opposite direction. The ferret followed suit and ran off after the dog. A moment later Odin trotted out back in his one-eyed black cat form. He leapt up on the gravestone where the bag of nuggets sat undisturbed. He shoved his head into the bag and tried to pull it back out, but the bag got stuck around his neck. "Astrid, a little help here."

"Really, you take on devil dogs but a paper bag gets the best of you?"

He threw his head from side to side, trying to knock it off. "No." His words were muffled like he had something in his mouth.

"Drop the nugget then try." I leaned against the nearest stone, needing to regain my strength.

Just as I was about to walk over to him and take the bag off his head, the church rubble lurched. And the front doors flew off and out. They landed on the ground, sending clumps of grass flying up. Hecate stumbled out of the door, her dress smoked in all different places and her perfect blond hair now frizzed out from her head like she'd put her finger in a socket. She pointed a finger toward me.

"You have got to be kidding me." I held my hands out, ready to call my magic once more.

"Now that's how you do it!" she yelled across the field.

"What?" I held off.

She smiled and clapped her hands together. "You want to be a boss bitch witch. Well, there you go." She patted the flames out that gathered on her dress.

I took a step back as she got only a few feet away. "Don't come any closer."

She froze. "Astrid, that's what I've been waiting to see."

"Say what now?"

"Power, pure powers." She clasped her hands to her chest. "Well done."

"Is this some kind of trick?" I glanced at Odin, who

managed to get the nugget out and was now trying to swallow it down in one bite.

She shook her head and held up two fingers. "Scout's honor. You have proven yourself."

"Good, now give me Beckett back." I put my hands on my hips. "So we can continue on our journey."

"Oh, you didn't think it was going to be that easy, did you?" A dark chuckle escaped her lips, sending a chill down my spine. "You have to *want* it."

"What the hell are you babbling about? Want what?" I was so confused. I fought, she approved. Apparently I proved myself and now I had to *want it.*

"You'll see." She chuckled once more then snapped her fingers in my face.

My head lulled back on my shoulders and I collapsed to my knees. The damp dirt seeped into my pants and I fell forward. My cheek smacked into the mud and my eyes fluttered. Exhaustion overcame me and I fought to stay awake. This wasn't right. We'd fought. I'd won. She was supposed to freeze then explode into a million pieces.

"Not my daughter, you biiiiii—" My words came out sluggish and I couldn't finish my sentence.

"Aww, isn't that cute. You think this is some kind of movie." She squatted down low and met my eye. "This is real life, Astrid . . . or is it?"

What? I blinked against the exhaustion and watched as she spun around and walked away. Her cloak billowed out behind her. Dimly I knew this was how people ended up dead. They passed out at night in strange places. Like freaking graveyards. The world became hazy and I could no longer fight my eyelids.

CHAPTER 48

"*Y*ay, happy birthday, Astrid!" Tilly reached up and plopped something on my head. "Make room for the birthday girl."

What was this? I sat up and glanced around at the inside of my father's stretch limo. How did I get here? My birthday was weeks ago. I reached up and felt the pointy edges. "A tiara? Really, Til? No, I'm not wearing this."

"Too late now." She wrapped her hand in my jacket and yanked me back, then tossed a white sash over my head. "Now we're ready."

When I looked at the other people in the limo I was faced with Brody-brad? And his goons. I hadn't seen them since the night of my birthday. This night? I tried to pull the sash over my head. "And I'm definitely not doing this."

Tilly grabbed it and jerked it back into place then spun me around and shoved both of her hands into my shoulders, forcing me out of the limo. I tripped forward and barely caught myself before I ate pavement. *That was close.* I tugged my skirt down into place and pulled my boots up higher on my thighs. My breaths came in light puffs of white fog. *This is the worst déjà vu ever.* Winter was coming and the chill seeping into my skin was proof it was just around the corner. November was one of my favorite months in New York and standing on the corner waiting for everyone to pile out of the limo gave me a small chance to enjoy it. I looked up at the hotel, admiring the exterior, when a flash of blue light coming from an alley caught my eye.

I spun toward it. "Beckett." It was his portal. Any second now he'd come out of it. I stood waiting. Tilly led our little group toward the door, but I couldn't force my feet to move. This was the part where Beckett came out and stopped a fight for me. This was the first time we met. He had to be here.

Tilly spun back around. "Astrid, come on."

I shook my head. "I'm just going to wait for Beckett."

She wrinkled her nose and shook her head. "Who's Beckett?"

Ice shot through my veins and I stood still as a statue shivering in the night. What the hell was happening? Why was it my birthday again? Did that magic asshat erase what happened? Only one way to find out. I called my magic to my hands . . . nothing. *What?* I tried again . . . nothing. No dark tide, no rolling power, no gold smoke. I shook my hands, trying to force it to work.

Tilly stomped her foot. "Come on, you're being weird, let's go."

"I got this." Brody-brad rolled his shoulders and cracked his neck. He walked over to me and threw his arm over my shoulder, pulling me toward the door. He walked like he was the king of the world in his black dress pants, light blue button-down, and dress shoes. I almost felt bad for him, almost. He had no clue about the world, and I was going to let his cocky ass in on the secret as soon as possible.

I ducked out from under his arm. "Yeah, why don't you get yourself."

I shoved him forward and walked over to Tilly. I hooked my arm with hers. "Come on, let's go."

"Are you okay?"

"Do you honestly not remember Beckett? Or

Warwick?" We walked past the line of waiting club goers and the bouncer opened the velvet rope for us. My heels clicked on the marble floor as we headed straight for the club elevator.

"Did you fall and hit your head when I wasn't watching? I have no clue what you're talking about." She pressed the button for the top floor. The doors slid shut and the elevator lurched upward.

I shook my head. "No, I'm fine." How could she not remember?

The doors slid open and I walked out into the club. The base thumped against my chest. The sound of bottles being tossed into garbage cans mixed with the music. I marched across the dance floor and around the blue velvet seating areas, out past the floor-to-ceiling windows, and to the terrace. A chill ran over me all the way down to my spine. What the hell was this? I walked to the area where I spotted Beckett gazing up at the stars last time. I stopped outside the VIP area and glanced around, looking for him.

"Astrid." My name was so faint among the thrum of the music, but it was his voice and I knew it. I spun in a circle and there he was like a faint hologram standing in the middle of the party, reaching for me. He looked over his shoulder and was dragged back. The sight faded and I stumbled after him.

I tripped into the crowd of people as I searched for Beckett. A set of strong arms flew out and caught me. "Hey, everything all right?"

"Yeah, fine." I shrugged out of his arms. When I looked up to where I'd spotted Beckett, he was gone like a mirage in the desert.

The guy ducked his head to meet my eyes. "Can I buy you a drink?"

He was tall and beautiful in a metro stylish kind of way. He was tall and fit with a slim sleek build. His skin was smooth and wrinkle free. He had to be my age, maybe just a bit older. He gave me a wide, dazzling smile then pulled his long hair up on the back of his head into a messy man bun. He wore a navy blue suit and white button-down shirt that was open at the collar, exposing his tan skin.

"I don't drink." I pushed past him and he reached for me. Then ran his fingers over my wrist.

When I spun back around, he wrapped his hand all the way around my wrist. "Try the wine. It's delicious."

My panic ebbed and I sighed, feeling relaxed for the first time since I got here. His touch was so calming. "It's my birthday."

"Well, happy birthday, beautiful." He leaned back on the bar and the lapels of his jacket opened. He reached back toward the bar and grabbed a glass of red wine. He held it in front of him and swirled it around. "My own personal vintage. It's delightful to the senses."

He lifted the glass under his nose and inhaled sharply. Then held it out to me. "A delightful array of floral yet sweet."

I sucked in the vapors and my eyes rolled into the back of my head. I swayed with the music. "Do you own this place?"

"In a sense." He took a deep sip. "I am the life of the party no matter where I go."

"Bold words." I felt so drawn to him, drawn to the party. Finally relaxed.

"Astrid . . ." My name came as a whisper on the wind and I glanced around once more. I was supposed to be looking for something.

"Try the wine." He shoved the glass at me. It sloshed over the side of the glass and dripped on my shoes.

I pushed it back at him. The wine fell over the side of the glass onto his pristine white shirt. The red stain spread over it, ruining his outfit completely. I took a step back from him. "What is it with you and the wine?"

He spread his arms out wide. "I'm Dionysus. Why wouldn't I like the wine?"

"No, this isn't another test!" I stepped up and shoved him in his chest. I held my hand up to summon my magic but nothing came to me.

He threw his head back, laughing. "What are you going to do to me? Stare me to death?" He shoved away from the bar and towered over me. "Face it, without your power, you are nothing."

I turned on my heels and threw my shoulders back. I was Astrid Lockwood, the last warlock of my line, and once I got my powers back I was going to deliver the ass kicking of his life. I headed back toward the VIP section where Tilly sat with the rest of our crew. Ten feet from my friends and Brody-brad got up from the seating area and walked over to me. He threw his arm over my shoulders and yanked me in close to his body. His cologne was like a slap in the face. *Wait, it's going to happen soon. The blood moon will come and with it my powers.* His jacket scraped my cheek and I tried to duck under his arm, but he clutched me even tighter. *Five more minutes.*

He held his drink in the hand he had wrapped around me. As he stumbled back toward our area, it sloshed over the side of the glass and spilled down my jacket. "Slumming it, I see."

His words slurred together and I craned my head away from him. "Come on. Let me go. You're drunk."

"Now why would I do that?" With one hand behind my head and the other pressed to my chin, he turned my face up toward his then slammed his lips down on mine.

His teeth hit mine and pain surged through my mouth. I ducked under his arm and spun out of his grip. The glass he was holding fell to the ground and shattered. I wiped my hand across my mouth, trying to rub the burning flavor of alcohol from my lips. He wasn't the fresh minty flavor I'd grown accustomed to.

I shoved him in the chest, only moving him back an inch or two. "What the hell?"

He took another step toward me and reached for my arm. I leaned out of the way. My muscles shot tight with anger and I felt something shift inside my chest. I glanced up toward the sky. The blood moon! My moon! It was coming and so was my dark tide. "Back off!"

"Just one little kiss." He took another step toward me.

Something in me snapped and I hauled my fist back then slung it forward. My knuckles cracked across Brody-brad's face. Golden magic exploded from me as the moon turned a dark red. The club goers all screamed and ran from me. I lifted my arms up and smoke traveled across the area toward where Dionysus stood.

"Oh Dion!" I yelled over the panic of the club. "Let me buy you a drink."

My power flooded around him and he lifted off the ground, hovering in a ball of my magic. I sauntered over to him and stood directly under him. "Let's stop playing. Where is Beckett?"

"I don't know who that is."

I snatched the wine glass from his hand and smashed it on the ground. "I'm done with this! You Greeks think you're going to be in charge of everything and this isn't any of your business. So give him to me or else."

"Or else?" He snorted. "Don't threaten me."

"Who's threatening?" I threw my arm out and the wine bottles at one end of the bar shattered to pieces, leaking wine all over the floor.

The smile dropped from his face. "Hey! Stop!"

I let my power crawl down the bar, ruining one bottle after another. They popped like firecrackers, raining down glass and wine. "Shall I move on to the white?"

"Okay, fine!" He held his hands up in surrender. Then pointed to a door that looked like a bank vault that hadn't been there moments before. "He's in there."

"If you're lying." I reached up, grabbed his arm, and spun him in the bubble where I held him. "I will come back and I will ruin everything you love."

"And they wanted to teach you to embrace your nature. I'd say you damn well fit the freaking warlock profile, you wretch." His face turned a bright red.

I left him hanging there in my magic I turned on my heels and sauntered over to the vault door. I grabbed one of the oversized bars and yanked it down, spinning it. The mechanism on the inside slid and the door clicked and began to swing open. I waved to him. "I know."

I yanked the door open and stepped over the threshold, leaving the party behind. I glanced around at the walls lined with metal safety deposit boxes. An empty pallet sat in the middle of the floor. "What the hell?"

I spun to turn back toward the club, but the door swung shut, locking me in. *Great, just great.*

CHAPTER 49

ASTRID

I hauled my leg back and kicked out at the solid metal door. Bang, bang, bang. The metal rattled but didn't budge. This was something straight out of a movie, with the marble tiles, horrible overhead lighting, a single table, and empty pallet. "Dionysus! When I get out of here I am going to ruin all your freaking vineyards. Wine be damned!"

"Yeah, see, I wouldn't recommend that."

I turned to face the man standing behind me. "Where'd you come from?"

"I'll keep this quick, well, because I don't like you. Or your little friends who like to throw people off of platforms into the Amazon because of one harmless prank." He was average height, about five-foot-ten, slender, with light brown hair parted down the middle of his head. The straight locks fell onto the sides of his face like a '90s boyband wannabe. He didn't even look up from his cell phone. His thumbs flew across the screen in a blur of activity.

"I'm sorry, my friends? Listen, bud, I have no idea who the hell you are, but I'm guessing you have some kind of stupid task for me to do." I crossed my arms over my chest and leaned back against the door.

He paused and his head snapped up. When he turned those eyes on me, I leaned away from him. They weren't the eyes of a normal human or any other supernatural I'd seen. Within those chutney-colored eyes was a swirling mass of silvery flecks that held untold secrets from the ages. "I'm Hermes. I swear they teach you nothing."

"Well, apparently you're here to teach me something." I rolled my eyes. "So let's get it over with."

He pulled up his khaki shorts and the winged tattoos that ran up his calves fluttered. "I got places to be. The holiday season is coming, and prime doesn't run on its own."

"Fine, then let's have it." Something told me I wasn't going to beat the lesson out of him.

"I want all of the loot that's in here to be on the pallet and then you'll get your little boyfriend back." He looked back down at his phone. "Off you go."

"Seriously, you want me to rob a bank to pay for the ransom to get Beckett back?"

"If that's his name then yup." He hopped up on the table, still looking at his phone.

I threw my arms up. "This is stupid."

"Duh," he answered in a valley girl voice.

"Then why do I have to do it?" I shoved away from the wall and moved to stand before the pallet.

"If you did your homework then you'd know I'm the king of thieves. I don't need a reason." He glanced up at me. "Are you gonna do it or not?"

"Yeah, okay, fine, I'll do it." This felt so wrong. I was going to rob people to get Beckett back. Would he do this for me? Was this the right thing to do?

I held my hands out and at the same time all the locks snapped out with one resounding click. Hermes dropped his phone. "Impressive."

The doors all few open and stacks of money, coins, jewels, and stock certificates floated out. They all spun together around the room in a slow tornado with the pallet at the base. Hermes hopped off the table and stood in the middle of it. "As annoying as you are, you'd come in handy. This is going to be a beautiful relationship."

Say what now? No, I didn't want to be a thief and definitely didn't want to have any kind of relationship with hipster Hermes. If Beckett were here, would he do this? The second I asked myself the question I knew the answer right away—a big resounding no. He'd find another way. Just because we were warlocks didn't make us evil. "No."

"What?" He stopped gazing at the spinning fortune. "What do you mean no?"

Gold smoke seeped from my hands and I forced all the money to go back to where it belonged. The money, coins, jewels, and everything else flew into the deposit boxset and one by one they slammed shut with a metallic thud. I twisted my hands and all the locks slid back into place as if I'd never been here. "No, Beckett wouldn't want me to do this. To take the easy way out. That's not how magic works."

"Ugh, are all of you so goody-goody?" He threw his arms up. "First that crazy one with the silver sparkles and now you with your golden bullshit. Who can stand teenagers?"

"Just send me wherever it is you are supposed to send me. Because I'm not doing it."

He towered over me, a supernatural more powerful than I was, crazier than I was, and here I stood defying him. He marched over to one of the lock boxes and pressed his finger to it. The lock opened and the box popped out. "It's fine. I didn't need all of it."

He pulled the metal shoebox looking thing out and unclasped the front of it. When he popped the lid open, there was a single shining object inside. He reached in and pulled it out so quickly I didn't get a look at it. He shoved it into his pocket. "All I wanted was this."

"So are you gonna let me go?"

"Yeah, yeah, mission accomplished. You passed." He waved me away. "Be gone with you."

"Wait, wha—" Blaring alarms filled the silence and echoed off the metal walls around me.

"Damn."

"Hermes! Get me out of here." My pulse raced as the lights went out and I fell into darkness. "Hermes?"

Nothing. "This isn't funny."

The alarm cut off and the temperature in the room went from feeling like I was standing in an air-conditioned cell to a hot, sultry jungle. The lights slowly rose like a dimmer switch being turned up. I took a step back and heard the distinct click of something under my boot.

"I suggest you don't move. Unless you want that leg to blow off."

I froze on the spot and sighed. "Oh shit."

CHAPTER 50

ASTRID

$\mathcal{I}$ stood in the middle of an open field with a giant of a man before me. Muscle on top of muscle on top of muscle. He had to be nearly seven feet tall, with a dark military haircut, his jaw hard and angular. A permanent five o'clock shadow covered his face and his eyes were a deep death-like onyx. The world rattled around us as bombs went off, yet he stood unmoving above me. His chest was bare all but for the golden chain lying across his chest holding a crimson cape in place. The sun overhead blared down on us and drops of sweat rolled down his torso. Army fatigue pants hung from his hips. Instead of the standard green camo his was a combination of black, white, and red. He had a helmet tucked under one arm and a sword strapped around his waist.

He glared down at me. "Land mine, hazard of the job."

He turned on his heels and his cape billowed out behind him. He marched across the battlefield toward an army who shared his flair for attire. Except they all had their helmets on and circular shields up. They banged their swords against the shields in a rhythmic drumming, boom, boom, boom. As he approached he lifted his arm and they all broke out into deafening war cries. On the opposite end of the field a line of robotic . . . butlers? Stood still as statues.

"Um, excuse me." I waved my arms, afraid to move to set off the bomb beneath my feet. "Get me off this thing."

The caped man marched through the throng of warriors up toward a stack of boulders at the back of his battalion. With three big steps he was on top of the boulder to watch over the fight. He threw his arms out to his sides and tilted his head back, screaming at the top of his lungs. "I . . . am . . . Ares!"

His battalion erupted into screams and the opposing army stood still and silent. A shadow passed over my head. My eyes widened when a golden chariot being pulled by six winged metal Pegasus flew overhead. Another man, the same size as Ares but burlier than built. He had a thick red beard and longer shaggy hair that matched. He tilted the chariot to the side and pointed an axe down toward his opponent. "Brother! This will be the last time!"

Brother? The metal robot butlers, the mechanical Pegasus, everything was clicking into place. *Hephaestus.* He spun the axe in his hand and more of those robotic butlers walked out onto the field to join his ranks. Click, clank, clack, metal ground against metal so much so that the sound flooded my ears. I bent down and pressed my hands to my ears, trying to block it out. But I was trapped here. If I moved, I blew up. If I stayed put, these arms would clash right over my head.

"I never touched her!" Ares chuckled. "This time."

Hephaestus threw his head back, screaming, "Charge!"

"For all the glory, leave it on the battlefield! You either win or die!" Ares held his sword up. "Forward!"

The ground rumbled beneath my feet. I watched as they both ran toward each other and I stood in the middle of it all. *I'm gonna die.* The first to go were headed right for me and I couldn't move. That dark tide rose up in me and I let my magic flow. As the first two men dove to meet over my head, I fired my magic off and it exploded like a bomb. A mushroom cloud of power threw them both back toward their own sides. The man plowed through Ares' side like a bowling bowl. *Strike.* The metallic butler smacked into the line, knocking several of them over. They clanked and fell one after another.

The rest of the armies paused for a single second, watching my power, then they charged at each other once more. *Crap, crap, crap.* My heart thundered in my chest and then they slowed, running in slow motion toward each other. "What the hell?"

A woman strolled across the field between the two encroaching armies. Her flowing blond hair blew in the wind. A band of gold leaves sat across her forehead. She wore a cottony toga that was draped over one arm and in the other she held a horn filled with gold coins. Pink pixie wings fluttered on her back with each step she took. When she came to a stop in front of me, she dropped the horn of gold at my feet. "Whoa, that was one hell of a walk and that thing is heavy."

"Umm, hi." This day had been way too long and way too strange for me to lose my cool now. Especially with a ticking time bomb under my feet.

She hunched over and sucked in a deep breath. "Nice day, though."

"Yeah, for a walk in a . . . battlefield."

The soldiers continued to move toward each other inch by inch.

"Yeah, it's so weird for you to end up here. Unless someone, say me, brought you here instead of where my sister wanted you." She looked over her shoulder at the warriors. "But also, like why would Matteaus leave you here?"

"Wait, your sister? And Matteaus, does that mean . . . ?"

"You're back on track, yup. My sister, she likes to mess with things that shouldn't be messed with." She extended her hand out toward me. "I'm Fortuna."

I took her hand and shook it. "And Nemesis is your sister?"

"Yep. Kind of annoying, isn't she?"

"I mean, I guess you could say that." I looked down at my feet and back at the war. Coming off as ungrateful was not something I wanted to do at this point, especially because she was the only one who might actually help me.

"You don't have to sugarcoat things with me. She messed things up. I'm here to fix it. Like two sides of karma." She grabbed up a single coin from her horn. "She took something from you."

Hope sprang in my chest, but I didn't want to show her or anyone else. If there was even a chance for me to get Beckett back, I wanted it . . . and I wanted it bad. I held down my excitement. "She did."

"Right, okay." She tossed the coin high up into the air and let it flip end over end. It burst like a mini fire-cracker and rained down toward the ground. Little sparks gathered on the ground at my feet and swirled upward, revealing first his black combat boots, then his dark blue jeans and narrow hips. Flat stomach visible through his white T-shirt, tan skin, and then his beautiful face. He gave a wide bright smile and jumped toward me.

I held my hands up, stopping him. "Wait."

He froze. "What?"

"Oh, she's got a little problem there." Fortuna pointed toward my feet. "She'd go boom."

"No, Astrid." He dropped to his knees and wound his arm around my leg. Shock waves went through my body having him this close, with his fingers pressing into my thigh.

Fortuna squealed. "Aw, you guys are the cutest. I really must be off now, though." She motioned to the oncoming war. "You all got this, right?"

Beckett gazed up my body. "Yeah, we got this."

"Excellent." She grabbed up another handful of coins and tossed them over her head. As they fell to the ground she disappeared among them. Life flew back to real time and the armies screamed as they charged toward each other.

Beckett held his hand over my foot. Blue smoke filtered from his palm underneath it. "Okay, I think I got the bomb down."

"You think?" The warriors were only yards apart.

"I know." He rose to his feet and wrapped his arm around my waist. He twisted his body to the side and dragged me with him as one of the metallic robots dove over my head and landed on one of Ares' soldiers, ripping at her face and arms.

Beckett drew his blade from the holder on his lower back and held it at the ready. He pulled me forward, and we ducked under two men sword fighting. I jumped over another man diving for my leg.

"I'm getting really tired of this."

One of Ares' men spear tackled Beckett around his waist, knocking him sideways. I tripped over another body and fell into a puddle of mud. "Ugh, you've got to be kidding me."

It was caked in my hair, across my face, and down the left side of my body. I lurched to my feet, shaking clumps off my fingers. A robot knocked into my shoulder and another into my side. I was thrown about like a rag doll. "That's it!"

I threw my hands up and magic spilled out of me.

Both armies flew off the ground and hovered in the air. Wind tore through the battlefield. The sky darkened, clouds rolled in, and I held them all there like my playthings. Beckett jumped to his feet and threw both of his arms out. Two streams of magic shot across the battlefield. He looped Ares with one stream and Hephaestus with the other. Then yanked them both to the center of the battlefield.

Ares tossed his cape back over his shoulder and yanked his helmet off. "What is the idea of this?"

I dropped their battalions to the ground and held them there. "I have no idea why Matteaus wants us here, but he sent us for a reason. And I'm thinking it's to stop this little battle you have going on."

Hephaestus vibrated with anger. "How dare you!"

Beckett sighed. "Oh, we dare."

There we were, two warlocks and two of the most powerful beings to ever walk the earth. I'd just gotten my powers and Beckett was only one warlock. I moved to stand beside him, not knowing what to do or say. Ares pulled his sword and pointed it at Hephaestus. "If I can't smite your army, I will take you down myself."

Hephaestus grumbled, "You can try."

"What is this about?" I stood between all of them, a tiny person among giants.

Hephaestus pointed his axe at Ares' chest. "He knows what he did."

"For the last time *she* came for *me*." He snickered. "Literally."

"Bastard." Hephaestus swung out with his axe, aiming right for Ares' head. Ares held his sword up, blocking the blow.

The air sizzled and I staggered between the two of them. I held my arms out to my sides, stilling them with my power. "You over there."

I pointed five feet farther back on my right. I lifted Ares with my magic and plopped him down. "And you over there."

I used my power to force Hephaestus back to my left. The two of them narrowed their eyes at me. "Oh no, you don't."

They froze, each fighting against my hold. Their bodies quaked with the effort. It took just as much effort to hold them in place. "If I let you go, you promise not to attack each other?"

"For a time." Ares lowered his sword.

"Perhaps for ten minutes." Hephaestus dropped his axe to the ground where it stood straight up and was the same size as me.

Yeah, that's not intimidating at all.

"What the hell is going on with you two? You're brothers!"

"My wife is not to be trifled with! Not now, not ever!" Hephaestus shoved his hand in his hair and pulled at it. "Yet he will not desist."

Ares shrugged. "Like I said, I can't help it if she comes for me and tells you about it."

"Hold up. This is about Aphrodite?" I crossed my arms over my chest and they both looked at me like of course it was.

"My brother has a temper." Ares said so smoothly and for a moment I could see why Aphrodite would go after him. He was the original bad boy, with a body of sin to match.

"Right, says the dude who's known for loving war." I rolled my eyes. "This is ridiculous. This fight has been going on for what, hundreds of years?"

They both nodded and I threw my hands up. "Really, did either of you stop and think that she's doing it to you on purpose? I mean, the woman is known as the ultimate lover *of everyone.*"

"Did you just call my wife a whore?" Hephaestus puffed up like a peacock and his face turned a bright red that nearly matched his ginger beard.

"Buddy, if the shoe fits. This is crazy. You all are fighting just to fight. You need to stop and think about what you're doing, and what is going on around you. I bet you didn't even consider that this might be someone's property."

I turned toward Beckett. "Am I right?"

"Yup." He nodded and gave me a weird look.

"So impulsive. You two need to learn to controlllll-llll . . . oooohhhhhhhhh crap." I let my words fall off and muttered, "Not to be so impulsive."

Beckett chuckled and I bumped him with my shoulder. "Shut up."

Then it hit me. The whole point of me being in this battle was not to learn how to fight because I was already a fighter. But to learn when to not, to control *my* own impulses. I shook my head and took a small step back to look at the devastation around me. All because these two couldn't get their shit together. They'd done it in a field and I'd done it in the middle of New York. "Ugh, impulse control."

A wide smile spread across Ares' face and he shoved his sword into the sheath. "Well done, little warlock."

He reached behind his back and pulled out a small box. He tossed it toward me then turned toward his brother. "Still want to have a go?"

Hephaestus pulled a tiny piece of metal off the end of his axe and handed it to me. "Tell Matteaus this makes us even for that little time I tried to keep some of his students. So we're good now."

I wrapped my hand around it and looked up at him. "What?"

"Nothing." His voice was gruff with finality. "Solved now, that's all you need to know."

He faced Ares. "I win, you stay away from my wife."

"For a time." Ares turned and marched back toward his troops. That cape billowed out behind him and I stood waiting for him to come back, but a moment later Hephaestus spun on his heels as well and marched back toward his side.

"Wait." I turned in a circle. "Where are they going?"

Beckett grabbed my elbow and tugged me toward the other side of the field. "Their mission is accomplished, but they're not going to stop now."

"But wait. Shouldn't we stop them?"

"Do you think they'll stop?" He pulled me a little bit faster.

"No, you're right. They taught me the lesson Matteaus assigned them. I don't think they'll stop just because of us." Behind me Ares shouted orders to his group.

"Add those pieces to the crown and let's see where it takes us next."

"Says the guy who hasn't been thrown all over the

place in the past few hours." I opened up my hand to look down at the tokens. The one Hephaestus handed me was a tiny hammer, not the kind you used on nails but the kind a blacksmith used. I reached up and placed it in the crown. The vines wound around it, sucking it up and making it a part of the crown Persephone gave me. The crown that'd stayed tangled in my hair. Then I flicked the little wooden box open that Ares gave me. There among the black velvet cushion was a tiny golden spear. So small I had to pinch it between my thumb and forefinger. The vines on the crown stretched down for it, reaching. Within seconds it wrapped around the spear and yanked it up into the crown. The moment it connected a wave of dizziness overcame me and I knew we were being transported. It was worse than Beckett's freaking portals and I hated every minute of it. *Don't puke. Don't puke.*

CHAPTER 51

ASTRID

*M*y body twisted and turned through the air. Beckett's portals held that blue color like diving into a swimming pool and drowning in magic. But this was pink and like walking through the perfume section of a department store. Floral fragrances assailed me from all directions. I swung around trying to find my footing or which way was up. But there was no up only around. My stomach pressed outward and nausea rolled up my throat.

I dropped and landed in something fluffy and full of blankets. I lay there with my arms over my head, sucking in a breath to try and stop myself from puking on the floor. The bed dipped and Beckett dropped in beside me. I lay there breathless, staring at myself in the mirrored ceiling. Velvet blankets curled underneath me and a pillow cushioned the back of my head. My hair fanned out around me and the crown tangled in my hair even more.

The heart-shaped bed sat across from a whirlpool bathtub that stood on its own. Wall to wall pink carpet covered the room and I never felt so out of place. "Where are we?"

"No idea. Where do you think we are?" Beckett sat up and I noticed for the first time that he was dressed only in his blue jeans . . . and nothing else. Heat bloomed in my chest and I just wanted to feel his skin against mine.

I glanced down at myself and nearly all my clothing was gone too. I lay there in my bra and leggings. I wasn't embarrassed, he'd seem me in a lot less than this, but why? Why was I here in this? "What the hell?"

"Maybe Matteaus decided we need a break." He ran the back of his fingers over my cheek. A light smile played on his lips and the depths of his ocean eyes drew me in. "I'm good with it."

I loved being this close to him, loved the freedom of not hiding anything from each other. "I can't see why he'd drop us here, in this love shack, but I'm not going to object."

"Me neither." He turned on his side to face me.

Then reached up and grabbed a piece of my hair and tried to unwind the crown from it.

"What are you doing?" Loose strands got caught in the branches and the crown wound itself tighter to my head. The tugging pain singed my scalp. "Ouch! Maybe give that a rest for a sec."

"Just wanted to make you comfortable." He shrugged and dropped his hands. His voice was so smooth like a calming balm. "That's all."

I laid my hand over his chest and felt the soft rhythmic beat of his heart in my fingertips. "Oh yeah? Don't you think we need to get going?"

He placed his hand over mine and held it there for a long moment. My heart soared. "Not yet. We should stay just a bit longer."

"Why?" I didn't want to go either.

He leaned in closer and his breath fanned over my face. We were so close I could feel the heat rolling off his body. "Maybe I just want to spend some time with you before we have to get back to our lives."

This wasn't like Beckett. He was always duty before personal stuff. But here he was lying with me cuddling in a huge bed. I threw my leg over his hip. "Maybe for just a few minutes."

"That's it, just relax." His fingers were firm on my

leg as he ran them higher and higher up my thigh. I wasn't used to Beckett's touch, only in my dreams, but I'd never felt him be so dominant with me. Desire bloomed and I wanted him the same way I knew he wanted me.

He wrapped his hand behind my knee and pulled my leg higher on his hip. We were nearly nose to nose. "Just one kiss."

I wanted it, wanted him. I leaned in then paused. We were on a mission. Each one had a lesson, so what was the lesson here? He tried to take my lips and I pulled back, pressing my hands to his chest. "Wait?"

"What?" His eyes darted toward the door. "We have all the time in the world. It's just us."

I swung my legs over the side of the bed and stood up. "We have stuff to do. Get my magic back, get to Matteaus. We can't just give in to desire."

Beckett jumped up from the bed and crossed to me. He grabbed my hands in his and pulled me to him. "But we could for just one second."

"No." I shook my head and tried to squirm out of his grip.

"Astrid." My name was a prayer on his lips, and I wanted to give in, but something in my gut told me not to. He yanked me to him and slammed his lips over mine. *Chocolate*... he tasted like chocolate. Deep, rich, and delicious chocolate.

Ice ran through my veins and I froze on the spot while he mushed his lips against mine. I held my mouth still then pulled back from him. My clothes were in a ball just next to the door and I lurched for them. I grabbed my sweater and yanked it down over the crown. It pulled at my hair, but I didn't care. I had to get out of here.

Beckett followed behind me. "Where are you going?"

"I'm leaving."

He grabbed my arm and yanked me back. "Don't you want to stay with me?"

"Buddy, I don't even know who the hell you are. But you sure as shit aren't my Beckett." I pulled my arm free from him.

In an instant the Beckett before me morphed into something else, someone else. This guy was beautiful and not in the bad boy surfer way I liked. No, this guy was straight out of a teen movie. With midnight hair combed back from his face, piercing blue eyes, and a jaw so chiseled I could cut glass with it. His lips were full, pink, and begging to be kissed. He stood before me in a black silk robe and matching pants that hung open from his body perfectly, exposing his muscled torso. His lips parted in a breath-taking smile that showed perfect white teeth.

He grabbed my hand once more and held it to his lips. "What gave me away?" He met my eye as he kissed the back of my hand.

"I know the way you taste," I mumbled in captivation at his sexy deliberate moves.

He chuckled. "Excuse me?"

"I just know Beckett." I pulled my hand from his grip. "And you are not him. Who are you?"

He took a small step back and bowed. "Eros, cupid, son of Aphrodite. Depends on the day, really."

"Well, Eros, I'm out of here." This time I did grab the doorknob and yanked it wide-open. I marched out into the hall and paused. Doors, so many doors going in both directions. It was like a bad hotel that never ended.

Eros walked out behind me and leaned against the doorframe. "Welcome to a Hotel California of a sort. You can check out anytime you like, but you can never leave."

"That's cute." I narrowed my eyes at him and held out my hand. "Now if you'll give me my token and my Beckett, then I will gladly be on my way and you can continue with whatever you've got going on in this place."

"Mother said you'd be difficult, but I assured her I'd get the crown from you and I don't like letting her down." His eyes drifted to the top of my head. "Though I didn't expect it to be magically bound."

My eyes locked on the thin chain around his neck I hadn't seen before. A little heart with wings coming out of it hung between his pecks. Before I could think I reached out and snatched it off, breaking the chain clean off . Eros grabbed at it, but I tossed it up into the crown before he could get it back. The vines did the rest of the work, winding around the heart and pulling it into the magical confines of the crown tangled with my hair.

"Thanks." I spun and ran down the hall. "Beckett!"

Eros ran after me. "You'll never find him."

"Beckett!" I yelled even louder. How was I going to find him in the house of doors? I knew he was somewhere in here but where? I stopped and closed my eyes for a moment, letting my magic flow. In my mind I pictured a big compass pointing in the direction I would find Beckett. When I opened my eyes there was a compass in my hand and the damn arrow was pointing due north. I ran toward it. The arrow banked left down a hallway and so did I. A large pane of glass sat at the end of the hall and when I reached it, the arrow spun to the right toward the last door in the hall.

I didn't know what I was going to find. All I knew was Beckett had to be okay and he was behind that damn door. Eros jumped in front of it and held his arms out to his sides. "You might not like what you see."

"I don't care." I opened up my hand and shot magic straight at him, knocking him down the hall.

I shoved the door open and froze. Beckett was strapped to a four-poster bed by thick red sashes. No wonder Eros could morph into him perfectly, because he lay there in nothing but his low-slung jeans. His feet and hands were spread and bound, a sash tied around his head, gagging him from saying a word. But the worst part of it all was he wasn't alone. No, he was surrounded by five—*five!*—girls who looked like me. Five Astrids all in different outfits I'd worn over the past few weeks. It was like looking in five mirrors. Two hung from the bed post at his feet. Two lay on either side of him on the bed and one, the worst one, straddled his hips.

"What in the actual . . . you know what? I don't want to know."

Beckett's head snapped up and his eyes bugged out.

The muscles in his body coiled with tension as he screamed at me through the gag in his mouth. His face turned an angry shade of red and he opened his hands. Blue smoke poured from his palms and fell down the sides of the bed.

"Screw this." I threw my magic in with his and the Astrid clones flew away from him, pinned up against the wall.

Beckett's magic wound up the bed and snaked around his bindings, untying them one by one. He pulled his arms free and sat straight up in the bed then yanked his gag out. "Where the hell have you been?"

"Where the hell have I been? How about what the hell have you been doing?" I dropped the Astrids to the floor then grabbed his clothes from the pile next to the door. The same pile where mine had been. I threw them at him as he climbed from the bed.

Beckett caught them and tugged his shirt over his head. "I woke up like that!"

"You and me both." I waited as he slid his feet into his combat boots.

He froze. "Wait, what?"

"Eros, we are wherever Eros' layer is." I glanced down the hall and saw him storming toward us.

"You guys didn't . . ."

I wrinkled my nose at him. "Ew, no." Eros was closing in. "We need to go."

I pulled him out into the hall and Beckett stood there looking from Eros to the glass window behind him. "How do you feel about jumping?"

"Anything is better than going back into any of those rooms." The door across the hall clicked open and a beautiful woman stepped through. She shook her head at Eros and he stopped dead in his tracks.

"Hi." She smiled and I swear she was the most beautiful person I'd ever seen. Her blond hair flowed in shimmering waves down past her hips to the back of her knees. The sun had kissed her skin to a perfect tan and her sparkling emerald eyes made me want to lean into her and do what, I didn't know, but I was having a hardcore girl crush at the moment. She wore a baby doll T-shirt that exposed her entire stomach. Across her bust in glittering pink rhinestones it said "heartbreaker." Her jeans were so low I was sure I was going to see something I didn't want to if she twisted the wrong way. She reached into her back pocket and handed me a piece of notebook paper folded into a little square.

"Hey, can you give this to Matteaus when you see him?" Her voice was light tinkering that was so sweet to my ears. She looked past me toward Beckett. "I would give it to you, but I doubt you'll survive."

"What?" I glanced from the women to Beckett and back again.

Beckett ground his teeth together. "Lucky I don't give a shit about anything you say, Aphrodite."

She did a little wiggle then slid the note deeper into my hand. "Your boy needs to learn some manners."

I grabbed the note and slid it into the side of my combat boot. "There, I got it. Now let us go."

The door Aphrodite had just come out of opened once more and a man with long raven hair stepped out. The deep widow's peak at the top of his head gave his face a severe, angry look. He was only a few inches shorter than Beckett, but I could feel the power rolling off of him. Long black cloaks flowed from his shoulders down to the ground. But there was something about him that looked familiar.

Beckett stiffened beside me and held his hands at the ready. "Dario."

"I prefer Mr. Malback." Fast as lightning he reached out and yanked me toward him. He spun me around and pressed my back to his chest. A flash of silver and he had a knife to my throat, pressing to the side of it. A sharp sting pinched the side of my neck then I felt the warm trickle of blood down my skin.

My heart raced and I found myself getting more pissed off by the second. I wasn't scared. Beckett was here and I had my powers. Powers I'd learned how to control. "What the hell, Aphrodite? This is supposed to be Matteaus' quest. You're supposed to listen to him."

"He never gives me what I want, so why should I give him what he wants? Besides, when I choose a side I like to choose the winning side." She shrugged and patted Dario on the shoulder. "Make it quick."

She left us all standing there to go back into the room. When she walked through, I spotted a cloaked figure out of the corner of my eye. I couldn't tell if it was male or female, but the feel of power rolled toward me. The person motioned for Aphrodite to sit and she dropped down on the bed like a trained dog and the door clicked shut.

Beckett took a step back and held his hands up. "What do you want, Dario?"

"Such a simple question for such a complicated answer." He clucked his tongue. "I want nothing more than for things to stay as they were intended to be. The way Alataris intended them to be before you all got in the way."

"You mean before we killed him?" Beckett snickered. "No."

He pressed the knife to my throat hard and I felt

the point of it go deeper. "Um, Beckett. Maybe we don't piss off the madman."

Dario's fingers dug into my arm. "Listen to her. Only one of you has to die here and she seems rather important to you."

I struggled against his hold. "Go, Beckett, the warlock world needs you."

He shook his head and spread his arms out wide. "And I need you."

Dario tossed me to the side and took one large step toward Beckett. He planted his foot and kicked him square in the chest with the other. He flew back toward the window, which shattered on impact, and Beckett flew out backward. Freezing air whipped through the open window and I lunged forward, reaching for him. "Beckett!"

Dario spun and pointed his knife toward me. "You're next."

He drew the knife back about to stab me. I spun and ran toward the window. Two steps and I swan dove out after Beckett. We were on a sheer cliff face and he looked like a limp rag doll as he fell. One large shard of glass pierced his shoulder and crimson blood seeped across his shirt. I tucked my arms into my side and forced my magic to propel me faster toward him.

The ground rushed toward us as I collided with him in midair.

His eyes rolled in his head. "Astrid."

"Portal, Beckett. NOW!" My words were laced with power and a single blue orb fell from his hand. It was small and we both might not fit, but I pulled him in tight to me and we fell through it in a twist of bloody limbs. I didn't feel the twists and turns. All I knew was we were both falling and at some point either we'd die or stop.

The portal opened into a room and we crashed into the middle of a bed . . . his bed. I scrambled to his side. That piece of glass was nearly ten inches long and protruding through his back and from his shoulder. His head lulled to the side and his eyes were closed.

I patted him on the cheek. "Beckett, come on, Beckett!"

Nothing. He was ghostly white and his breathing was shallow. "Oh God."

I ran to the dresser and grabbed a towel then wrapped it around the glass, making sure not to move it. Tears fell from my eyes as my body quaked from head to toe. "Somebody help me!" I screamed so loud it ripped at my throat.

Footsteps barreled toward Beckett's room and my eyes grew focused on the blood seeping between my fingers and spreading over the bed sheets below us. "Don't worry, they're coming, Beckett. They're coming, just hold on."

I threw my head back and screamed as tears poured down my face. He was going to die with my hands coated in his blood. "God help me!"

CHAPTER 52

ASTRID

 ive hours later...

I SAT with my back pressed against the wall and my knees up. I rested my arms over my knees and stared at my hands. Beckett's blood dried over my fingers long ago, yet I couldn't bring myself to leave to clean up. Niche, Zinnia, Cross, and Matteaus shoved me out of the room when they arrived and I sat here waiting. The door clicked open and I jumped to my feet, ready to race back to his side. But Matteaus filled the doorway. He held his hand out and motioned for me to back up. His lips were pressed into a hard line and his brows were drawn low in a grave expression.

I took two small steps back and sucked in a hitched breath. "Oh God, is he? Is he . . . ?"

"He's going to need a lot of recovery time, but he'll live." His large black wings twitched and for a moment I thought I saw his eyes swim with unshed emotion. "He's going to live. Niche got all the glass out and he's patched up. Zinnia is feeding him a shit ton of magic to keep his vitals up. You might want to go in there later and give her some. Speaking of which." He handed me an empty glass orb. "Here you go."

I reached up and grabbed it with both of my hands. "But it's empty."

"You always had most of your power, Astrid. Zinnia only took a very small amount in the beginning so you would live through you ascension and to motivate you to learn to control yourself faster. Now you have it all. Congratulations."

After all this time it didn't seem to matter anymore. Beckett was injured and I had to be with him to help him recover. "Thanks." I tried to step by him. "Can I see him?"

"Just a second, Astrid. I need to know what happened to him. This was supposed to be a mission of lessons. No one was supposed to die or come so close to it." He crossed his arms over his chest and waited.

"Let's just say your Greeks tend to do whatever the hell they want and Aphrodite was no different."

His brow furrowed deeper. "Aphrodite? She wasn't supposed to be there."

"Neither was Nemesis, Hecate, Dionysus, Hermes, or Fortuna. Although Fortuna was helpful." I was anxious to get to Beckett and my words spilled out.

"I will kill all of them." He growled.

"By all means feel free. All of them were a pain in my ass!" I said a little too loud, but I wanted to get this over with. "But at the end with Eros, Aphrodite showed up and asked me to give you this." I pulled the note from my boot and handed it to him. "Then she gave both of us to Dario Malback."

Matteaus grabbed the paper and curled his fist around it. "Hold that thought." He opened the door and crooked his finger. "Cross, front and center."

Cross walked out the door looking pale and worn out. "Yes?"

"It's time." Matteaus opened his phone and held it to his ear. "Phoenix, come up and bring Ophelia."

Cross jumped on the balls of his feet. Only moments ago he looked completely worn out, but whatever Matteaus just said got him all amped up. Two sets of footsteps came up the stairs and Tuck rounded the corner followed by Ophelia. Tuck's face was deadly serious. "Is he?"

I reached out and placed my hand on his shoulder. "No, he'll live thanks to Zinnia, Niche, Matteaus, and Cross."

He let his head fall back and he sucked in a deep breath. "Good, that's good, we need him."

Matteaus nodded. "We need all of you, which is why it's time to send Ophelia and Cross on a man hunt."

Ophelia rolled her shoulders and cracked her neck. "Who's the target?"

"Dario Malback. He's the one who tried to kill Beckett and nearly succeeded." He placed his hand on Cross' shoulder. "Are you up for this? I can send someone else."

Cross gave him a single nod but kept his eyes locked on Ophelia. "I'm ready. It's about time I fulfill my end of the pact, isn't it, O?"

She reached out and wrapped her hand in his shirt and yanked him to follow her as she turned away. "This is gonna be one hell of a wicked hunt."

Matteaus turned toward Tucker. "You going to be okay without them for a while?"

"Oh yeah, it'll be good to take out the leader of the warlock resistance." Tucker nodded.

I could almost pity Dario . . . almost. Whoever Ophelia was going after didn't stand a chance against a girl like that. "Guys, I'm not sure he was the leader."

Matteaus sighed. "I wish you were wrong." He opened the note Aphrodite gave him then crumpled it up and threw it to the ground. Without another word he walked away from the two of us.

Tucker motioned to the door. "Have you been in yet?"

"No." I shook my head. "I'm going in now." I hesitated just outside the door, terrified of what I was about to see.

"Let's go in together?" He grabbed the knob and pushed the door open then motioned for me to walk in first.

The smell of antiseptic smacked me in the nose as I walked into the room. Niche stood on one side of the bed and Zinnia on the other. Silver magic flowed from her to Beckett in winding streams. When she spotted me, she dropped her hands and sucked in a deep breath. Dark bags hung under her eyes and she staggered toward Tucker. He caught her around the waist and held up at his side. She smiled down at me. "Well done, Astrid, you completed your task."

"And nearly got Beckett killed." Guilt sat heavy in my stomach and I hated the feel of it.

"No." She shook her head. "He's alive because of you."

Her sleeves were rolled to her elbows and blood covered her fingers the way they covered mine. But there around her wrist was a tattoo I'd never seen before. I didn't know why my eye was drawn to it, but it reminded me of the one I'd shown Beckett a long time ago. "Is that a tat binding you to your powers too?"

I moved to Beckett's side and grabbed up his hand. When no one answered me, I glanced back at them. "What?"

Zinnia forced a smile on her face. "Oh no, this, it's my soul mate mark. Links me to this guy. He's got the same one. Show her, babe." She gave Tuck a little hip bump.

Tucker smiled and moved her toward the door. "Maybe later. I'll be right back, Astrid. I'm just going to get her some place to rest."

"She can take my room." I pointed down the hall. *Wait, I don't live here anymore.* "Down the hall."

As the two of them left, Niche followed behind them. She tossed her mane of red hair over her shoulder and pushed her glasses up her nose. "He's going to be okay, just needs to rest and heal now."

"Thank you." I sat there holding his hand in the

silence. I watched the easy rise and fall of his chest. Every breath he took brought him closer to being better. The warmth of the room seeped into me and I tugged my sleeves up. There on my wrist was the mark Beckett told me linked me to my orb. But the orb was done now and I still had it. My pulse quickened as a thought hit me. *Can't be.* I tugged up his sleeve and there on his wrist was the exact same mark.

Two lines, one thicker than the other with two circles going through them on the base of his wrist. Ours were identical, his a bit larger than mine, more masculine. A small smile spread on my face and it explained so much. Why I was so drawn to him, why he frustrated me more than anyone, and why he evoked such strong emotions. We belonged to each other. He was mine and I was his. I chuckled and new tears ran down my cheeks. I leaned over and pressed a small kiss to his wrist right over the mark.

I froze. *Hold up. He knew . . . he knew the whole time and he didn't tell me.* Why would he not tell me? Why keep this a secret? Why lie? I dropped his hand and sat up straight. Of all the times he told me we had to be honest with each other, we had to trust each other. *Hypocrite!* I wanted to yell, scream, and cry all at the same time. How could he do this? To me? To us? He kept them hidden with his own magic so I wouldn't know, so no one else would know. Was he ashamed of me? Of us? My head swam with a thousand questions he couldn't answer. Questions he could've answered.

I rose from his bedside and began to pace back and forth at the foot of the bed. After everything we'd been through, we were in a good place. A place I thought was a new beginning for us. How could that be when it was all based on a lie?

I froze at the foot of his bed and called upon my magic. "If it's lies you want, it's lies you'll get."

I wasn't angry. I was livid. And after all of Matteaus' lessons I learned to control my impulses. I wouldn't fight or scream at him. My power crept across the bed toward his wrist. It wrapped around it and the soul mate mark was hidden just the way he'd hidden mine. I wound it around my own wrist and masked mine as well. If he wanted it to be a secret then a secret it would remain. If he wanted lies between us then lies there would be. I was calm, cool, and collected. This wasn't a time for impulse, this was a time for tact, plotting . . . total control.

"So many wicked lies you tell, my love . . . two can play at that game. I am, after all, a warlock . . ."

ASTRID FINALLY HAS her soulmate mark and knows what it means. What will happen when Beckett wakes up? How will Astrid handle his secrets? Find out in book three of *The Royals: Warlock Court, Wicked Lies.*

CLICK HERE to pre-order *Wicked Lies.*

My power doesn't lie but everyone else does...

* * *

CURIOUS ABOUT WHERE Cross and Ophelia? Will they find Dario? Or will they come to a new agreement? She loves to torture him, but he likes it. Find out how their manhunt goes in *The Royals: Witch Court Novella, Wicked Hunt*.

CLICK HERE to order *Wicked Hunt*.

I'll do everything in my power to take him down...

* * *

IF YOU'D LIKE to come join the fun and madness in my FB group. Where we talk about anything and everything join us. Just CLICK HERE.

* * *

WANT to see how it all started with Tuck and his Knights? Where you can get your first real glimpse of Beckett. Great news- it's FREE! Just sign up for my newsletter and get your copy of Wicked Trials today for free.

CLICK HERE For Wicked Trials.

This power chose *me*...

Within the supernatural world of Evermore everyone prays their child will be born with the Mark of the Guardian for they have unparalleled strength, intelligence, and *power*...but they have no idea what it's actually like. I didn't wish for this *gift* and I definitely don't want it. I was born a prince, I already had it all. This Mark on my neck stole all of it from me and forced me into a dangerous life I'd gladly trade away if I could...

But now the Witch Queens have ascended and it's time to try and defeat the evil King once and for all. For over a thousand years his cruelty has spared no one as his torturous power grows stronger. He must be stopped now, before his reign destroys everything and anything in his way. So I must push aside my dreams of returning home to the family that cast me out. I must step up and claim the power that chose me. I *must* enter the Trials and become a Knight in the Witch's Court.

There's only one way to prevent the tyrannical king from destroying everything I love...I must become the one thing he can't beat.

IF YOU MISSED out on season one The Royals: Witch Court now is your chance to read the complete season from start to finish in one beautiful package.

CLICK HERE to get The Royals Boxset.

ALSO BY MEGAN MONTERO

The Royals: Witch Court

Wicked Witch

Wicked Magic

Wicked Hex

Wicked Potion

Wicked Queen

The Royals: Witch Court Boxset

The Royals: Warlock Court

Wicked Omen

Wicked Wish

Wicked Lies- Coming soon

ABOUT THE AUTHOR

Megan Montero was born and raised as sassy Jersey girl. After devouring series like the Immortals After Dark, the Arcana Chronicles, Harry Potter and Mortal Instruments she decided then and there that she would write her own series. When she's not putting pen to paper you can find her cuddled up under a thick blanket (even in the summer) with a book in her hands. When she's not reading or writing you can find her playing with her dogs, watching movies, listening to music or moving the furniture around her house... again. She loves finding magic in all aspects of her life and that's why she writes Urban Fantasy and Paranormal.

Learn about Megan and her books by visiting her website at:

Www.meganmontero.com

Made in the USA
Las Vegas, NV
03 April 2021